HER ENEMY AT THE ALTAR

Virginia Heath

Published in Great Britain 2016
by Mills & Boon, an imprint of HarperCollins*Publishers*
1 London Bridge Street, London, SE1 9GF

ISBN: 978-0-263-91716-1

nd
ainable
rm to the

When **Virginia Heath** was a little girl it took her ages to fall asleep, so she made up stories in her head to help pass the time while she was staring at the ceiling. As she got older the stories became more complicated—sometimes taking weeks to get to their happy ending. One day she decided to embrace her insomnia and start writing them down. Virginia lives in Essex with her wonderful husband and two teenagers. It still takes her for ever to fall asleep…

Mills & Boon Historical Romance

That Despicable Rogue
Her Enemy at the Altar

Visit the Author Profile page at millsandboon.co.uk.

For Katie.
And all of the other beautiful tall girls out there.

Chapter One

A London ballroom—November 1815

He was surrounded by the usual gaggle of giggling girls who found him charming. Fortunately, mused Lady Constance Stuart as she watched him from the opposite side of the ballroom, she was not one of them. Like his father, Aaron Wincanton had hair as dark as night and a heart as black as sin, and Constance was predisposed to hate him with a vengeance. But there was something about Aaron Wincanton that had always grated. Perhaps it was his cocky arrogance, or perhaps it was the way he constantly flirted with any woman in possession of a pulse, or maybe it was simply the fact that he was the most irritatingly handsome man in the room, but whatever it was she had developed a deep well of loathing reserved especially for him.

The gaggle of silly girls all stepped back at his command and Constance watched in reluctant fascination as Aaron Wincanton held an unopened champagne bottle upright in his palm. He had obviously procured a sword from someone and held it aloft in his right hand with far more flourish than was necessary. The blade glinted in the light of the chandeliers above, attracting even more attention to the exciting spectacle at the edge of the dance floor. He lay the flat of the blade against the side of the bottle and his mewling disciples began to count out loud in squeaking excitement. 'One… Two…'

On three he slid the blade swiftly upwards against the glass, slicing off the cork and the neck of the bottle in one, deadly clean cut. Foaming champagne spilled from the top of the bottle like a fountain and the audience all held out their wine glasses for him to fill or clapped at the audaciousness of the trick.

As if he knew that she would be watching him, his eyes languidly lifted and locked on hers. Before she could look away, he was already smiling smugly and winked at her in that oh-so-arrogant way of his that suggested that he just *knew* she had been staring at him again. It was galling.

Irritated beyond measure at the man, and at

her own stupidity at being caught gawping at him yet again, Constance forced her eyes to another part of the ballroom. The part that she had been deftly avoiding. For the third time this evening she spied her new fiancé, the Marquis of Deal, leering down Penelope Rothman's ample cleavage. Despite the fact that her father had already instructed her to ignore it, explaining that a good wife understands that a husband might—from time to time—seek the company of other women, Constance still struggled to do so. She and the marquis had been engaged less than a fortnight. And he had chosen her over Penelope. Surely he could keep his urges under control for such a short period of time out of respect for his future wife?

Unless this was a bitter taste of the life she was destined to have with the man? Despite the fact that the marriage had been arranged, Constance had hoped that they might find some sort of happiness together. Secretly, she had nurtured the belief that he might, one day, actually fall in love with her. That the Marquis of Deal would see beyond the hard exterior she had always presented to the world as a defence mechanism, find some beauty in the unruly, unsubtle, red hair that did its own thing and the tall, gangly, unimpressive figure, and uncover the real woman who lay beneath. The one who felt things a little too deeply and worried constantly that she was not quite good enough. What an idiotic, hopeless fool she was to have such a ludicrous dream!

Deal would never love her. It was no secret that her father had increased her dowry as a sweetener to lure him and Penelope Rothman *was* considered to be the diamond of the Season. It was humbling to realise that the Marquis of Deal had chosen his future bride pragmatically and solely for economic reasons. That is where his attraction to Constance started and stopped. Connie's vivid appearance could never tempt him in the same way that Penelope's golden hair and ethereal beauty did. She was merely a better financial prospect. It was still Penelope he really wanted and no amount of money would change that. Her eyes flicked back towards Aaron Wincanton and she saw him watching Deal and Penelope briefly before his gaze locked with hers again. She could tell by his bland expression that he also knew that her fiancé preferred petite blondes to gangly redheads. *Everybody* preferred petite blondes to gangly redheads.

The surge of disappointment was so sudden that tears threatened to form and hell would have to freeze over before she allowed anyone see her cry. Constance quietly disentangled herself from her mother's group and slipped away to an empty alcove. Once she was composed she would give Deal the sharp end of her tongue and remind him of the behaviour expected of a gentleman. She might well be able to overlook his indiscretions in time, a very long amount of time, but that did not mean that she wanted to witness them as well. Besides, she reasoned as she watched festivities from a distance, nobody was likely to miss her—least of all her devoted marquis. As always, her dance card was woefully empty, aside from the occasional polite invitation issued from older family friends and the first waltz that she had already danced with her indifferent fiancé. She was now doomed to spend the rest of the evening with the matrons and the wallflowers. As usual.

It had always been that way. Ever since her come out six years ago, she had been doomed to watch every ball from the far side of the room. A situation that had been made much worse by the unfortunate, but incredibly apt, nickname that she had been given by Aaron Wincanton on the night she had been introduced at Almack's. Of course, it had caught on almost immediately and Connie had learnt of it when she had overheard another group of debutantes laughing about it in the retiring room. Thanks to Aaron Wincanton, from that moment on she had been referred to scathingly as the Ginger Amazonian.

The first year had been mortifying. Only her pride had got her through it as she had stoically ignored all of the whispers and giggles, and tried to be grateful for the pathetic trickle of fortune-hunting suitors that still tried their luck. She knew that she looked ridiculous and ungainly up against the other girls. Nobody knew better than she how very unappealing she was. There had never been another debutante who had the audacity to grow to six feet. Nor was there one with feet so enormous that the cobbler had once bragged that he made the biggest slippers in London. The debutante pastels further washed out her already pale complexion and she positively towered over all of the other women—and most of the gentlemen as well. She endured every feeble joke about her height by laughing politely, even though she wanted to smash her fist in the face of the next person who asked her what the weather was like up there or suggested that she slept in a greenhouse.

In an attempt to blend into the background, for a few months she had even took to standing with her knees bent at all times. While this served to make her appear shorter when stationary, the effect was spoiled the moment she had to move because she found it far too painful to attempt to walk, or heaven forbid dance, in a crouch. Besides, as her younger brother had laughingly pointed out, her crouched gait was oddly reminiscent of that of the apes at the Royal Menagerie. She gave up squatting after that. It was bad enough being compared to a giant female warrior. She did not want to ever have to endure a simian nickname and would not put it past Aaron Wincanton to come up with something even more insulting, like the Giant Ginger Gorilla. Heaven forbid!

The second year Connie was more prepared. If she was going to be compared to a mythical warrior she might as well act like one. Nobody would ever witness her lack of confidence in her own attractiveness ever again. She had learnt to watch the proceedings with a detached and slightly disdainful air, as if she would never deign to lower herself by courting the interest of the eligible gentlemen in attendance or attempting to make friends with the silly gossiping girls. She was better than that. Lady Constance Stuart never fluttered her eyelashes over her fan, or giggled or swooned or simpered. Lady Constance Stuart proudly loomed over any gentleman who had the audacity to be shorter. She also wore bold colours to set off her copper-coloured curls to best effect. Turquoise, emerald and, if she was feeling particularly unattractive, crimson became her preferred colours of choice. They were no longer merely gowns; now each dress was a statement of defiance. She might well be an ugly wallflower, but that did not mean that she had to be a shrinking violet. Connie had been doomed to stand out wherever she went so she gave the impression that she was comfortable with that by purposefully sticking out wherever she went. But she loathed it nevertheless. Almost as much as she loathed her wild red hair, pale skin and beanpole body.

Lady Constance Stuart earned the reputation for having a sharp tongue and used it to wound if the need arose, which it did with less frequency as the seasons passed. She was formidable, like a true Amazonian, and the character she had created was now so convincing that sometimes Connie could forget how much it all hurt and how much she hated being relegated to a curiosity rather than a woman.

Out of the corner of her eye she spotted her fiancé brush his fingers over Penelope Rothman's perfect cheek and whisper something close to her ear that soon had those perfect cheeks blushing a very pretty shade of pink. Enough was enough. Lady Constance Stuart would never silently condone such insulting behaviour. She was going to talk to her fiancé and lay out some rules.

Connie regally walked towards the Marquis of Deal, where he was stood still fawning over Penelope. 'My lord, if I might have a private word?' She fixed him with a pointed stare and watched him blink in surprise at her icy tone.

'Of course, my dear.'

Connie headed purposefully towards the French windows that led out to the terrace and heard him follow. Despite the chill in the air, there were several other guests outside so she made sure that they were all well out of earshot before she turned around and faced him. Out of deference for the two inches of difference in their respective heights, Connie crouched until she could stare pointedly in his perfect blue eyes before she spoke. There really was no delicate way of putting it.

'Your behaviour this evening has humiliated me. I am your fiancée. We are newly betrothed. It is insulting that you should continue to flirt with other women in public. If I am going to be your wife, I expect to be treated with some respect.'

Her comments appeared to startle him. 'How exactly have I been disrespectful? I danced the first waltz with you. I have spent several minutes in your company. Surely you are not put out by my socialising with my friends? It is the norm for married or engaged couples to not linger in each other's company at social events. People would talk if we did otherwise.' The Marquis of Deal gave her one of his benevolent smiles. The one that set off the dimple in his square chin to perfection and made his blue eyes twinkle against his thick, golden hair. The man was far too handsome and far too aware of it. 'Although I do find your jealousy flattering, it is quite misplaced. I can assure you that Penelope and I were simply having a brief and platonic conversation.'

'It was hardly brief. She has dominated your time for at least the last hour and people are beginning to notice.' Aaron Wincanton had certainly noticed. 'In the future I would prefer it if you avoided cosy chats alone with Penelope, or any other unattached woman for that matter, out of respect for me.' Connie had hoped that Deal would feel ashamed of his behaviour. Instead he looked angry.

'It is not your place to tell me what I can and cannot do, madam, and I will thank you to remember it. Do you seriously expect me to avoid all contact with other women? I have already discussed this at great length with your father and he assured me that you understood that our arrangement was more about convenience than convention.'

Hearing that spew from his mouth was like a slap in the face and Connie balked. 'Do you have no affection for me whatsoever?' She had hoped that he had some and that the tiny seed would grow and she hated herself for that as well. Silly, needy fool!

Deal stared back at her as if she was quite mad. 'Ours is an arranged marriage, Constance. It is based on an agreement that is mutually beneficial to both of our families. I thought you understood that? I am doing you a huge favour by marrying you! You have been on the shelf for years and nobody else wants you. To be perfectly frank, you should be grateful for that and stop all of this nonsense. I will give you my name, a home of your own and a child or two to keep you company and secure the succession. In return, I have promised your father my support.'

A home of her own? What exactly did that mean? It certainly did not sound as if he wanted to share it. So much for her hopeful dream of a happy marriage. 'And then what?' she asked boldly, although she suspected she already knew the answer. Deal did not want her. He never would.

'And then we will both live our lives exactly how we want to! You will stay with the children in the country, of course, but as long as you are discreet I have no objection to you doing as you please once you have provided me with an heir.'

Connie was starting to feel a little queasy. Surely her father had not agreed to this? He had sold her off as a brood mare to a man who had no intention of being more than a temporary husband. 'And I am to accept the fact that you will continue to live the life of a bachelor in town?'

At that he looked her up and down with obvious distaste and then his expression turned to bemusement. When he finally spoke it was the final nail in the coffin of her foolish dreams.

'What else did you expect, Constance? Surely you did not think that I would miraculously fall in love? With *you*?'

Chapter Two

Aaron had seen her face change almost imperceptibly just before she had hurried out of the ballroom and found himself watching the Marquis of Deal with downright disgust. Whilst it hardly mattered to him that Lady Constance was marrying a libertine, he could not help feeling a little exasperated at the man's behaviour. To consort openly with another woman when your fiancée was in the same room was worse than poor form, in his opinion, especially when the woman you were consorting with did not hold a candle to the one you were apparently betrothed to.

Constance Stuart might well be snooty, disdainful and disapproving towards him, that was only to be expected when they shared such an unfortunate history. But to others she was always the epitome of what a proper lady should be. Yes, she might well be aloof and in possession of one of the sharpest tongues in Christendom, but she had a way of carrying herself that set her apart from so many of the other young women of the *ton*. And with her height and willowy figure and all of that red hair, she was certainly distinguished. Added to that was her obvious intelligence and innate grace, combined with a rare and spectacular smile that lit up the room. Not that she ever bestowed it on him, of course, nor could he conceive that she would ever have cause to, but he could imagine that such a smile must make the recipient of it feel as if the most glorious sunrise had been created only for him to enjoy. Yet Deal preferred to humiliate the girl by fawning over the Rothman chit. And Aaron had never met a more scheming, manipulative and shallow creature in all of his life than Penelope.

Remembering his purpose, he turned back towards Violet Garfield and feigned interest. If he was going to propose to the girl, he had to at least appear to care about whatever it was she was currently wittering on about. Two hours into the ball and already he could feel his mask slipping. Being Aaron Wincanton was becoming exhausting.

Once upon a time being the charming and slightly mischievous rogue had come as naturally to him as breathing, but he had left that effervescent young man behind somewhere on a battlefield in Spain and he doubted they would ever cross paths again. The new Aaron Wincanton found no joy in balls or parties, nor did he find it in intimate gatherings or quiet solitary contemplation either. He did not deserve to feel joy any more. Most of the time he felt burdened. The rest of the time, if he was lucky, he just felt numb. He caught Violet looking at him as if she expected him to say something. He had not been listening and he did not want to offend her. Out of habit he turned on the charm. 'Violet, when I am with you I wish the minutes were hours and the hours were days.' They certainly felt like that.

As he had expected, the inane platitude worked wonders and she started to chatter afresh, with such gusto that all he had to do was listen and nod. A few seconds later and Aaron found his mind wandering again—it made him feel quite unsettled. He had hoped that he could convince himself that he might be content with Violet. There was no doubting that she was very pretty, which was a bonus, but much as he liked her poor Violet bored him senseless. Unfortunately, she was also an heiress—with a staggeringly large dowry—so beggars, like him, could not be choosers. The estate needed funds fast and his father wanted him to start producing the next generation of Wincantons while he was still alive to see it. Therefore, Aaron needed to step up and propose to Violet. And he needed to do it tonight.

But before he did, Aaron definitely needed a bit of peace and little Dutch courage. With nothing stronger than ratafia at the refreshment table he excused himself from the conversation and wandered out of the ballroom to see if he could find something suitably fortifying to drink alone elsewhere.

At the furthest end of the darkened hallway he found the empty library. Empty, except for the full brandy decanter and the one solitary redhead sat on an immense sofa and staring sightlessly into the fireplace. For a moment he considered turning around and looking elsewhere for sanctuary. The very last thing he needed was a dressing down from Lady Constance Stuart, even if he hoped that such encounters would eventually lead to an introduction to her brother, when he would broker the idea of an end to the silly feud that threatened to bankrupt him. His nerves were shot as it was and he needed a rest before he forced himself to become Aaron Wincanton again. But something about the way she sat, with her shoulders uncharacteristically slumped, made him dither. Perhaps they both needed the comfort of a sparring match this evening?

'How clever of you, Connie,' he said to vex her, 'to find a place where we will not be disturbed.'

Her startled head whipped around and Aaron thought he saw tears shimmering in her green eyes but, if he had, she covered them quickly with her usual frostiness. The shocked expression dissolved into a harsh frown instantly.

'You are like a bad smell, Mr Wincanton, which always seems to follow me around.' She stood stiffly and glared. 'I was hoping that, for once, you would leave me in peace.'

'And where would the entertainment be in that? I look forward to our little exchanges, Connie. I find your disdain refreshing when I am so admired by all wherever I go.'

'So you seek me out for your entertainment, then? Does your father know that you regularly converse with a Stuart?'

'No more than your father knows that you engage in discourse with a vile Wincanton, I will wager.' Aaron gave her a cheeky wink because he knew that nobody else ever dared to flirt with her and he watched her eyes narrow in annoyance.

'But I do not seek you out, Mr Wincanton. That is the difference. I could happily go to the grave and never exchange another word with you. Therefore, I must conclude that I must hold a particular fascination, or pose a particular challenge, to you. Does it bother you that I am immune to your flirtatious charms? Does my obvious distaste wound your frail ego?'

She gave him a withering look that only spurred him on further. When she was riled those green eyes hardened to cold emeralds and her red hair crackled copper in the firelight. It was a sight to see and one that might send a lesser man running for the hills. But Aaron was made of stern stuff. He had fought Napoleon, for goodness sake, so he could survive a war of words with this fiery redhead. Besides he had an ulterior motive that he could not ignore. He needed to improve relations to put an end to the costly feud between their two families, and so far Constance Stuart was the only Stuart who would deign to speak to him. 'Why don't you admit it, Connie? You find my persistence exciting. Too many men treat you like a marble statue with their dull politeness, the rest bore you because they are terrified of your sharp tongue.

But I am different. I make your blood run hot. I suspect I might even fire your passions.'

The man was as mad as he was insufferable. In a strange way Connie was grateful that he was here. She could take out all of her hurt and anger on him. At least then she would not feel so utterly despondent and powerless. 'Do not flatter yourself, Mr Wincanton. You fire my temper, not my passions.'

'How many times must I ask you to call me Aaron? After all the jolly conversations we have shared these last two months, surely it is time that we dropped the formalities, Connie?'

He knew perfectly well that her name was always Constance—her father disliked informality of any sort—and that she would never, ever give him permission to use it. He was also the only person in the universe who ever shortened her name to Connie. She despised his familiarity even though she quite liked the name. 'In case it has escaped your notice, *Mr* Wincanton, we are mortal enemies. Have you forgotten the fact that the Stuarts and the Wincantons have been at loggerheads for nigh on three hundred years?'

'We have? I confess I have forgotten what all of the fuss is about now. Why should we care about an argument that happened almost three hundred years ago? I would prefer to hold out an olive branch and declare a truce.'

'Indeed. And I suppose we should simply brush under the carpet the despicable behaviour of your father, only a few years back, where he swindled mine out of land that should rightfully have been his?'

He merely brushed that away with his hand. 'A misunderstanding, Connie. Nothing more.'

At times his irreverence did amuse her, not that she would ever let him see that. Nobody ever spoke to her like Aaron Wincanton did. No one else dared. 'Then there is the unfortunate incident that occurred between our grandfathers. What did your foul grandfather do to mine again?' She tapped her chin as if in deep thought. 'Ah, yes! Now I remember. He shot him dead in a duel on Hampstead Heath.'

'To be fair, my grandfather only did that after your grandfather seduced his wife. And it was a proper duel with rules and seconds. It is hardly my fault that your grandfather did not have the good sense to try to dodge the bullet.'

Connie waved away his warped logic. 'Such things cannot be overlooked. If my father caught me talking to you, he would disown me. Yet here you are again, Mr Wincanton. Bothering me.'

It had been like this for the entire Season.

Ever since he had returned from Waterloo, in a blaze of glory, he had sought her out. Despite the bitter and long-running feud between their two families, the Stuarts and the Wincantons had managed to co-exist in society very well by pretending that the other side simply did not exist—despite the fact that their ancestral estates were right next door to each other. They were always invited to the same functions and happily imagined the other to be invisible when in a social setting. Society understood this perfectly. Thus, there were never any public scenes and there was certainly never any attempts at conversation. It was a system that worked very well because it had been that way for centuries. Until now.

Unfortunately, Aaron Wincanton, heir to the house of Ardleigh and all-round blackguard, had no respect for tradition. It had been two months ago when he had first started to speak to her—and to her alone. It was never done openly, of course, or in front of any member of her family or his. But at every function he managed to catch her by herself at some point, no matter how much she tried to avoid it, and each time he did he would flirt a little and try and make her smile. Sometimes he would be loitering near the retiring room just as she came out, other times he would find her in an alcove or he would appear behind a potted palm or at her elbow at the refreshment table. And now he was here, in this remote library where she had sought sanctuary, and he had almost seen her cry. That was a situation Connie found the most intolerable.

Yet he merely shrugged in response, as if all of that bad blood did not matter, and then fixed her with his unusual and intense gaze. Unusual because only when you were up close could you see that his eyes were almost russet brown surrounded by a ring of dark, melted chocolate. Those eyes could be very unsettling at times, as if they saw too much. 'Has it occurred to you, Connie, that our situation might be similar to that of the Montagues and Capulets? History might dictate that we be enemies, but apparently fate wants us to be friends—or perhaps more than friends?'

'You are aware, Mr Wincanton, that Romeo and Juliet are fictitious and therefore not really pertinent to our situation? But as I recall, things ended very badly for both Romeo and Juliet because they did not listen to their fathers, so perhaps they should have ignored the will of fate, as you put it. The ending might have turned out very different if they had simply let things be. However, you do seem to be missing the point.

Juliet welcomed Romeo's attentions. I do not welcome yours. And in case it has escaped your notice, Mr Wincanton, I am engaged to be married and happy to be so.'

'How can you be happy to be marrying a man who has shown more attention to Penelope Rothman this evening than he has to you?' As soon as the words came out of his mouth Aaron regretted them. He felt even worse when he saw her frown turn into an expression of raw pain before she attempted to cover it. 'I am sorry, Connie. That was uncalled for. I apologise unreservedly.'

'Pay it no mind,' she said with a shrug of bravado that did not ring quite true. 'The Marquis of Deal has had a little too much to drink this evening and Penelope Rothman is trying to incite my jealousy, and failing. It must be quite galling for her to lose her most favoured suitor to the Ginger Amazonian.'

She looked him dead in the eye as she said this and saw him wince. He still felt guilty about calling her that, more so that the nickname had stuck. But he had been young and foolish back then and she had dented his pride. He had never meant for her to ever hear it. Or for her father to respond with such malice. It had come as quite a shock to come back from years of fighting

Napoleon to see how dire the situation between their two families had become. His own father had become so obsessed with the feud that he had almost bled the estate dry in his attempts to get revenge on Connie's father.

'For what it is worth, I am sorry that I called you that, too.'

She gave him a regal and cold smile that did not touch her eyes and stood slowly. At her full height her face was almost level with his. The woman must be close to six feet in height, he mused, as she loomed in front of him, perhaps a little more. 'I can assure you, Mr Wincanton, that I have never really given it a passing thought.'

Then, to the apparent and total horror of both of them, she promptly burst into tears right there in front of him.

Aaron felt like a total cad. At a loss as to what else to do with a crying woman who was evidently not usually prone to crying, he rushed towards her and pulled her into his arms. 'There, there, Connie,' he murmured ineffectively as she buried her face into his neck and wept noisily, 'I genuinely am sorry for calling you an Amazonian. It was most ungentlemanly of me.'

'I am not crying because of that, you idiot!' Her brief flash of anger was still peppered with tears, but it did make him feel better. At least this rare and noisy display of emotion was not specifically directed at him. The poor girl was clearly upset at Deal's callous behaviour.

'I am sure Deal's flirting means nothing,' he said, not believing his own words. Deal was a shameless philanderer and one who liked to brag about his many conquests.

'Hardly nothing. It means that he prefers her charms to mine,' she sobbed. 'And who can blame him? Penelope is so beautiful. Everyone says so. And I am pale and plain in comparison, with hideous freckles and my figure is as flat as a washboard. And I have all of this ghastly carrot-coloured hair.'

Clearly, he had inadvertently kicked a hornet's nest. Aaron could feel her slim shoulders shaking as she wept and felt the most peculiar urge to hunt the Marquis of Deal down and give him a well-deserved punch on the nose. 'For a start your hair is glorious. Your skin is not pale, as such. Think of it more as alabaster. The freckles on your nose are quite delightful. Really they are. I have never understood why freckles are considered unbecoming. And you are not as flat as a washboard. You have a lovely figure.' He could feel the gentle flare of her hips beneath his hands and there was definitely something interesting pressed against his chest that his body was responding to—against his better judgement and his black mood. What on earth was the matter with him? This was Constance Stuart. Constance *Stuart*.

Connie lifted her face from his shoulder and looked at him through puffy eyes, her expression the very picture of anguish. 'If I am so lovely, then why has he not even tried to kiss me? Answer me that. We are engaged after all.' She looked positively distraught. 'The man finds me repulsive. He has as good as said so.'

Further proof that Deal was a blasted idiot, Aaron realised. She felt splendid in his arms. It was nice to be able to look a woman in the eye, for once, rather than have to look down at her. Connie was a pleasant armful of woman who apparently fitted against his big body perfectly. And she had a brain. Nobody could ever claim that Constance Stuart was a dullard. Sparring with her was always one of the highlights of any ball. The sultry smell of roses tantalised his nostrils and overwhelmed his senses, giving him ideas that he had not had in a very long time. How on earth did Deal resist her? Her full mouth was all red and swollen and positively ripe for kissing. If she were his fiancée he would not be able to stop himself… Before he could think about it, Aaron dipped his head and did just that.

The moment his lips touched hers he quite forgot everything else. She sucked in a breath of surprise at his impertinence, but did not push him away, so he brushed his lips over hers again. And again. His arms wrapped around her possessively and he pulled her closer still. Initially, she stood stock still, then he felt her breath catch. But then her lips opened slightly and she sighed. When she pressed her mouth tentatively against his, Aaron lost all sense of reason and kissed her like a starving man.

Kissing Aaron Wincanton was nothing like she expected kissing to be. Not only did she feel it on her lips, but she felt it in her legs as well. They were oddly unsteady. A million tiny goose bumps appeared all over her body and every nerve ending tingled involuntarily with awareness and need. Connie did not notice the passing of time or exactly when the kiss changed into something more visceral, but one moment she was stood in his arms upset and the next she was almost reclined on the sofa, her hands fisted in his dark hair and his large, warm palm sliding over the silk of her stockings until it rested scandalously on the bare skin above her garter. It felt glorious to be wanted this way and by a man who had no interest in her dowry or her prospects.

He was kissing her.

Connie.

And she could tell by the way his breathing was ragged and how his heart hammered against his ribs that he was as lost in the kiss as she was. The feelings and sensations created by this intense passion was so unexpected, so overwhelming, that she was transported by it all to a place that she had never been and never wanted to leave. Finally, she was attractive and desirable to someone. She felt beautiful and womanly and alive.

She had not heard the library door open nor had she heard several people pile in until it was too late.

'What the hell is going on here?'

The angry voice of the Marquis of Deal had her sitting up and pushing Aaron unceremoniously to the floor while she did her best to put her skirts to rights. Her father stared at her coldly from her fiancé's left and a very smug-looking Penelope Rothman stood at his right.

'This is not what it looks like,' Connie stuttered wide-eyed and frantically glanced at Aaron for support. His face was taut as he stood up, but he said nothing as he helped her to her feet.

'Your daughter has been compromised.' Deal turned to her father in disgust. 'I will not have her now.'

Her father turned back to her with something akin to hatred burning in his usually cold eyes. 'You have disgraced our family, Constance!'

Connie felt nauseous, dizzy, the floor having been completely ripped from beneath her feet, and totally stunned. How could this be happening to her? Several other guests began to spill into the room to watch the dreadful scene unfold and she could hear more outside, shouting for others to come, too. Among their number she recognised her younger brother, Henry, and her mother. Both of their faces were pale with shock. Her mother looked close to tears. Behind them came Aaron's father, Viscount Ardleigh, the assembled crowd parting like the Red Sea as he entered the room.

No doubt he saw his son's dishevelled hair and the undone buttons of his coat. Connie did not want to think about how she appeared to their audience—but if it was anything like Aaron then she suspected she looked completely wanton and guilty of acting upon those urges with unbridled enthusiasm. One heavy lock of her shocking red hair hung guiltily against her cheek where he had removed the pins that held it. All around her, women were whispering behind their fans with outraged glee.

The oldest Wincanton took in the scene slowly. After an age his eyes rested upon his eldest son. 'Well played, Aaron,' he said with a note of pride. 'And I thought you did not have it in you.' Then he threw back his head and began to laugh.

Chapter Three

Connie had a vague recollection of being ushered out of the ballroom. She remembered the carriage ride home with perfect clarity, though. It had been terrible. Her mother had sat in brittle, terrified silence, her brother Henry had been pale and stunned. Her father had been incandescent with rage, spitting out profanity after profanity as he railed against her with more force than usual. In the end, his rantings all boiled down to one thing: he thought her a stupid, ungrateful whore and she was dead to him. She was to pack her bags and leave in the morning and never darken his door again. Even now, several hours later, Connie still felt numb. One ridiculous and ill-conceived moment of weakness and her life was in ruins and she had absolutely no idea what she was going to do or where she was going to go.

As soon as they had returned home, a maid had been sent up to her room to help pack her things and then left her to sleep. Two trunks and a bag were now stacked in the corner of her bedchamber, but Connie had not slept. She had spent most of the night relieving the awful events and could still not understand how it had all gone so horribly wrong. But she was very clear who was responsible.

Aaron Wincanton.

He had purposefully taken advantage of her when she had been vulnerable in some petty act of revenge. The man had clearly gone out of his way to ruin her.

A maid knocked on the door timidly. 'You are required in his lordship's study, my lady. I am told to tell you not to dally.'

It was barely past dawn and already her father wished her gone. With a heavy heart, Connie stood and made her way downstairs. The study door was closed so she tapped upon it before entering. Her father had never appreciated being interrupted at the best of times and now was definitely not that. His voice was curter and colder than usual. 'Enter.'

'You wished to see me, Father?' Connie looked down at her hands rather than see the disappointment in his eyes. Even so, his next words were brutal.

'Do not refer to me as that again. As far as I am concerned I have no daughter.'

Connie's eyes snapped up and only then did she notice Aaron Wincanton standing stiffly in the furthest corner of the room. She could not work out what emotion was clouding his eyes as he walked towards her and neither did she care. Automatically, her hands curled into angry fists at her side. Were the Wincantons so callous that one of them had to witness her entire ruination? 'What is *he* doing here?'

Her father did not look at him. 'He has come to request your hand in marriage and, under the circumstances, I have granted it.'

'I will not marry him. I hate him!' Connie spat the last words directly in her despoiler's face.

'That is as may be,' her father continued, sounding bored with the entire conversation, 'but your mother prefers that I do not throw you on to the streets, so this solution suits us well enough. You made your bed, Constance, when you lifted yours skirts for him.'

'I did not—'

Her father cut her off with a raised hand. 'Half of the ballroom witnessed it. Whether you did, or did not, consummate the act makes no difference. That you would allow this…this…' his head whipped towards Aaron for the first time and regarded him with absolute disgust '…this Wincanton to touch you when I had arranged the perfect union between you and Deal, it beggars belief. But you did and now you must live with the shame and the consequences. He has arranged a special licence and the pair of you will be married within the hour.'

Connie felt her legs give way and staggered backwards to steady herself on the arm of the sofa. 'No! You cannot make me. I am past the age of majority. You cannot force me to marry anyone that I do not choose to.'

'Yes, I can, Constance! The alternative is I throw you out on to the streets with nothing but the clothes that you stand up in.'

'I would rather that than marry a Wincanton.' Connie stalked to the door, refusing to look at either her father or *him*. Both men were vile.

'Then do so on the understanding that I will toss your mother out alongside you. If she had done a better job of chaperoning you, then this would never have happened. You have always been as wilful and difficult as you are unattractive—and she has always given you far more credit than you were due. I have no intention of listening to her bleeding-heart pleas for your safety and I hold her equally as responsible for the disgrace that has been brought on to our family by your actions.'

Connie turned to her father in abject disbelief and met his stony stare with one of her own. Was the man truly serious? Surely he was bluffing? Was he truly callous enough to throw them both out in order to get his own way?

Bile rose in her throat when she realised that he was. The Earl of Redbridge's word was always law and, in matters concerning the feud between the Stuarts and Wincantons, that law was cast iron. Both her mother and she were inconsequential. As long as he had an heir to pass it all on to her father would be content. Connie risked a glance at Aaron. He was still watching her intently, his jaw set and his dark eyes angry, but she did not know if that anger was directed at her or her father.

'Then bring in the priest and let us get this travesty over with.' Connie was beaten. He could see it in her eyes. It was as if all of the light had gone out of them. She might be brave and bold for herself, but her loyalty to her mother was too strong to ignore. Aaron wondered what that bond felt like. His own mother had died shortly after giving birth to him so he had never grown up with the unconditional love of at least one parent. His own father and the Earl of Redbridge had a great deal in common and both were apparently hard on their children. He had almost stepped in to defend Connie, but realised that her father would likely throw them both on to the street immediately and if that happened she would never marry him. He could not leave her to the harshness of such a life on her own.

Connie's father marched to the door and spoke quietly with a footman, so Aaron took the opportunity to speak to her.

'It will be all right, Connie. I promise,' he whispered quietly as he gently clasped her hand with his own. She snatched it away as if she had been burned.

'Do not touch me! I despise you, Aaron Wincanton. That will never change.'

Whilst the words hurt he could not blame her for them. This whole, sorry situation was all his fault. He should never have gone into the library in the first place. He had made her cry. And he had instigated the kiss that had ruined her. No wonder she hated him. He hated himself as well—but that was nothing new. He was supposed to have proposed marriage to Violet Garfield and saved the future of the Wincanton estate. Instead he had made another huge mess and ruined yet another innocent person's life.

From the moment his father had patted him on the back in front of that room full of people, and congratulated him for getting one over on the Stuarts, Aaron had vowed to make amends for this latest transgression. But when he had seen Connie stumble out of that library with her life in ruins, the guilt he had felt had been so overpowering that he could barely stand in the same room as himself.

'I knew my heir would not let me down,' his father had crowed when they were finally left alone. 'Now no man will want her.'

Aaron recognised the truth in those words. Society was fickle and the transgressions of a woman would never be overlooked. If he did not make it right, then Connie would be shunned and doomed to an empty life of spinsterhood. 'I will marry her,' he had suddenly declared.

'You will not. I forbid it. I will not have my bloodline sullied with a Stuart!'

'It cannot be helped. I ruined the girl. It is my responsibility to marry her.' Aaron went to walk to the door.

'It is not your responsibility. The world is full of ruined women who should have known better. Once the dust has settled you could still propose to Violet Garfield. You are too good a catch for her to ignore.'

For the briefest of moments Aaron seriously considered the wisdom of his father's words. Violet Garfield's money could save them. Just as quickly he discarded the thought. He might well be a Wincanton, but the army had taught him about his responsibilities. It was his duty to do right by Connie. He had wronged her and he would not let her pay the terrible price alone. Aaron had ruined enough peoples' lives already, he did not need another on his conscience. The guilt from all of his previous sins was already too heavy to bear.

'I will offer myself as Constance Stuart's husband and let her decide.' He sincerely hoped she would turn him down—despite her unfortunate family connections she deserved a better man than him, but it had to be her choice.

'If you do, then I will…'

'You will what, Father?' It was a familiar threat that he had lost patience with long ago. 'You cannot disinherit me. The estate is entailed. You can throw me out until you die, which we both know will happen sooner rather than later, and I will survive well enough until then.' Aaron stalked towards his father and loomed over him. 'Take comfort that I inadvertently ruined a Stuart, Father. It is the only satisfaction that I will allow you to take from this whole sorry mess.' Aaron turned to leave.

'You are soft, like your mother. She had no backbone either. But, as I have always said, bad bitch—bad pup. And now you would bring another bad bitch into our house.'

Aaron spun around and practically growled into his father's face. 'If Connie will have me, then she will be my wife by tomorrow and you will treat her with the respect that position deserves. I promised you a grandson within the year. What difference does it make whose belly he comes from?'

He had stepped away then, frightened by his own need to cause the man who had sired him physical pain, and had stalked out into the street in search of a cleric senior enough to issue him with a special licence. Only then did he seek out her father. He had been surprised that the man had so readily agreed—but now, seeing the way the earl treated his only daughter, he was not surprised at all. The earl was determined to make Connie pay for the shame she had brought down upon their family. To add insult to injury, the Earl of Redbridge only agreed to the match if Aaron agreed to take her without a penny—which of course he had. He might desperately need the money, but that was hardly Connie's fault. What better way to make her pay than to make her marry the enemy and disown her completely? Like his own father, the Earl of Redbridge was so fuelled with bitterness and hatred from the feud that he could not see past his own nose. Both men were tyrants. Both men made his flesh crawl.

Connie was now sat hunched on the sofa, looking defeated and disgusted in equal measure. Aaron had no idea what to say to her, so he sat in a chair close by and waited. Neither spoke. What was there to say? They were doomed to be stuck with one another now and neither one of them wanted to be with the other. Fortunately, they did not have to wait long. A very nervous-looking vicar arrived. He blinked awkwardly at the pair of them through the lenses of his thick spectacles. 'May I see the licence?'

Aaron handed it over and the man scanned it quickly. 'Everything appears to be in order. However, I cannot help but notice that the two of you do not look quite so keen.' He was peering kindly at Connie, but it was her father who answered him.

'That is simply natural bridal nerves. My daughter is as keen as I am to begin the wedding formalities.'

The priest did not look convinced and was

still looking from Aaron to Connie with concern. 'We will need some witnesses.'

'They are waiting in the next room,' the Earl of Redbridge said curtly. 'I shall fetch them and you can get it over with.' He walked towards the door and then slowly turned back and spoke to Aaron directly as if his daughter was not there at all. 'I shall not be returning. Once the ceremony is over with, get that girl out of my house. I wash my hands of her. She is your problem now. And she will be a problem. She always has been.' And with that he left.

'It might be prudent to wait a bit.' The priest rested his hand gently on the back of Connie's. 'Perhaps in a few days all will seem clearer. This marriage is particularly fast.'

She shook her head without looking at the man and then retreated back into herself. Several ashen-faced servants filed in and stood uncomfortably in the room. Connie stood next to Aaron stiffly, staring off into space and struggling not to cry.

'Do you, Constance Elizabeth Mary Stuart, take this man, Aaron Phillip Arthur George Wincanton, to be your lawfully wedded husband?'

Aaron held his breathe until Connie nodded once.

'I need you to say the words, Lady Constance.'

There was a long pause. Aaron watched her hands fist at her sides and a myriad of emotions cross her face. After an age she turned to him with an expression of complete hatred.

'I do.'

She mumbled the rest of her vows as if in a trance. In his haste, Aaron had forgotten to buy a ring and was forced to use his own signet ring as a wedding band. It swamped her delicate fingers and looked completely wrong on her hand, as he supposed he did too. Everything about this marriage was wrong. At best they were strangers, at worst sworn enemies.

As the first rays of the sun filtered into the study the vicar declared them man and wife. He did not suggest that Aaron should kiss his bride. Even the vicar realised that Connie would rather kill him than kiss him. But it was done. What had possessed him to follow her into that library last night he could not say, only now they both had an entire lifetime to regret his impulsive decision.

'Come, Connie,' he said with a sigh of resignation, 'it is time to go.'

Chapter Four

Aaron did not sit in the carriage with her as they travelled directly to Ardleigh Manor, instead he rode his horse alongside. While she was grateful that he had the good sense to realise that she really had nothing whatsoever to say to him, and probably never would have, it meant that she was left alone with her own thoughts and fears for hours on end.

Ardleigh Manor.

Whilst she had seen it almost every day of her life from her bedchamber window, the Wincanton estate was completely unfamiliar to her. It might well neighbour her father's land, but that might as well be the moon now, it was so far away. She was completely and irrefutably estranged from her family. Her father had made that quite clear. Never again would she while away the hours chatting to her brother, Henry, or her mother, nor would she ride her own beloved horse again, nor would she experience the comfort, smells and cosiness of her childhood home. Although she doubted that she would miss her father—she had been a disappointment to him from the moment she had been born—each of those losses was a cruel blow. Connie felt as if her heart had been ripped from her chest and shredded, and there was not a thing she could do about it. She felt raw and broken, wronged and ashamed.

And so very angry that she felt as if she might burst from the way it boiled and curdled in her gut. She had let her mask slip in front of Aaron Wincanton, of all people. The man who had cursed her with that dreadful nickname, had seen how much it had hurt her, how it continued to hurt her because she had never been the kind of woman that men fancied, and that the only husband she could get was either bought or trapped into marriage.

Connie heard the sound of gravel under the wheels of the carriage and forced herself to look out of the window at her new home. Up close, Ardleigh Manor was larger than she had realised. The symmetrical, classically designed front appeared stark white against the night sky, the windows glowing warmly with candlelight.

If it had belonged to any other family than the vile Wincantons, she might have considered the house pleasing to look at, rather than menacing, but as the carriage came to slow stop outside Connie physically steeled herself to go inside.

An austere butler and a small round housekeeper stood waiting just outside the open front door. Connie rudely ignored her husband's proffered hand and made her own way down the short steps to the floor, all the while staring up at the enormous double-front door looming menacingly from ahead. To all intents and purposes those doors represented the gates of Hell, although in this scenario Ardleigh Manor was Hell and Aaron Wincanton was the Devil incarnate. Connie had no idea if she was a lost soul or a genuine sinner. The truth was she was likely a bit of both. Aaron had instigated her ruination, but she had welcomed his touch, silly desperate fool that she was. It was galling to have to acknowledge her part in the incident, but she would not meekly accept her fate. Aaron Wincanton would rue the day he had used her to get revenge. Of that, she was certain.

The stern butler stepped forward. 'On behalf of the staff, may I offer you our congratulations, Mr Aaron? I am Deaks. This is Mrs Poole. Welcome to Ardleigh Manor, Lady Constance.'

It was the first time she had been referred to as a Wincanton and hearing her new name made Connie feel queasy. Out of ingrained politeness she inclined her head towards the servant. It was hardly his fault that she was here.

'I have prepared the suite of rooms that you requested, Mr Aaron. I hope they meet your satisfaction, Lady Constance. There is also a light supper ready if you are hungry.'

Connie shook her head and then remembered her manners again. 'Thank you, but I am not hungry. Mr Deaks… Mrs Poole.'

'It has been a long day,' Aaron interjected, 'If you could have my wife's luggage brought up, Deaks, I believe she would prefer an early night.'

'Certainly, sir.' The butler turned to Connie with a smile and she knew exactly what was coming. 'Excuse my impertinence, madam, but you are tall, aren't you?' Mrs Poole, to her credit, rolled her eyes at this and nudged him unsubtly in the ribs.

Connie glared at him in response until he withered. Usually she would endure the crass stating of the obvious with a brittle smile. Tonight she did not have the strength. Aaron stepped in and rescued the butler from the frigid atmosphere she had created. 'Thank you, Deaks,

Mrs Poole. That will be all.' The butler bowed stiffly and then stood to one side.

Without touching her, Aaron guided Connie into the house and up an ornate and sweeping marble staircase. 'I am sure that you are finding all of this very daunting. I know I am.' He smiled at her a little awkwardly. His face fell when she remained stoically silent. 'I have put you in my mother's old rooms. They look over the gardens. Attached is a small sitting room. I thought you might appreciate a little privacy whilst you become familiar with your new home.'

They were walking to the end of a long hallway. Aaron opened the double doors and stepped back to allow her to go inside first. The feminine parlour was actually very pretty. A roaring fire had been set in the fireplace, around which were arrange a cheerful old-fashioned sofa covered in boldly striped satin brocade and two comfortable matching chairs. The walls were papered in a subtle lemon-coloured stripe while a large picture window dominated the wall. Connie nodded, grateful that she would have a place where she could sit away from this awful family. Away from the man who knew that she hated being tall and ugly. The man who had seen her cry. The man who had married her out of pity when no one else would because she was so unattractive.

'I have arranged for my father to stay in London for the next week so that you can settle in.' Aaron might have told the old man to stay away, but there was no guarantee that he would comply. 'As the new mistress of Ardleigh Manor, some of the staff will expect to take instructions from you. Mrs Poole will introduce you to the cook and the staff tomorrow.' He could not help noticing that her green eyes were hard emeralds again and her mouth had begun to curl into what appeared to be a snarl. 'Unless, of course, you would prefer to postpone that until you feel more comfortable.' Despite the fire, the temperature of the room felt as if it had dropped several degrees since she entered it.

'Through here is the bedchamber.' Aaron opened the internal doors for her self-consciously, aware that he was rambling to fill the excruciatingly painful silence, and then his voice trailed off as he saw that the servants had already turned down the bed. *Both sides* of the bed. They barely knew each other and now they were stood alone in a bedchamber. The big, canopied mattress mocked him from the centre of the room. It was designed for two people to share, yet he had no idea if they would be sharing the thing tonight. A wedding night was the expected conclusion of a wedding day, he supposed, but as theirs had been so acrimoniously arranged with such speed he would not blame her if she wanted to wait a bit. They *were* little more than strangers.

'You have your own bedchamber,' she asked abruptly, staring at the bed as well.

'It is down the hallway.' Good grief—was a conversation ever more uncomfortable and stilted as this one?

'Good.' She turned her face towards his and he saw the venom in her pretty face. 'You are not welcome in this one.'

Aaron slowly nodded in sympathy, oddly relieved that he would be spared the ordeal tonight. They were both still so shocked to find themselves married, they hardly needed the added burden of enforced intimacy now. 'I did not think you would want me here just yet. I believe we should get to know each other a little bit first, before we…ah…'

'I will never *want* you here. Be under no illusion that those feelings will ever change. They won't. The thought of your hands on my body makes me feel ill. The only way it will happen is if you force me and even then I will not lie meekly under you like a dutiful wife is supposed to. I will scratch and claw and scream my hatred for you so loudly that all of the servants will hear it!'

Well, that certainly left his position in doubt, Aaron thought, reeling, although he supposed he deserved it. He had a particular talent for ruining lives. 'I am sorry for the way things turned out, Connie. I never meant for this to happen.'

Her hands fisted and for a moment he thought that she might strike him, so vivid was her anger. 'How dare you lie to me? Do you seriously expect me to believe that a vile Wincanton would not seize the opportunity to ruin the only daughter of his sworn enemy? You planned it, Aaron Wincanton! You came to the library intent on compromising me. Intent on revenge.'

The woman clearly had a penchant for the fanciful if she could think that, although she was overwrought, so he replied calmly in the hope she would see reason, 'I most certainly did not. I will admit I went into the library because you were there, and with hindsight I realise that was a reckless and stupid thing to do, but I never intended anyone to know about it.'

Her hands went to her hips. 'Oh, really? And I suppose you expect me to believe that your seduction, followed by the convenient arrival of my fiancé and both of our fathers, was also accidental? I am not a fool, Aaron.'

He could understand that it looked bad. 'I

did not go to the library with plans to seduce you, Connie.'

'Then why did you?'

It was a fair question and one he was not sure he could properly answer without admitting how precarious his financial situation was. He ran a hand roughly through his dark hair in frustration. 'I suppose I kept seeking you out because I hoped that it would eventually lead to a conversation with your brother. I want to build some bridges between our families. I thought that, in time, as the next generation we might find a way to end this petty feud. I never meant for anything more than that.'

'Of course you didn't.' She was flouncing around, her long legs making short work of the distance from one wall to the next, and dramatically gesticulating as her mouth dripped sarcasm. 'You spouted all of that Romeo and Juliet rubbish and it *inadvertently* gave you romantic ideas. Then you kissed me, because you were so caught up in the *magic* of the moment and so dazzled by my *obvious* beauty—and then invited an audience to witness it, you snake!'

His own temper was roused now. Likening him to a snake was uncalled for. 'You kissed me back, as I recall, and with a great deal of enthusiasm, too. You are not completely without blame in this. My waistcoat did not undo itself, Connie. As for the audience, I was as shocked as you were when they all turned up.' It was then that he had realised that his own carefully laid plans for the future had been shattered as well. Now they were destined to be penniless and miserable together.

She planted her hands on her hips and gave him one of her imperious glances. 'How very *convenient* for you.'

Aaron saw red. Literally. He had never understood that expression until that moment. But to see her stood there so piously, as if she had not kissed him back with so much fervour that they had both lost their heads, while throwing ludicrous accusations at him, then sarcastically discounting every explanation he tried to make—well, it was too much. That ill-timed kiss had ruined much more than Constance Stuart's reputation, it had ruined the lives of every impoverished tenant on the Wincanton land.

'Convenient? Have you gone quite mad?' He found himself marching towards her and looming over her in a way he had never, ever done to another woman in his life. His hands were fisted tightly at his sides to stop him from grabbing her by the shoulders and shaking her until her teeth ratted inside that smart mouth of hers.

'You think that this marriage is *convenient* for me? Of course it isn't. This is a marriage of great *inconvenience* to me, Connie. In fact, it is an unmitigated disaster. I was about to propose to Violet Garfield! Now I am stuck with you instead.' Violet might well be as dense as a suet pudding, but at least she had a cheerful disposition and looked at him with glowing admiration. Constance Stuart was tart as a lemon and looked at everyone as if they were beneath her. Especially him. Well, he was quite done with it.

'Answer me this, Miss Sanctimonious: if I constructed this whole ruse, in an attempt to bring about your ruin in petty revenge against your awful family, then why the hell did I not leave you to suffer it alone? Surely that would have been the greatest revenge possible for a *vile* Wincanton? Leave you compromised and doomed to endure the censure of everyone alone. Yet I did not. Against my father's wishes, and against my own better judgement I might add, I left that ballroom straight away and procured a special licence. And then I married you. I gave you my name and my protection. I gave you a home. A truly vile Wincanton would have seen you thrown on the streets, as your own father planned to, and laughed at you in the gutter!'

She gaped at him then, lost for words, but he

was not done and she had it coming. He could not remember the last time he had unleashed his temper with such unchecked fury. He had long ago stopped feeling personally aggrieved at anything, instead he accepted everything thrown at him as just punishment for all that he had done. But in this instance, although he knew he was largely to blame as he was in everything, she *had* to take her share of it. Yet she was still staring daggers back at him, completely unrepentant and totally aggrieved. Her self-righteous martyrdom enraged him further. Again he seriously considered shaking some sense into the woman or putting her over his knee and spanking her like the spoiled child she was.

In an attempt to calm his turbulent thoughts, Aaron started to pace backwards and forwards at the foot of the bed. Unfortunately, the more he paced, the more outraged he became at her accusation. His only crime had been a desire to end their expensive and destructive feud so that he could live in peace next door. He did not want to waste his life looking over his shoulder, like his father and grandfather had, waiting for, or plotting, the next attack. He had had a gutful of war and did not want to continue to fight one on his own doorstep. The only thing that came out of war was death and destruction. It was a pointless and futile state to be in. And expensive. Very expensive when the estate was practically broke.

He had harboured the ridiculous notion that by befriending Constance, and then in turn her brother, the silly feud would be done with once their fathers died. Meanwhile, he could use Violet's dowry to bring the estate back into profit, so that future Wincantons could live happily ever after even if he had to sabotage his own happiness to do it. Not that his happiness really mattered. Once he might have considered it important, before he had the ruined lives and shattered the dreams of his men and their families, now he had to make amends as best as he could wherever he could. And right now that meant protecting the livelihoods of all of the people that relied on the Wincanton estate. If that meant he had to marry for money and spending a lifetime married to a woman he was incapable of loving, then he had been prepared to do it.

But that lofty plan had backfired spectacularly. Violet and her dowry were lost to him for ever. Worse still, Connie's father would unleash fire and brimstone now that his only daughter had been ruined by Wincanton. Instead of healing the rift between their families he had created an even greater chasm, yet had no way of clawing his way out of debt. Aaron had taken Constance without a penny. No, indeed, there was nothing convenient about this marriage. Everything was considerably worse because of it. The very least she could do was muster up a bit of contrition.

Aaron found himself glaring at his new wife. Her pale face was pinched and her lips were so pursed they were almost non-existent. And she thought that he would be disappointed not to be invited to her bed! That he might resort to forcing her to consummate the marriage! Quite frankly she would have to drag him there kicking and screaming, no matter how much his father wanted a grandson.

'Be under no illusion, madam, I am thoroughly appalled to be your husband. To think that I am now doomed for all eternity to spend my days shackled to you till death do us part—God help me, Connie!' Aaron marched to the door before striding back again to issue his parting salvo. 'And as for not wanting me in your bed? *Pah!* What sort of a man would willingly want to bed a shrew like you? I would sooner go into battle again!' He was glaring down at her, but still she refused to be cowed. When her hands planted themselves on her hips again it was like a red rag to a bull. How dare she? His index finger began to jab the air. 'You are my wife now and you *will* do your duty if I decree it. And if I can bring myself to touch you, Lady Constance, *you* will provide an heir!'

Aaron slammed the door with such force that the windows shook and stalked towards his own bedchamber. Unsurprisingly he did not sleep well. But for once his sleep was disturbed, not by the usual incessant nightmares filled with blood and body parts, but by dreams involving a statuesque redhead who made his blood boil and his loins ache.

Chapter Five

A maid brought her breakfast on a tray the next morning. 'Mr Aaron has told me to inform you that he has gone out for the day. If you need anything, Mr Deaks will see to it.'

Connie smiled at the girl politely and accepted the tray while her stomach growled in protest. The hot bacon smelled delicious, despite the fact that it came from the Wincanton kitchen, and reminded her that she had not eaten in over twenty-four hours. Perhaps once fortified she might be able to sort out all of her tangled and mangled thoughts and emotions. At least she was rid of *him* for a few hours.

Their fight yesterday had bothered her more than she wanted to acknowledge. Some of the things he had said rang uncomfortably of the truth, as galling as it was to have to face the reality she had never resorted to lying to herself.

She *had* kissed him back. And enjoyed it. She could have slapped his face, she could have run screaming from the room, she could have left it the very moment that he had arrived. There were so many things that she could have done to have avoided her current predicament—but she hadn't. She had stayed, cried like a baby and confessed all of her deepest darkest fears about her lack of attractiveness to the man who had given her that awful nickname. She had let Aaron Wincanton put his arms about her and she had revelled in the security of his warm embrace.

She had been so needy then, so pathetically vulnerable, that it made her want to scream just thinking about it. Then she had surrendered to his lips greedily the moment they had touched hers and practically melted. Whether that surrender was because she had been feeling unsettled and off kilter after hearing the Marquis of Deal reduce their betrothal to merely a financial settlement or whether it was because she had been so grateful to imagine that a man might actually find her attractive, she could not accurately say. Whichever it was, it did not excuse the fact that she had kissed him back and therefore had to take a small portion of the blame for the situation that she now found herself in.

But she would only take a small portion of the blame. Aaron Wincanton still held the lion's share. He had instigated the kiss. Although, in the cold light of day she was forced to acknowledge he really had gained nothing but grief in marrying her. Marriage was such an extreme thing to do for revenge that it seemed highly unlikely that he had gone to such a length to upset her family. If that was the case, he had been noble and to think otherwise was simply being petty.

And she still hated him for what had happened and how pathetic he had made her feel.

Now she was married to him and living in his house. As staggering and distasteful as Connie found that, there was no getting around it. The realist in her knew that continued outright rebellion was futile. She was his wife. The law dictated that she must abide by his rules. Despite all of his bluster last night, she knew in her heart he would never force himself on her, no matter what the law said about it. His behaviour had, in the main, been more than decent. He was so decent that he might even let her leave, but she really had nowhere else to go.

Her father would never allow her back so there was no point fleeing there. Her father also had a cruel streak that meant that she would not put it past him to punish her mother or younger brother if they offered her sympathy. Connie was not prepared to take the risk.

She had friends. Most of them were long since married and it was unlikely that any of their husbands would condone harbouring the runaway daughter-in-law of Viscount Ardleigh. She had no money, so leaving was out of the question until she could afford to do so. She supposed that she could steal something of value and leave in the dead of night, however then she would be a fugitive and the consequences of that were too terrible to seriously contemplate. That left her with two options. Stay and make the best of it, knowing that she would never be the woman he truly wanted, or stay and continue to fight. Neither appealed.

There was one potential light at the end of the tunnel. An annulment. But for that she would need Aaron's consent. Granted, she would still be a scandal and an outcast from her family. Her father was unlikely ever to consider taking her back—but he could hardly put her mother on to the streets if Aaron dissolved the marriage. It would simply be another vile thing that the Wincantons had done—as long as her father believed that the situation was not her fault. If her father still refused to mend the breach, she supposed that she could earn a living somewhere. Perhaps she could teach in a school for ladies or become a governess? If she changed her name and went very far away, she could manage.

Connie had only married Aaron because she had been forced to do so and he had only married her out of a sense of duty after he had compromised her. If that alone was not grounds enough for an annulment, then failing to consummate the marriage would guarantee it. And she would be free of seeing the disgust and disappointment on his handsome face at being tied to such an unattractive, giant of a woman—if she could convince her new husband to start the process.

The most sensible course of action would be to ask him. There was the slight chance that he would be quite open to the suggestion. He had called their union *'a marriage of great inconvenience'* so she seriously doubted he would want to remain married to her for ever, any more than she did him. Especially as he had had his sights set elsewhere. But an annulment would bring about another dreadful scandal and he might be reluctant to weather another. And he was hardly going to agree to anything sensible that she suggested whilst they were at loggerheads. He would dismiss it out of hand just to vex her.

Neither was she prepared to apologise for her behaviour towards him last night. The only thing that she had left was her pride and he had said some very hurtful things, too. He might not have called her unattractive, but his angry words had confirmed how unappealing he also found her. Hadn't he stated that he had no desire to bed her and he had called her a shrew? Even more humiliating was the fact that while he was shouting at her she found herself quite excited by his temper. Nobody ever stood up to her and most men avoided her. Aaron had gone toe to toe with her, his face mere inches from hers, so close that she could feel the heat of his body. The intensity and passion whirling in those dark eyes lit a fire within her that burned slowly, causing her body to hum with awareness and her mind to recall how wonderful it had felt when all of his passion had been directed at her in another way.

Her lips even tingled at the thought of touching his again even though she was outraged by everything that came spewing out of his mouth—until he had demanded that she would have to do her duty by him. Then she had been suffused with a heat that had nothing to do with the temperature in the room and everything to do with the way that the sheer presence of this man was making her feel. Had he kissed her right then, her traitorous body would have happily let him. Perhaps her needy heart would have, too?

But he left then, abandoned her to her own devices in a strange house surrounded by strange people consumed with equally strange thoughts. What if she did have his baby? Would that be so terrible? A family of her own to love and care for?

Of course it would, because he had already made it quite clear that he didn't actually want *her*. He was stuck with *her*. She was a burden to him, too, just as she had been to her father and to her indifferent fiancé. Nobody, it seemed, really wanted *her* at all. Like the Marquis of Deal, Aaron had reminded her that she was not the sort of woman that roused a man's passions and Connie was not prepared to let him see that she desperately wanted to be that woman for someone—even if that someone was *him*. The longer she was forced to stay here, the harder it would be to hide that need from him.

That meant that the only course of action left to her which left her with her pride intact while freeing him of his terrible burden was a mutually agreed annulment. Maybe later, when all was calmer and less fraught between them, could Connie bring up the subject?

* * *

By the time the maid brought her a lunch tray, Connie's small private sitting room was beginning to feel like a dungeon. Her new husband had failed to materialise all morning and Connie had had enough of waiting for him. Despite their fight, she would have thought that basic good manners dictate that he should show her around the house and introduce her to the staff. Seeing as he had failed in even that simple chore, she decided to acquaint herself with her surroundings in spite of him.

There was nobody on the landing when she finally plucked up the courage to leave the room. Connie allowed herself a brisk snoop around upstairs, quickly opening doors and poking her head inside. There were a great many bedrooms, although the majority were not in use. At the furthest end of the east wing there was a monstrosity of a bedchamber that smelled of acrid tobacco smoke. The enormous four-poster bed was draped in a gaudy tartan fabric. Staring out from every angle around the walls were the stuffed heads of many animals. Stags, boar, badgers and even a lone wolf's head watched her with their glassy, lifeless eyes and Connie shuddered involuntarily. This was a not a room where a decent person could get a good night's sleep and she sincerely hoped it was not her new husband's room.

She dashed back down the hallway to the other side of her suite of rooms and began to look into the rest of the rooms. Just two doors down from her was another bedchamber that was obviously in use. Next to the neatly made bed was a pile of books. The one on the top had been laid face down, open. A pair of wire-rimmed spectacles were discarded next to it. Thrown over the washstand was the very coat she had seen Aaron wear yesterday. Realising that this must be his room and burning with curiosity, Connie stepped inside and quietly closed the door behind her.

This room smelled pleasantly of bay rum and fresh air. Despite the wet cold of autumn, one of the windows was cracked open, but a fire burned in the grate. His personal items were stood in a tidy row on a tall chest of drawers. Idly she ran her fingers over a comb and picked up a pair of cufflinks. They were plain gold and unfussy. Aaron Wincanton was no dandy. She slid open the top drawer. The first thing that struck her was how organised it all was. Small, open boxes were filled with an array of items. One held tie pins, again, plain and not ostentatious, another more cufflinks. The drawer beneath was filled with plain, white cravats. All lightly starched, suggesting that he had no time or patience for some of the complicated and frothy knots that were currently all the rage.

The enormous oak wardrobe beckoned and, without considering whether she should or shouldn't, Connie pulled open the doors. A pristine line of snowy white shirts sat on one side. Stark black and navy coats on the other. He was always immaculately turned out and his austere clothing tended to make the more adventurous outfits of other gentlemen look a tad foppish. She might dislike a great many things about Aaron, but she could not fault his dress sense or the way he filled out his clothes.

Connie wandered towards the stack of books and read the title of the one he had been reading: *The Complete Farmer or General Dictionary of Agriculture and Husbandry: Comprehending the Most Improved Methods of Cultivation...* It hardly promised to be a riveting read. She picked it up and scanned the open page. As the title suggested it was indeed a dictionary, although the definitions of each term covered several pages and were accompanied with diagrams. The open pages were explaining, in great and laborious detail, the concept of ploughing. The spectacles were a surprise and she could not help wondering what he looked like in them. Knowing Aaron Wincanton, he no doubt looked quite splendid in them. He had a tendency to look splendid in everything. The wretch.

As she went to put the book down she noticed the name of the book beneath. *The Complete Works of William Shakespeare.* There was a bookmark slotted between some pages so Connie opened them. Then her eyes narrowed. The words 'For I am born to tame you, Kate!' stared mockingly up at her from the top of the page. The rogue was reading *The Taming of the Shrew*!

Aaron ignored the light rain and slowly rode around the furthest perimeter of the estate. Feeling cold and damp was preferable to marching back into battle with his new wife. His father often accused him of avoiding confrontation or adversity—and perhaps that was true—but in this case it seemed the prudent thing to do. Besides, Connie was only one of his mounting problems.

The estate was another one. The fields were all empty of crops, something that did not really surprise him seeing as it was the middle of November, but they were also choked with weeds and something about that really did not seem right. Surely they should be ploughed like the tenant farms already were?

Not for the first time, he wished he had paid more attention when his grandfather had tried to teach him about estate management. The old man might well have been a vindictive and tyrannical man, but he had known everything there was to know about farming—especially how to turn a profit from the land. His father had always preferred to delegate the task and Aaron had been so determined to leave and join the army that he had never shown any sort of interest. Now he was back, and would soon be in charge of the estate and wholly responsible for the many people who depended on it, his lack of knowledge bothered him.

What Aaron could not quite get to grips with was the fact that the price of wheat was fixed, yet they were falling deeper and deeper into debt every year. Obviously, he had asked his father. Unfortunately, Viscount Ardleigh was so arrogant and so absorbed with besting the Stuarts next door that he failed to acknowledge there was even a problem. He was happy to leave all responsibility for the farming to his estate manager while he plotted and planned and schemed against the Stuarts in his study. Mr Thomas, the estate manager, was as elusive as fox and probably just as wily. Aaron did not warm to the man at all. Unfortunately, his father would not have a bad word said about him.

Mr Thomas was responsible for the enormous parcel of land his father had bought while Aaron was fighting in the Peninsula. The viscount refused to allow Aaron full access to the estate accounts—not that it had stopped Aaron from snooping in the ledgers when his father was not around—and as far as he could make out, things were now very dire indeed. The unnecessary purchase had created a massive void in the coffers that they had not recovered from. The land in question did not even border the Wincanton estate. It sat to the south of the Stuart estate, which probably explained why his father had paid ten times what the plot was worth just to get it. That the Earl of Redbridge had also desperately wanted the land had made his father even more reckless with his money. He was so pleased to have snatched it away from the Stuarts that he had apparently failed to notice that all those additional, ridiculously expensive acres were good for nothing. The soil was so thin it was barely a film upon the hilly rock beneath, so nothing would grow upon it. It had been a total waste of good money that had set them on the road to ruin. Each year since, they had failed to turn a healthy profit. Or, for that matter, any profit at all.

Aaron turned his horse towards the small hill. From the top he got a good view of the Earl of Redbridge's estate and there all the fields were dark brown from ploughing. A fortnight ago he had seen men sowing seed in the land ready for next year. Why were his fields still idle? Perhaps the fact that they did this task so much later was the reason why their wheat crop had been so sparse last season?

It irritated Aaron that he did not know the answer to these questions. It irritated him more that he had no control over any of it either way. Not yet at least. Until his father died, he would not relinquish his control and Aaron could do nothing but watch the decline and wait. Except now, when his father did die, Aaron would not have the funds to fix things or to branch out into more modern investments. Thanks to his disadvantageous marriage.

Just thinking about Constance Stuart put him in a bad mood and he had no idea what to do about her. He had tried to be pleasant yesterday and had hoped that she would realise that they were both now stuck in the same boat and that she might come to appreciate his noble gesture. He had hoped that they might, in time, find a way to be able to co-exist without wanting to kill each other. After last night, he found that prospect less likely. The woman had no intention of making any form of compromise and trying to get her to see reason was exhausting. After hours of soul searching he had come to the conclusion that the best thing that they could do for the time being was avoid each other. At least until the dust had settled.

To that end, Aaron had been actively avoiding her all morning. He had ridden over every inch of the estate, was cold, soaking wet and the beginnings of hunger was gnawing at his belly. He wished he had had the foresight to bring some food and a blanket out with him, so he could have camped outside all night. He had slept quite soundly under the stars in worse conditions than this. Unfortunately, Connie would see such behaviour as cowardice rather than a tactical retreat and he was not prepared to give her that satisfaction. Clearly too many people had kow-towed to Constance Stuart for far too long and he was not going to be one of them. He had never run away from a battle in his life. Reluctantly, he turned his horse towards home and hoped for the best.

Chapter Six

Connie whipped around, startled when the bedchamber door suddenly opened, but she was too angry with him to apologise for invading his privacy. Without thinking, she tossed the leather-bound volume of Shakespeare at him and it hit him squarely on his sopping wet head.

'What the devil!'

Her hateful husband glared at her murderously as he rubbed his temple and Connie glared right back undaunted. 'You were reading *The Taming of the Shrew*! *The* Taming *of the* Shrew! Did you hope it would provide you with a few pointers on how to deal with me?'

Connie stalked towards him, wielding another book. To his credit he did not back away from her. Far from it, in fact. He met her in the middle of the floor and stared right back at her with his hands planted on his hips as if she did not frighten him in the slightest. His confrontational stance reminded her that he was significantly larger than she was, something that was uncomfortably unfamiliar and quite intoxicating. He topped her by a few inches in height, but in width there really was no comparison. The dark, caped greatcoat that he still wore made him loom even larger and his expression was thunderous. Connie felt like a brittle sapling stood next to a mighty oak tree and was forced to raise her chin to look him in the eye. And they really were magnificent eyes. Her mouth went dry as she stared into the outraged depths of them.

'The thought crossed my mind.' Up close, she could see flecks of gold shimmer in the irises. 'Why are you in my bedchamber, Connie?'

How could she admit to wild curiosity about *him* without sounding pathetic? 'I like to know my enemy!'

His dark hair was beginning to curl at the nape of his neck where it was wet. For some inexplicable reason Connie felt the urge to brush the droplets of water from his skin, but stopped herself. What on earth was the matter with her? This man thought her a shrew. Why did she desperately want to touch him?

'Did you find anything useful?'

His expression had changed. He no longer appeared quite so angry at her behaviour, more amused. As if he knew that she had wanted to know more about him. His arrogance, combined with the awkward realisation that he had seen through her bravado, rankled far more than his temper did.

'You read boring books.' What an utterly pathetic and insipid response. Connie felt her cheeks redden at the banality of the insult. His eyes flicked briefly to the weighty tome on farming still on the table before the ghost of a smile touched his lips, mocking her.

'That particular volume is spectacularly dull, I will grant you that, but monstrously heavy. I suppose I should be grateful that you had the Shakespeare so readily at hand. *The Complete Farmer* might have killed me.' He rubbed his head for effect and then shrugged out of the heavy wet coat. After depositing it over the arm of the washstand Connie watched in alarm as he made short work of also removing the wringing, limp cravat around his neck. He had started unbuttoning his waistcoat when she stopped him.

'What exactly do you think you are doing, Mr Wincanton?' Surely he realised that undressing in front of a lady was grossly improper. Part of her hoped he would continue.

'I am taking off this wet shirt, Lady Constance *Wincanton*. This is *my* bedchamber after all. All of my dry shirts are in this wardrobe here, although I dare say you know that already seeing as you have been rifling through my things.'

Connie opened her mouth to refute everything he had just said and promptly closed it again when she realised he had a point. She was in his room and she had been poking through his things. And much as she hated being Lady Constance Wincanton, that was also now her name. Instead of a pithy set down, more banality spewed from her mouth. 'I was merely familiarising myself with the house because you had failed to do so.'

'I would be happy to give you a tour of the place as soon as I put on a clean shirt.' To her utter dismay he was already untucking the one he was wearing. She caught the briefest glimpse of the skin of his abdomen and it was dusted with dark hair. Her eyes fixed to that area in the hope that she would see more of his body before she tore them away, disgusted at her own wayward thoughts.

'Then kindly wait for me to leave. I have no desire to watch.'

'I wouldn't mind if you did. You might find it entertaining. Or educational.' He shot her such an astute glance, his dark eyes practically smouldering, that she felt herself blush even hotter. He had known that she was looking at him wantonly. How mortifying was that? But then again, he was probably quite used to women looking at him and lusting after him. Not that she had been lusting exactly, it was more out of curiosity. Perhaps it was lustful curiosity? The man was devilishly handsome and knew it. In that wet shirt he looked delicious. It clung to his broad shoulders and chest, giving her a tantalising glimpse of the strength and power of his body. In places the fabric was almost transparent so she could definitely see that there was more of that intriguing dark hair that her fingers ached to explore.

Again she found her eyes drifting below his neck, but as she dragged them reluctantly back to his face the arrogant wretch was grinning unashamedly. Connie wanted to cover her burning face with her hands and curl up into a ball. She managed to paste a haughty expression on her face before she turned around and prepared to exit the room with as much fake dignity as she could muster. Lost for any suitable words, she stalked towards the door and yanked it open. She could still hear his deep chuckle after she slammed it shut behind her.

* * *

Constance did not blush prettily, Aaron realised. She positively glowed with abject mortification. Every inch of her visible, milky white skin had turned a most florid shade of pink. Two circular crimson spots had formed on her cheeks, as if they had been painted on with a brush, and her delicate, swanlike neck was covered in angry blotches. And with her vivid red hair already escaping the confines of its pins, tiny strands floated around her head like sparks rising from a bonfire. She had managed to create an entire spectrum of red above her neck in just a few seconds. Aaron had never seen anything quite like it.

She certainly had not looked anything like the ice maiden he had taken his vows next to or the firebrand he had fought with last night. Nor had she sounded like one. The woman who had just stormed out of his bedchamber was a completely different Constance altogether and one he doubted many people had ever seen. Rumpled, flummoxed, innocent Connie was a delight and Aaron could not help wondering if she blushed all the way down those glorious long legs of hers to the tips of her toes. Now that was a blush he would pay good money to see. To think he had brought about such an unexpected transformation just by attempting to take off his shirt—well, that was just too funny. He had only done it in the first place to remind her that she was overstepping boundaries and to get her to leave. Who knew that regal, haughty, argumentative Miss Stuart was easily embarrassed?

Not Miss Stuart, he corrected, she was Lady Constance Wincanton now. She had been positively outraged to have been called that, too. Those were two little things he would squirrel away as ammunition for the future. Aaron had a feeling he was going to need it. When he had sneaked past her room earlier, in a rare display of complete cowardice, he had just congratulated himself on his stealth. Then she had thrown the book at him.

Literally.

He had not expected that. The irony of that book's title was not lost on him either. Connie could be quite shrewish when she put her mind to it.

But she was a blushing shrew. A shrew who was so loyal to her family that she had agreed to marry a man that she despised. A shrew who had cried in his arms because her fiancé was an idiot and one who had kissed him as if she had been born to do it. Despite all of the inconvenient aspects of his hasty marriage to Connie,

Aaron could still not keep his mind off that kiss. His mind had wandered back to it repeatedly during his ride this morning and each time he caught himself thinking about it he was smiling. It had been such a long time since any of his smiles had been genuine that he had quite forgotten how invigorating one could be. And it had been a most spectacular kiss.

Catching himself smiling wistfully again, Aaron snatched a clean shirt from the wardrobe and then wound a fresh cravat around his neck. He wasn't entirely sure that he could tame Connie, even if he wanted to, but he did need to find a way that they could live together. At least in the short term. He had made his father a promise. He might not want to father a child, but he wanted to put his father's mind at ease. It was the least he could do after everything he had done. He had taken a life so it seemed only fair that he should make one.

Back in her own room, Connie frantically dabbed her hot face with cold water. How she hated being a redhead. Her pale skin provided no camouflage for the embarrassment that had flooded her face and he had seen it. Why did fate keep allowing Aaron Wincanton to see her when she was at her least composed? He had seen her tears, witnessed the first bloom of her passion, been present when her father had cruelly berated her and now he also knew that she was a complete innocent in all matters pertaining to men. At the grand old age of four and twenty, the mere prospect of seeing a man without his shirt on had sent her running for the hills red-faced. All of her perfectly constructed, haughty, uninterested and unflappable façade had disintegrated in seconds and, to add insult to injury, she was more than a little peeved that she had not been brave enough to stand her ground and feast her hungry eyes on the wretch's nude torso. And that wretch had first called her the Ginger Amazonian. It was all too humiliating.

His knock at the door came too soon and Connie forced some steel into her backbone before she went to open it. Aaron completely filled the door frame and was smiling. Just that made her silly pulse speed up. His hair was still slightly damp, which encouraged it to curl up boyishly at the ends, but he was perfectly turned out in a fresh white shirt and dark black coat. He looked exactly like the arrogant and handsome devil that he was and she felt so very unattractive in comparison. Aside from the unflattering pink tinge to her face, her hair was a complete disaster and was wilfully refusing to do as it was told. Connie had never been any good at pinning her own hair into submission, but without a maid of her own she had had no other choice this morning and it showed. She was not really surprised that he had no interest in bedding her. Who would?

'Are you ready for your tour *Mrs Wincanton*?'

'Do not call me that!' It made her sound like his property, which she was, damn him.

'But you continue to call me Mr Wincanton, so I was merely trying to be polite. As you are constantly reminding me not to call you Connie, I confess I am now at a loss at what to call you—perhaps *wife*?' His lips were curving upwards in an expression that he probably knew made him appear to be charming.

'My name is Constance.' Her voice sounded suitably clipped as she gave him her very best imperious stare. It usually withered the most insolent of gentlemen but it only served to make Aaron Wincanton grin. Of course, that drew her eyes to the twin dimples that appeared on either side of his irritatingly perfect face, providing her with two more thing that she wanted to touch. And taste. Good heavens, where did that thought come from?

He was still smiling. 'I dislike the name Constance. It comes from the word constancy. That does not suit you at all.'

'Constancy means steadfast and resolute. I am both of those things.'

He appeared to ponder this for a minute. As he was still blocking the door Connie had no option but to stand and wait for him to finish whatever it was he seemed intent on saying. He smelled delightful.

'I looked the word up in the dictionary. It has many meanings, and whilst I agree you can be stubborn…'

'Steadfast and resolute,' she corrected automatically.

'Constancy also means that something remains the same, no matter what the circumstances. You, *Mrs Wincanton*, are a seething cauldron of different emotions. I never quite know which to expect from one moment to the next. You are as changeable as the weather. Therefore, I simply refuse to call you Constance. Which leaves me in a bit of a quandary. You do not like *Mrs Wincanton* and I could not help noticing that you winced a bit when I affectionately called you wife. So that leaves me with Connie, which was always my preferred choice.'

Connie was still reeling from being compared to a *seething cauldron of emotions*, but worried that he might elaborate on that observation more if she did not concede, so she rolled her eyes and looked down her nose at him. 'Call me what you will.'

Finally, he stepped away from the door and offered her his arm. 'Shall you call me Aaron or *husband*? Or perhaps *my dear* or *my darling*?' His voice had dropped conspiratorially, giving it a seductive edge that set her traitorous pulse fluttering faster. Why did the man always have to resort to flirting? He must know that it was unsettling. Connie had never quite known how to react to it from anyone at the best of times, seeing it as a ruse to get to her dowry or as something disingenuous that was only done because that particular gentleman flirted out of habit. But from him, it was even worse. Whilst he did have a habit of flirting with every woman, he certainly was not flirting with her to get her dowry. It was too late for that. But when Aaron flirted with her, he had a way of staring deeply into her eyes as if he wanted to see into her very soul and truly understand her, which was a completely ridiculous notion. As if he cared one way or another about her soul. But he did have an intensity in his eyes that made her wonder nevertheless. It made her feel all at sea and so pathetically grateful that he had bestowed her with some attention that she did not quite know herself at all.

She limply took his arm, but avoided looking at him. It was easy to picture his smug expression well enough as she felt another ugly blush stain her wan face. 'Lead the way, *Aaron*.'

And now he had just seen her be petulant, too—and she just knew that he was smiling.

Chapter Seven

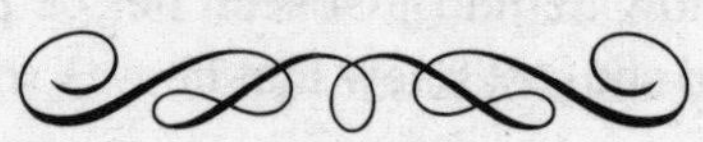

Fortunately, their paths only crossed briefly for the next few days. Connie wiled away the hours reading or embroidering in her own little sitting room, a place that had become both her sanctuary as well as her prison, and longed to go outside and ride as her new husband did. Aaron, on the other hand, disappeared for several hours every morning, surveying the estate. It apparently took up a great deal of his thoughts as well because if he was not out riding around it, he was ensconced in the library or his bedchamber reading about farming methods or animal husbandry or some other such endeavour. But he never invaded her private space and she never invaded his.

Connie was hopelessly lonely. She missed her mother and her brother dreadfully and was desperate to speak to them, but the one letter she had written, and risked sending to Redbridge House, had been unceremoniously returned unopened. The Wincanton servants were polite but understandably wary of her and, because she did not have a particular maid designated to her yet, Connie's only real conversations occurred with her husband. As they were still virtual strangers, and had been brought up to be mortal enemies, those conversations were hardly meaningful.

They met every evening for dinner, and occasionally over lunch, in the small family dining room. When they did, their interactions followed much the same pattern. He would flirt and she would parry haughtily until the pair of them were issuing mindless barbs to top the other. With nothing else to do, those interactions had quite become the highlight of Connie's miserable day. Aside from that they had little to do with one another. Connie had not yet plucked up the courage to broach the subject of an annulment.

A maid disturbed her foray into self-pity. 'Viscount Ardleigh requires your presence in his study, Lady Constance.'

Connie had been dreading the return of Aaron's father. Now it appeared that he was here. 'Is my husband back from his ride yet?' Bizarrely, she did not want to face the viscount for the first time without Aaron, although it was a sorry state of affairs that she desperately wanted his comfort at all when he had made it quite plain he would never want hers.

'Not yet, Lady Constance. Shall I send someone out to find him?'

Connie shook her head. Viscount Ardleigh would see that as cowardice on her part. No matter how terrified she really was about meeting that dreadful man on her own, she would rather walk over broken glass barefoot than let him know that. The last time she had laid eyes on the viscount he had been cruelly laughing at her ruination in front of a room full of onlookers and congratulating his son for doing it. She had been stunned and ashamed.

Vulnerable.

Pathetic.

This time, he would see the unyielding and defiant Constance Stuart.

With a deliberate lack of haste, Connie rose and made her way to the study. It was a room she had only glimpsed from the hallway and, like his bedchamber, Viscount Ardleigh had decorated the walls with the heads of dead animals. She found his love of taxidermy both disturbing, and a little intimidating, but fortunately it was only confined to those two rooms. Outside the door, Connie drew herself up to her full height and composed her features into an indifferent mask. First impressions were important and this one would serve to set the tone of her relationship with her father's worst enemy.

'Enter.' The voice was deep and stern, not at all like his son's seductive, mellow tones that turned her to pudding. Connie grasped the handle and glided inside with her hands folded primly in front of her and her nose ever so slightly in the air because, despite her unfortunate marriage, she was still a Stuart.

'You wished to see me, my lord?' Because politeness dictated that she defer to his title, she inclined her head as little as possible, then looked him straight in the eye. The first thing that she noticed was how like Aaron he was, except much older. The once-dark hair was now more grey than black—but the eyes were almost exact replicas. Almost. Where Aaron's were warm and filled with mischief Viscount Ardleigh's were hard and cold.

'Come closer, girl, so that I can get a proper look at you.' Her new father-in-law made no attempt to disguise the fact that he was looking her up and down. Connie did her best to endure his scrutiny stoically. 'You are so very tall close up, aren't you? But not a dead loss. You have quite good birthing hips and you look fertile enough. Turn around, girl.'

It was like being an insect under a magnifying glance and Connie refused to lower herself further. 'I am not an exhibit in a side show, my lord, therefore I will not turn around and behave like one.'

His grey eyebrows lifted slightly at her refusal. 'You have spirit, I will give you that, Constance Stuart, but I cannot pretend to be happy about this match. I had never thought to have to tolerate a Stuart under my roof. But Aaron is stubborn and I suppose your womb will do as well as any other woman's. However, I must say I am pleased that your betrothal to the Marquis of Deal did not come to fruition, so I suppose I must be grateful for that. Your idiot father must be spitting feathers.' His sharp, angry laugh grated.

There were a hundred spiteful retorts that she wanted to make so it was difficult to know which of his points to take umbrage with first. 'I can assure you, quite emphatically, my lord, that I will not be the mother of *your* grandchildren.'

To her delight that seemed to bring him up short and he glared at her. 'The servants have told me that you keep to your own chamber at night. That will have to stop, missy. I want a grandson!'

'And I want to be a million miles away from you and your dreadful family. It seems that both of us are doomed to have to deal with some disappointment.'

Aaron had not been having a particularly good morning, not that any morning started particularly well any more. He had woken himself up with his own screaming an hour before dawn, drenched in sweat and tangled in the damp bedcovers. As usual, completely shaken and exhausted, he had crawled out of bed straight away to escape the images that haunted him. Bitter experience had taught him that he would not go back to sleep again, not with his heart pounding like a blacksmith's hammer against his ribs and the horrifying memories so fresh in his mind that he could smell the metallic tang of blood as if he were still surrounded by it. Covered in it.

When he had first started having the nightmares after his regiment had stormed Ciudad Rodrigo, Aaron had thought that they would only be temporary. As the war went on, the business of keeping the rest of his men safe had occupied most of his time, the dreams still plaguing him infrequently. They had been awful when they came, but he had been able to separate them from his daily horrors, almost as if he had locked them in a box to keep them for another time. Unfortunately, his box bore a striking similarity to Pandora's. As soon as his feet had stepped back on to English soil it had opened and steadfastly refused to close again. Every painful, horrifying memory had gushed out, demanding atonement. The nightmares were incessant and vivid, coming nightly with alarming regularity. To begin with it had bothered him. Now that he had been home for a few months when so many of his comrades had been left behind to rot in foreign soil, he accepted the nightly ordeal as penance. Under the circumstances, he deserved the torture. He had caused death, therefore like every murderer he should pay.

This morning, Aaron had washed and dressed quickly, saddled his own horse and had been galloping across the estate as the sun's rays first appeared over the horizon. The exercise never made the horror disappear, but it did serve to exorcise the worst of it from his mind so that he could function. Just after dawn he had collided with one of the estate's tenants and the man was not very happy. Once he had noisily aired his grievances Aaron conceded that the man made a valid argument. Apparently, under the terms of his tenancy agreement he had to grow whatever crop the estate wanted him to grow and had to use the seed given to him. Quite rightly, he had wanted to know why the promised seed had not yet been forthcoming, especially as it should have been sown weeks ago. Aaron wanted to know the answer, too, and had promised the poor fellow that he would seek out Thomas, the estate manager, but the man was nowhere to be found.

It confirmed all of Aaron's worries about the future of the estate. He might not yet be an expert on farming, but even he could see that they were unlikely to turn a profit if their crop was so late in the ground. With a growing sense of foreboding, and to have more proof to take to his stubborn father, Aaron had spent the rest of the morning and most of the afternoon checking on the other tenants. All had similar complaints—however, for many the lack of seed was merely the tip of the iceberg. It also appeared that while their revenues were consistently falling each year, the rents that they were charged were rising significantly. Many farmers complained that they were close to not being able to afford to continue. Already, several farms lay abandoned, their fields choked with weeds that would not make any money. Such gross mismanagement was not going to turn around the estate's ailing fortunes any time soon.

Aaron walked his horse into the stable yard, tired and completely worn down, but broke into a run the moment he spied his father's carriage parked outside. The old man had come home early to spite him and probably to cause mischief. The last thing he wanted was his father rubbing Connie up the wrong way, especially as she was showing some signs of civility towards him. Both of them needed a mediator when they collided or likely all hell would soon break lose. Unfortunately, as soon as he stepped foot in the house he heard his father practically roar and realised that he was too late. Hell had already broken and was running loose all over his father's study with its arms waving.

Aaron skidded to a halt outside the open door just in time to witness his fiery wife standing toe to toe and eye to eye with his snarling father. Her elegant hands were curled into her signature angry fists at her sides and Aaron found himself scanning the immediate vicinity for heavy objects in case she was tempted to throw something again. The woman had an excellent aim and a very strong arm. 'I see you have already met?' he said breezily as he walked towards them, smiling as if nothing whatsoever was amiss. Both sets of eyes swivelled angrily in his directions, but neither dropped their combative stance.

'Your wife needs to learn her place, Aaron!'

'Your father needs to learn some manners!'

Someone had to behave like an adult. 'Sit down, the pair of you.' To emphasise that his words were an order, not a request, Aaron forcefully pointed at two empty chairs with each of his hands.

Connie sniffed, but retreated regally to one of the chairs, sitting primly as if butter would not melt in her tart mouth. His father looked a little blue around the gills and his breathing was more laboured than Aaron wanted to hear, but once Connie was sat he reluctantly did the same. He was going to have to tell her, he realised, and hope that she understood. As difficult and beastly as his father was, he was in no state to endure daily combat, no matter how much he might deserve it.

'Has anyone rung for tea?' Convinced that the answer was going to be no, Aaron walked towards the bell pull and gave it a hefty tug before sitting down himself. 'I appreciate that this is an awkward time for all of us,' he began with forced calmness, 'but we are a *family* now and, therefore, we must find a way to live together peaceably.'

'Then I suggest that your father desists from treating me as if I am a brood mare up for purchase. He has done everything except check my teeth!' Connie's usually plump lips were drawn into a thin line and he could feel the outrage radiating off her, so incandescent was her barely controlled anger.

'She says that she refuses to have your children, Aaron. How dare she?'

Aaron felt his spirits sink from despair to despondency. How typical that the pair of them would go for the most controversial of topics straight away. Even the most skilled of diplomats would struggle to find a way out of this bed of thorns and Aaron knew that there was absolutely nothing that he could say, here and now, that would please both of them. Under the circumstances, that left him with only one option and he just knew that he was going to pay dearly for it.

'Connie, could you go to your room, please?' Aaron tried to say it as kindly, yet as adamantly, as he could, but still her smart mouth opened to argue. Much as he hated to do it, he held up his hand to stop her. 'I said go to your room, Constance! We will discuss this later.' And he would probably feel the full weight of *The Complete Farmer* on his cranium, too, but it couldn't be helped. Aaron had to separate them in order to deal with this issue effectively.

Connie's green eyes widened, then he watched them harden into sharp emeralds as she glared back at him with barely disguised contempt. She stood abruptly and flounced out of the room, slamming the door behind her exactly as a true shrew would.

Aaron turned to his father. 'How did you come to be discussing procreation with my new wife?'

The old man had the decency to look a little contrite. 'I merely mentioned the need for a grandson and she took it badly.'

Aaron sincerely did not believe it was quite as innocent as all that. Knowing his father's blunt way of speaking, he suspected he had probably been downright insulting. As usual, the stubborn old man started to bluster to cover his obvious guilt. 'I know that she has denied you your conjugal rights since you married, boy. The servants have told me. Do not bother denying it. I was merely setting her straight. I told her that she needs to open her bedchamber door and her legs for you promptly. The girl has to do her duty!'

'The poor girl has lost her family and her fiancé in one fell swoop, and been publically humiliated in the process. Do you not think that she might need a little time to adjust to her new situation first?'

This was met with belligerent silence.

'Connie is not a bad sort when you get to know her, Father. Yes, she is a little quick tempered…'

'And she's a blasted Stuart!'

'But she is also clever and I believe that she does have the capacity to be reasonable. Going forward, I must insist that you treat her with the respect that she is due—as your daughter-in-law. You can start tonight, at dinner, where I will expect you to be polite. And you will make no mention of conjugal rights.'

For several seconds his father stared at a spot just to the left of Aaron's face before he nodded curtly. 'Do you promise that you will get to work making my grandson?'

'I shall get to it immediately, Father. In the meantime, I think you should get some rest before dinner.'

'I am not a child, Aaron. I will not be mollycoddled.'

'If you will not rest voluntarily, I shall have to fetch the physician.'

Aaron rose as he watched his father glare at him. He could just imagine him considering if the threat was an empty one or not. They would need to talk about the estate later, too, and the likelihood was that conversation as going to be equally as difficult, perhaps even more so. Aaron needed to show that he could not be cowed. For good measure he folded his arms across his chest and glared right back at his father until the old man capitulated.

'Perhaps a little nap wouldn't hurt.'

Chapter Eight

Connie was in grave danger of wearing a hole in the rug with her frenetic pacing, but she was so furious she could not stop. She was not entirely certain which Wincanton she was madder at, his father for being so utterly obnoxious or Aaron for dismissing her so curtly as if she were the one in the wrong. It was probably Aaron. She certainly expected a little more of him. He had not even listened to her complaint properly before he had sent her away. How typical. Hadn't her father just done exactly the same thing? Well, if he thought she was going to take that sort of treatment lying down he had another think coming.

She spun around at the light tap on the door, ready for the fight, and watched it open barely a crack. Instead of Aaron, only his large hand squeezed in and it was waving a white handkerchief. The man was incorrigible! Surely he did not seriously think he could get around her with charm, not after he had so rudely dismissed her like that?

'Oh, just come in, you fool!' Already she could feel the sharp edge of her temper soften despite her determination to remain livid.

The door edged open slowly to reveal him standing there with the handkerchief of surrender in one hand while the other hand held a bucket over his head like a helmet. He surveyed the room with exaggerated wariness before he gingerly stepped inside, still holding his bucket armour about his head and looking, much to her utter consternation, quite delightful. 'I come in peace, Connie. Put down your weapons.'

It was such an unexpected sight that her first reaction was to laugh at the ridiculousness of it. Fortunately, she held the bark of laughter back. She would not be charmed by him. 'How dare you send me out of the room like that? I am not some servant that you can order around!'

'I am sorry. It couldn't be helped.'

'Of course it could. You should have told your rude and ill-mannered father off immediately. He said the most outrageous things to me.'

Aaron nodded contritely. 'He has a blunt way about him sometimes.'

The intense lustre in her green eyes reminded him of a stormy sea he had witnessed one afternoon off of the coast of Portugal. The water had been beautiful, mesmerising and deadly. A stark reminder of the force of nature. Now he was confronted by the full force of Connie's temper, which showed no signs of ebbing any time soon. Her shoulders were thrown back and her delicate pointed chin was already raised, ready to do battle. The stance left the lily-white curve of her neck exposed and he wondered how she would react if he gave in to the sudden urge to place a kiss at the base of it rather than argue with her.

'He said that I looked fertile! That I had birthing hips!' Her voice had risen several octaves and she had started to pace again, using her demonstrative hands to punctuate her words. She was all fire and heat and Aaron found that even in a temper he enjoyed watching her. 'He said that I had to open my…' All of the air rushed out of her lungs in one fell swoop as she swallowed the last word in complete outrage. A small blush of indignation bloomed on her cheeks. 'I have never been spoken to like that in my life!' She stopped pacing then and turned to him. Immediately her expression changed from fury to exasperation. 'Please take that stupid bucket off your head. I refuse to argue with a man who has a bucket on his head.'

'Then if you don't mind, I shall keep it on. I don't want to argue, Connie.'

She hesitated then, before she slumped down on to the chair behind her. All the anger and outrage disappeared and she suddenly looked so very sad and lost. 'I don't want this marriage, Aaron. It is all wrong and doomed to make us both miserable. I am so very unhappy. I want an annulment.'

He had not expected that. The sheer misery in her voice brought him up short. Her eyes rose to his and he saw the suffering and torment swirling in their depths. There were no jokes or clever remarks that would diffuse this situation and his heart ached for her. He lowered the silly bucket to the floor. 'I cannot agree to that, Connie. I'm sorry.'

Aaron's own legs felt oddly unsteady so he sat heavily in the chair across from hers. The very last thing he wanted to do was make her miserable, but he could tell by the way her face had paled, and her posture dissolved, that he had just condemned her to worse than misery.

'Why not? You do not want this marriage either. We were both forced into it. I could argue that my father used the safety and security of my mother as collateral to make me agree to the marriage and you could argue that you felt under an obligation to do the right thing as a result. It all happened so quickly. We have reasonable grounds, Aaron. It has to be worth a try. Please release me.'

Aside from the fact that the process was unlikely to be that simple, and there was a very good chance that it would be thrown out and they would be stuck with each other anyway, it could drag on for years, Aaron did not have years to do what he had promised. 'Please, Connie, do not ask me to do that. I cannot.'

'We both know that you would never have wanted to marry me under any other circumstances. You had your heart set on Violet. If our marriage was declared null and void, you could be free to marry whomever you wanted. I am sure Violet will wait for you.' There was a pleading edge to her voice that tugged at his conscience. 'And I know that your father would be pleased to see the back of me.'

And there, in a nutshell, was the rub. 'You are quite wrong there, Connie. My father would be quite devastated if we started such proceedings now.' Aaron realised that he had to be completely honest with her and had to hope for the best.

'Can I trust you with a secret?' She inclined

her head in acknowledgement, her eyebrows drawn together in confusion. 'He's dying, Connie.'

Instead of the relief or triumph he might have expected from a Stuart at this grave news, Aaron saw sympathy dart across her features and realised that telling her the truth had been the right thing to do. Underneath all of the fire and ice and sharp, acidic tongue Constance Stuart had a heart. Telling her actually felt like a relief. 'His health is in rapid decline and has been for some years. He did not tell me else I would have come home from the Peninsula sooner. The man believes himself to be invincible—but his heart is weak. He suffers from a lung condition that has significantly worsened in the short time since I arrived home. He firmly believes that he has at least a year left. I have kept the truth from him as it feels unnecessarily cruel to burden him with the reality, but his physician believes that he has a few months at best, although realistically he could go at any time. I know better than anyone my father's shortcomings, Connie, but I promised him a grandson. If we begin the proceedings for an annulment now, I will destroy all of the hope that he has for one while he is still alive and I will not do that.'

She was so silent that he could hear the bones

in her stays whisper as she breathed in and out. The breaths came in staccato bursts as she absorbed the enormity of the situation.

'I am to be made to pay the price for this. You would keep me here, against my will, because your father wants an heir?' Her eyes were suddenly dewy, but typically she merely inhaled deeply and gazed back at him proudly, refusing to give in to tears. 'Will you force me to have a child?'

Aaron felt the bile rise in his throat at the suggestion. In truth, he was not fit to be a father to anyone, but he would not admit that to anyone, least of all the delightful woman in front of him. 'Of course not.' Her slim shoulders slumped in relief. 'Even if you were to carry my child, my father will be gone before it could be born. But it matters so much to him that I would like for him to believe that there is a chance of one.'

That was a much better compromise, he realised. He would not have to face the expectation and responsibility of being a father, and the inevitable disappointment that would cause to the unlucky offspring. But if Connie would agree to the ruse, then his father would be placated and would go to his grave a happy man.

'You want me to lie?'

'If you consider making a man's passage from

this life to the next easier by telling him what he wants to hear as a lie, then, yes, Connie. I want you to lie.'

'Why should I? Your father hates my family. He could not have been more disrespectful towards me if he tried. I have no loyalty to either him or you. I would prefer to leave here and live on the streets than pretend to want that man's grandchild!'

She saw his anger then, even though he fought to hide it from her. His jaw clenched and Connie could see the tops of his knuckles whiten as he gripped the arm of the chair. 'Have you ever seen a man go to his death petrified and screaming for the things that matter most to him, Connie? Seen the panic and terror in his eyes when he realises that he has run out of time and that he will go to the grave without any sort of comfort? Have you ever heard grown men weeping like babies, pathetically begging you to fetch their mothers or wives or children so that they can see them one last time and then had to tell those men that you cannot help them? It is the most horrific thing, to see all hope die before death takes them. I have seen it and I wish every day that I had not. Had you seen it, too, then you would know that it is not such a terrible thing to lie to a dying man. Not if you give him hope. No matter how much I sometimes detest my father, I would at least spare him that torment.'

There was no lazy charm or bravado about the man in from of her. His pain was almost visceral and it shocked her to her core. Revealing it to her had also clearly shocked him. He appeared stunned at the enormity of what he had just confessed. Connie watched his Adam's apple bob as he swallowed and saw how ruthlessly he suppressed his anger, as if he were taking it all inside of himself before he turned to her again, the usual half-smile firmly in place, almost as though he were pulling on a mask to hide the real man beneath. 'Give me until then, Connie. Let me allow him to believe that we are man and wife in the literal sense and then, when he goes, I will move heaven and earth to secure you an annulment, if that is what you truly want. I promise.'

Of course, still stunned, she had readily agreed to his terms and he had thanked her and assured her that his father would be on his best behaviour going forward. Then he had left her, as if nothing meaningful had just passed between them and there was not an abyss of torment hidden behind his russet eyes. But Connie worried about what she had seen for the rest of the afternoon and wished that she was brave enough to offer him some comfort.

* * *

Dinner was a stilted affair, although Viscount Ardleigh remained polite, even though he made no secret of the fact that he was doing it under duress, and Connie allowed Aaron to bait her so that they could exchange a version of their usual sparring to relieve some of the awkwardness of the meal. She had excused herself after that, ostensibly to leave them to their port and male conversation, but she had found the whole ordeal quite draining. To know that you sat opposite one who was so close to death—who did not know that it was imminent, and conscious that he would be mortified to know that she knew that—had made the meal even more trying. But she had made Aaron a promise and would be rewarded with her freedom in due course. Once she had thought about it all, her compliance did seem a small price to pay.

However, Aaron's intense reaction and the emotion that she had seen fleetingly in his dark eyes made her wonder about the man she was temporarily married to. Connie requested a bath be drawn and spent the better part of an hour soaking in it and pondering that question. What did she really know about Aaron Wincanton?

All these years she had thought him to be one of those superficial but confident types. He had always been at the centre of any social affair, laughing, telling amusing stories and charming everyone from the crustiest old curmudgeon to the most invisible of wallflowers. Such things came so naturally to him. To think that he might have hidden depths beneath all of that ease and swagger, that he also might feel things a little too deeply and be wounded by events, was unnerving.

It was strange and probably showed her complete lack of understanding about war, but when he had come back home a few months ago and been heralded as a hero for all of his brave deeds in the battle against Napoleon, Connie had been dismissive. How like Aaron Wincanton to blithely go off to war and come back the darling of everyone and a hero to boot. The adoration of others had always been something that he appeared to achieve without any effort. She had always envied that about him. How could he be so confident and so charming and so comfortable in his own skin when she found such things so difficult? Aaron Wincanton always gave the impression that he tiptoed through life largely unscathed.

But he hadn't. *Have you ever seen a man go to his death petrified and screaming?* Imagining the horror of what he had described was almost too awful to contemplate, but she now knew that he had witnessed such things and that they had hurt him. Deeply. And he still carried all of that hurt around with him. She was sure of it. Connie had seen his pain with her own eyes, felt the power it had over him for a split second before she had watched him cover it as if it did not matter. Almost as if it had not happened at all. Like her, she now had to entertain the prospect that he also wore a face in public that was quite different to the one he wore when he was alone with himself. Oddly, she felt almost privileged to have seen that.

By the time that she was dressed in a fresh nightgown and sat on a low footstool in front of the fire so that her unruly, thick hair could dry, Connie was feeling quite unsettled. She supposed that it was unsurprising as it had been a taxing day. Despite the revelations about the failing health of Viscount Ardleigh and the new and burning questions she now had concerning Aaron's experience on the battlefields, at least there was now a light at the end of the tunnel. He had agreed to an annulment, even if she did have to wait a few months for the proceedings to begin. She could make plans for a new life somewhere where she was not a duty or a burden. That had to be a good thing, didn't it? As her husband was being quite generous, Connie made a silent vow to behave more benevolently towards him going forward. It must be difficult to sit by and watch the demise of a parent whilst pretending that all was well. If nothing else positive came out of this travesty of a marriage, at least she could ease his burden on that score just a little bit. She hated all of this forced inactivity and lack of purpose. It would be better to do something.

Connie tipped her head forward and drew her brush through the underside of her hair. It always took such a long time to dry. If she had had any sense she would have delayed washing it until the morning. Now, she would have to wait up another hour. The light tap on the door startled her at first, but assuming that it was a maid come to see if she needed anything before she retired for the night, Connie did not move from her spot by the fire.

'Come in.'

She heard the door open and footsteps approach, but the maid never said a word. Flipping her hair back to its proper place, Connie turned towards her with a smile.

Chapter Nine

Aaron had never seen quite so much magnificent hair in all of his life. Unbound, it hung all the way down to her waist in sensual, copper waves that positively glowed in the firelight as if they were burning from within like the hot embers crackling in the hearth. In places it was still slightly damp, he noticed, making some of the heavy tendrils appear almost chestnut brown in a sea of swirling red. Her skin was rosy from her bath and he found himself wondering exactly what lay beneath that chaste and proper nightgown.

'What do you want?'

Her initial smile had been replaced by a look of bewilderment. Aaron watched her eyes flick towards the cut-crystal balloon glasses he held in one hand, then to the brandy decanter he held in the other. It occurred to him that her hair and the brandy were much the same colour and both were enhanced by the firelight.

'If I am trying to pretend to my father that I am impregnating you, I cannot do that from down the hall. Besides, my father will be kept informed of our nocturnal habits by the servants. You are going to have to put up with my company every evening from now on. Just to put on a convincing show, of course.' In an attempt to divert his attention away from the alluring sight of her sat by the hearth and the embarrassing topic of the conversation, he set the two glasses on the small table near the sofa and began to pour a healthy amount of the amber liquid into them. Bizarrely, his hand shook slightly.

'Yes, of course. That does make sense.'

Aaron made the mistake of turning towards her as she slowly rose from her low position on the footstool. Fortunately, she was unaware of the fact that, with the firelight behind her, the gauzy material of the voluminous nightgown became more translucent. It no longer took his imagination to wonder what lay beneath. The dark silhouette of her lithe body was illuminated like a cameo. Aaron could make out the gentle mounds of her shadowed breasts, the trim waist and the seductive curve of her hip. His eyes moved lower, taking in the unbelievably long, shapely legs and felt his breath quicken. Unwanted images of those legs wrapped around him filled his mind and the memory of the silky feel of the skin on her thigh came back to haunt him, forcing him to take a large gulp of his brandy to cover his reaction. A little startled, he turned away from her and pretended to take in the room.

He sensed when she came up alongside him. The fragrance of her perfume wafted under his nose, exactly the same heady fragrance he had first smelled that fateful night in the library where they had lost their heads. The sultry undertones of rose were more intoxicating than the alcohol he held clenched his hand. Quite why she was having such an effect on him, he could not say. His body had shown no interest in any woman in the better part of a year. Apart from her. That one time. But now, apparently, it had decided to reawaken. Aaron hastily sat in one of the large armchairs to disguise the fact that half of the blood in his body had suddenly just rushed to his groin.

How inconvenient. For the sake of appearances, he would have to visit her here almost every evening for as long as was necessary to maintain the ruse. Was he now doomed to suffer through these visits in a state of complete and unwelcome arousal as well? He had promised the girl an annulment so he could hardly take her to bed. But he wanted to.

That came as a shock. He wanted to bed his wife and he couldn't. Fate certainly had a warped sense of humour.

Connie picked up the other brandy glass and perched in the chair opposite him, feeling at a distinct disadvantage. He was perfectly dressed, as usual, without a single dark hair out of place. She was naked under her nightgown, with all of her own unruly hair twisting into its usual tangle of brambles all around her shoulders. If she hastily plaited it now it would appear that she was bothered to been seen in such a state and he would find her vanity amusing. He would assume that she had wanted to improve her appearance just for him. Therefore, she had to appear as unaffected by this intimate intrusion into her private quarters as he was, despite the fact that she had never been so aware of her own body before or wished that she was wearing several protective layers of protective clothing under her nightgown. To cover her embarrassment, she took a sip of her brandy and felt the liquid burn a warm path down her throat. When the brandy hit her stomach she found the warmth it created there strangely calming, so she drank a little more. 'If we are going to be thrust together like this for the next few months, we might as well get to know each other better.' Clearly the drink was also making her bolder as well.

Connie watched fascinated as he cupped the bowl of the glass in his palm and swirled the golden liquid around. 'I agree. We can hardly spend the next few months arguing. That will soon become quite wearing. Shall we begin by asking each other some simple questions?' He was smiling that lazy, slightly flirtatious smile again. 'Shall I begin? What is your favourite colour?'

Connie answered without hesitation, 'Emerald green.'

'Like your eyes.'

He thought her eyes were like emeralds? Flattered, Connie took another quick sip of her brandy to cover the silly smile that threatened. 'What is your favourite colour?'

'I am not altogether sure that I have one—but I have become rather partial to red of late.'

The bubble of laughter escaped from her lips before she could stop it. 'You really are the most shameless flirt, Aaron. Do you practise it? Or does it come naturally?'

She watched him lean back into the chair and

make himself comfortable before he answered. 'In the spirit of honesty, I will admit that I used to practise it a great deal when I was younger. Now, I think most of it just spills from my mouth naturally. Out of habit'

'Do you ever mean any of it?'

She could see that her question surprised him because there was laughter in his eyes. Laughter in his eyes? What on earth was the matter with her to suddenly be so poetic? It was probably the brandy scrambling her wits. Just in case, she put down the glass.

'I mean everything that I say. Usually. As I am sure you do to.'

'*Touché*. Perhaps it is better if we ask questions about more practical topics. What did you win your medals for?'

For the briefest of moments his face clouded and then the clouds dispersed. 'Surviving.'

He did not elaborate and quickly changed the subject. 'What do you enjoy doing, Connie, when you are not railing at me, of course?'

'I like to read. Not the sort of learned tomes you do, but I enjoy novels. I also love to ride.'

A devastating smile split his face. 'You do? That is splendid. So do I. Perhaps we should ride together tomorrow?'

The suggestion pleased Connie immensely

and she forgot to behave in a uninterested and haughty manner. It would feel so wonderful to get out and enjoy the fresh air. She felt herself grinning in return. 'I would love that! I am curious to see the Wincanton estate.'

He told her then of all of the best places to ride on his land and of his great love of horses. She told him about how she had learnt to ride and described her favourite parts of her father's estate next door. In doing so, Connie felt suddenly homesick and desperately floundered for something else to talk about that was not as personal or as sensitive to her.

'Do you love Violet Garfield?'

He actually laughed at that. Amusement crinkled his eyes as he poured the last of his brandy down his throat. 'No, Connie. I tried to care about her and I actually find her sweet but, no, I do not love Violet.'

'Then why were you going to propose to her?'

There was an over-long pause before he answered and Connie noticed that he did not meet her eyes. 'My father wants a grandson and therefore I needed to marry someone quickly to ensure that it happened in time. Speed was of the essence and Violet appeared to be open to the idea. Why did you agree to marry the Marquis of Deal?'

'He asked me.' As soon as she uttered the words she regretted them. The brandy was loosening her tongue. Aaron sat forward in his chair, his dark eyebrows drawn together as he regarded her with undisguised interest.

'Really? That was the only reason?'

She had just admitted her desperation and her lack of suitors to Aaron Wincanton. Connie felt incredibly stupid and gauche, but tried to cover it with her usual haughty disdain. 'My father chose him. He thought it would be a good match. I am a pragmatist. I know that I am not the sort of woman who appeals to the majority of men and I had no desire to remain a spinster. Deal suited that purpose well enough.'

'So your heart was not engaged?'

'Not in the slightest.' It was then that she remembered how he had seen her cry when her fiancé had made his ambivalent feelings towards her plain and knew that Aaron did not believe her blithe words at all. At his look of disbelief, she deflected. 'Your father said that he was relieved when my betrothal was called off. Why would he care who I married?' That odd comment had niggled her all day. Ardleigh had laughed because her father must be *spitting feathers*. An odd turn of phrase that suggested that she was missing something.

Aaron had been about to take another sip of his drink, but the glass paused midway. There was bemusement in his expression. 'Did it not occur to you that your father had arranged your marriage to spite my father? You do know that the Marquis of Deal's estate borders the Wincanton estate to the south. Or did you think that was simply a coincidence?'

The awful reality was that she had never even considered it. She had been so relieved to have received an offer of marriage from a handsome and titled gentleman that she had never considered that her father had arranged her future so strategically. That realisation was accompanied by an overwhelming sense of disappointment. Not just at her own pathetic stupidity in being so hopelessly flattered by it all, but also in the way her father had manipulated the situation to benefit himself. No wonder he had urged her to ignore Deal's philandering. He had put his own desire to get one up on the Wincantons above the happiness of his only daughter. Once again, Connie had been made to look a fool in front of Aaron Wincanton, who had the nerve to be wearing an expression of pity. It suggested that he, too, knew that she was pathetic. She wanted to slap it off his face.

'How much longer do you need to stay here?

It has been a very long day and I am tired.' The words came out without any real venom, but fortunately he took his cue and stood.

'I did not mean to upset you again, Connie.'

'The only thing upsetting me is your continued presence. Whilst I have agreed to your request to maintain this charade for the sake of your father, do not take that to mean that I think any better of you, Aaron Wincanton. I still dislike you and would prefer to spend as little time in your company as possible until this marriage is annulled.'

Connie turned and walked swiftly towards her bedchamber door without a backwards glance. Only once she was safely on the other side, her back pressed against the wood, did she allow the tears of shame to fall.

Chapter Ten

The maid woke Connie early with a breakfast tray. 'Mr Aaron said that he will meet you in the stable yard at eight, Lady Constance.'

Connie considered sending the maid back with an excuse and then rapidly decided against it. She would not be cowardly and avoid him. At some point today she would have to face him so she might as well get it over with. Besides, she was desperate to get out in the fresh air again and did not want to squander the opportunity to go riding. He might never ask her again and she was not convinced that it was an activity that she would be allowed to do alone. She ate quickly, allowed the maid to pin her hair to within an inch of its life and then donned her favourite forest-green riding habit before she hurried outside.

Aaron was waiting for her in the stable yard as promised, a lively looking chestnut mare already saddled next to his horse. She watched his eyes scan the entire length of her body before he smiled lazily and wished her a good morning. He was probably thinking how gigantic she looked. The habit was cut to show off her willowy figure to its best advantage, but whilst she did like the way it made her appear to have curves, it also emphasised her extreme height. Her father had been most critical of the outfit, claiming that in it she appeared to be all legs and no bosom and that no man wants to be seen riding with a giraffe. Connie would not lower herself to crouching beneath the folds of the skirt in order to look more feminine. She already knew that he did not find her the least bit attractive, so why bother? Theirs was a temporary marriage, thank goodness. Nothing more. Defiant pride made her smile back with equal cheerfulness and Connie deliberately pulled herself up to her full height as she strode purposefully towards her horse.

He looked a little sheepish then, but fortunately made no mention of her former fiancé. 'I thought that we might have a side saddle, but alas we do not. Ardleigh Manor has been a house of solely men for too many years.'

A robust and proper gentleman's saddle was strapped on the mare's back and Connie blinked at it covetously. She had always wanted to ride astride. It always appeared to be so much more fun. On a side saddle she could never truly gallop fast and always had to be conscious of her balance and her ladylike posture. Riding astride was more daring, and thus far more appealing, however, for appearance's sake, she regarded the thing with distaste. 'I am sure that I can manage well enough.'

A groom scrambled forward with a riding block, but Aaron shooed him away. With a smug grin he cupped his hands so that he could bolster her foot. Connie purposefully ignored it. At times, there was great benefit in being so tall. One of them was that she certainly did not need anyone's help to get on a horse, especially his. Boldly, she placed one foot in the stirrup and then hoisted herself on to the back of the horse. Only once she was sat astride the saddle did the limitations of the tight riding habit present itself. The skirt had been designed to have as little bunched fabric as possible when she was perched on a side saddle. Therefore, there was precious little extra fabric to accommodate the width of her splayed legs on the top of the animal. The hem of the skirt had risen in protest, giving her new husband an excellent view of her calves, whilst the top of the skirt was stretched tight across her thighs and bottom. Desperately she tried to wiggle it down to no avail.

'Allow me.'

To Connie's complete consternation, Aaron reached up and manoeuvred the heavy fabric around her thighs so that he could cover the majority of her modesty. This operation took much longer than Connie felt was necessary and was made worse by the fact that she could feel the heat of his gloveless hands, all the way through the layers of skirt and petticoat, until an imprint of them was seared on to her very skin. Her ankles were still on full display to the world when he stepped back and grinned knowingly. At a loss of what else to do, and still feeling shaken by the effect of his touch, Connie thrust her nose in the air and stared out over the fields beyond.

Aaron mounted his horse quickly and the pair of them set off at a sedate pace out of the yard and up a well-worn path away from the house. Connie had to concede that even now, at the start of winter when all was at its bleakest, the woodland and meadow surrounding the estate was quite lovely. Aaron pointed out the occasional feature or entertained her with stories about scrapes he had got into as a boy. By the time they crested a small hill, Connie's horse was sufficiently warmed up and she was aching to feel the wind on her face.

'I will race you to that copse of trees.' It might not be ladylike, but it was hardly as if her father was ever likely to get wind of it and, even if he did, it really was none of his business any longer. There were some benefits to the estrangement after all. That thought made her feel much better, so she crouched low over the horse's neck and nudged him to go faster still. It felt marvellous.

Before Aaron was prepared, she had raced off ahead of him, a broad smile on her face and her body moving gracefully in the saddle as if she had been born to ride. He chivvied his own horse into a gallop, holding the beast back so that he could keep a short distance between them. In his mind he rationalised this behaviour as gentlemanly. It would make her happy to win. But in truth, from that position he could also enjoy the spectacular sight of her rounded bottom bouncing in the saddle, snugly encased in green velvet.

And he had thought that she looked splendid when he had first spied her in that outrageously bold riding habit. It had fitted her like a glove, highlighting the womanly curve of her trim waist where it met her hips. From there downwards was a slim column of green that went on and on until it hit the floor. The woman had legs that went on for ever. After catching an illicit glimpse of the shape of those magnificent legs last night, he had spent a great deal of time thinking about them. Before he had inevitably woken himself up screaming, he was certain that he had dreamt about them, too. He had certainly drifted off to sleep, wondering what it might feel like to run his fingers through all of that hair when he should have been thinking about how to salvage the estate. Connie had a way of permeating a great many of his thoughts since they had been thrust together. Even now. His morning rides had been a place to strategise about the future of Ardleigh Manor or contemplate his guilt—but there would be no strategising or guilt today. His new wife was too much of a distraction.

By the time they reached the trees they were both a little breathless. The ridiculously small hat that she had pinned on the top of her tightly bound hair was slightly askew, several copper tendrils had sprung free of their pins and were beginning to curl in the damp morning air. Combined with the victorious grin that lit up her eyes, the overall effect was simply stunning. It fair took his breath away.

What did not make any sense to Aaron was the fact that she had agreed to marry that wastrel Deal purely because he had asked her. That little snippet she had inadvertently let slip had occupied his thoughts a great deal last night and he still could not understand why she would sell herself so short this morning. Surely other men had asked? Connie had caused quite a stir when she had first come out, he remembered. Every young buck had been positively gushing about how glorious she was. One or two compared her poetically to a Titian painting but, he recalled with sudden clarity, when he had first seen her all those years ago he had thought that she was more like Botticelli's *Birth of Venus*, rising proudly out of a giant clam shell, red hair tumbling carelessly over her milky-white shoulders and looking positively ripe for seducing.

How was is possible that five years later such a fine specimen of womanhood was still on the marriage mart? Unless she had frightened all potential suitors off with her feigned haughtiness and uninterest. And it was feigned, he now knew. Connie used it as a disguise in much the same way he used his charm. He had seen her reach for the emotion last night when she had realised that her betrothal to Deal had been nothing more than a way of perpetuating the feud. He had watched her transform her features from anguish into indifference and had wanted to go to her and hold her, and tell her that she did not have to wear her mask with him. Except if he did that then she might expect him to do the same—a preposterous thought that he could never entertain. He had left then, knowing that it would be simpler if they both played the characters that made them feel safest, and had regretted it instantly.

The smiling creature riding next to him appeared not to be wearing her mask at this moment. Connie looked relaxed and happy to be outside. Aaron let her gloat about her victory as they rode around the trees to the empty fields behind, secretly pleased that he had made her happy with such a simple act.

'Why are your crops not planted?' she asked after a minute, taking in the acres and acres of nothingness.

'A very good question, Connie, and one that I cannot answer. I suspect my father's estate manager is an idiot.'

'I do not know a great deal about farming, but surely if the man is an idiot your father should dismiss him and hire someone more competent?'

Aaron gave her a wry smile. If only things were that simple. 'Unfortunately, my father will not hear a bad word against the fellow. Mr Thomas is credited with orchestrating the purchase of land next to your father's estate. Therefore, he is a genius according to my father.'

'Because nothing is more important than the feud.' She understood instantly and gazed off into the distance. 'My own father is much the same. His main priority always has been the feud, too. Nothing else matters quite so much. Not peace or harmony and definitely not daughters.'

Her face had clouded a little and he realised that she was thinking about her betrothal again, only this morning she was inclined to be more reasonable about it. That was another thing he had noticed about her. Her temper burned hot, but quickly disappeared. She did not hold a grudge very well and faced her own shortcomings head on. He envied that.

'I did think that you knew that Deal's land borders ours. I wasn't trying to be cruel last night, Connie.'

She brushed his apology away with a swat of her green-gloved hand. 'I should have realised it myself. The signs were there. Why else would a man like Deal agree to marry me? I am quite annoyed that it never occurred to me sooner.' But she had been so desperate to be a wife and a mother that she had ignored her better judgement, preferring to fool herself into believing he might miraculously grow to love her one day. As if a beautiful man like that would find something attractive in a gangly, ginger-haired giant. Connie doubted she would ever forget the look of disgust that had passed across her fiancé's golden features when he had explained why he had agreed to the betrothal. If ever she had needed clarification of how unappealing she was as a woman, then that had been it. Yet Aaron's words had also wounded. Perhaps more so. *What sort of a man would willingly want to bed a shrew like you?* She would spare him that ordeal because he had been honourable in marrying her. They rode in silence a little longer, side by side, neither looking at the other.

'For what it's worth,' he suddenly blurted with an irritated expression on his handsome face, 'I am glad that you never married Deal.'

Connie stared resolutely ahead because she did not want him to see how much talking about it hurt. 'I am sure you are. It would have been very inconvenient if my father's plan had succeeded. You would be surrounded by Stuarts and my father would have the upper hand once again.'

'Stop being daft, Connie!'

She could feel herself bristle at his harsh tone and was about to give him a set down when he surprised her.

'I do not give two farthings if this estate is positively ringed by Stuarts. I keep telling you that the silly feud needs to stop—and that I refuse to play any part of it. What I meant was Deal is a toad of a man. He's a gambling, narcissistic lecher. The man brags about his many conquests at White's and shows no regard or respect for the poor women he has seduced. I have always found him to be quite odious. You deserve better than that, Connie. And it irritates me to hear you sell yourself short by claiming you agreed to marry him simply because he asked.'

He looked irritated and that irritation on her behalf was very flattering. In case he saw that, she encouraged her horse to trot ahead of his before she allowed herself a little smile. She could not remember another man, save her brother, ever coming to her defence before. A little part of her heart rejoiced at that.

They rounded another copse of trees and the sight beyond brought Connie up short.

Redbridge House.

She could see it plainly in the distance, so near that she could just about make out the wisps of smoke coming out of the four large chimneys on its roof. If all of the fires were lit, then that could only mean one thing. Her family were in residence. The wave of longing was so swift and sudden that she could not hide it as he pulled his horse up alongside.

'You miss your family.'

'I miss my mother and my brother.' There was no point denying that. She did not care one whit about her spiteful, critical father.

'Perhaps you should write to them? I am sure that they would be glad to hear from you.'

It occurred to Connie then that Aaron was not keeping tabs on her, else he would have known that she had already tried. 'Then you do not know my father. I sent a letter a few days ago. It came back unopened.'

'Your brother and mother might think differently. Perhaps you should write to one of them.'

Connie turned her horse abruptly away from the painful view. 'I am sure my father would ensure that any letters would be intercepted before they got to the rest of my family. You were there, Aaron, when he said that I was dead to him. The man never backs down.' Once again she saw a flash of pity in his eyes and decided to nip it in the bud. 'Let us not talk about it any more. Discussing it is pointless and will only serve to spoil my ride.'

They meandered slowly back towards Ardleigh Manor, the mood somewhat more sombre than he had been. Aaron said little, which she was grateful for, and was apparently deep in thought. Two stable lads intercepted them in the yard and led the horses away and Aaron offered her his arm as they walked back towards the house. In the spirit of their awkward truce, she took it, trying not to enjoy the solid feel of him beneath her hand or remember how that arm had once held her with such passion.

The sound of another horse arriving behind them had them both turning. 'That is Mr Thomas,' Aaron said with a mixture of urgency tinged with disgust. He abruptly disentangled her arm from his. 'If you will excuse me, Connie, I really need to talk to him.'

He practically sprinted back towards the stable yard, leaving Connie rooted to the spot. Mr Thomas's eyes met and locked with hers. For an instant he appeared startled, then he inclined his head politely before turning his full attention back to Aaron as if nothing untoward was going on at all.

Except it was. Connie had seen Mr Thomas before. Many times. The last time had been a little over a fortnight ago, in her father's study.

Chapter Eleven

Connie had no idea how to react or what to do, so she went inside and quickly changed, wrapping herself in a warm shawl before heading back downstairs. Pretending to go out for a walk, Connie wandered nervously up and down the paths closet to the stables, looking for any sign of Mr Thomas and filled with an enormous sense of foreboding. There was more afoot here than she had been aware of and unexpectedly she found her loyalty torn. Eventually she saw him striding towards the building. Fortunately, he was alone.

'Mr Thomas! Might I have a word?'

He spun around and then gave her a slow smile before walking towards her, then bowed politely. 'Lady Constance, what an unexpected pleasure.'

'I hardly think it should be unexpected, sir,

not when we both know that you have dealings with my father. You must have realised I would seek you out and demand an explanation the moment I clapped eyes on you. Why are you here?'

'Have you told all this to your husband?' The man's eyes were suddenly cold and his expression, although trying to remain bland, was also hostile. It made Connie feel uneasy.

'Not yet.'

She watched his shoulders sag with relief before he pinned her with his gaze. 'Good. Let us keep it that way. I dare say he would get quite the wrong impression. I am merely of an acquaintance of your father's, though Viscount Ardleigh and his son might not be particularly forgiving of that relationship if they were to find out about it.'

'You are more than a passing acquaintance, Mr Thomas. You have visited Redbridge House at least once a month for several years. I believe that you are working for my father. He is using you to sabotage the Wincantons in some way. That is why the fields still lay idle, isn't it?'

The estate manager's eyes narrowed and his voice became clipped. 'I can assure you, madam, that I have no idea what you are talking about. I am simply an acquaintance of your father's. That has nothing to do with my position here. Occasionally, I might tell your father snippets of what the Wincantons are up to, in passing conversation, but that is hardly a crime.'

'Do you expect me to believe that your only purpose here is to keep my father informed of the latest gossip? I am not a fool, sir.'

His thin lips curled into a snarl as he watched her coldly. 'Your father would be very disappointed in you if he heard that you had interfered in his *personal* business, Lady Constance.'

'My father is already disappointed in me, Mr Thomas, as I am sure the whole world now knows, therefore I fail to see what difference my interference would make.' Connie turned on her heel and began to march away. She had to find Aaron and tell him.

'I should imagine that it is very painful to be estranged from one's family, Lady Constance.' Instantly, Connie's footsteps slowed and she turned back to the estate manager suspiciously. Mr Thomas merely smiled. 'You always did have such a strong bond with your mother. I have seen first-hand the strain this breach has put on her. I dare say she misses you as much as you miss her—and your father can be quite stubborn. However, I am certain that his poor opinion of you will change once he hears of your loyalty and discretion in this *delicate* matter.'

'I doubt my father would bend, sir, in which

case you are asking me to be disloyal to my husband for naught.' Why did she suddenly feel the need to be loyal to Aaron Wincanton? It was not as if she had any affection for the man or owed him anything. Yet she felt it just the same.

Mr Thomas was all charm and subservience again. 'Perhaps. And then again perhaps not. I was only with your father yesterday and he did *specifically* ask me to enquire about your health. He mentioned something in passing about how badly his wife was taking it all and he wanted to know if you were well cared for. I am to report back to him straight away if there is anything amiss.' He paused briefly to let this news sink in and when he next spoke it was conspiratorially. 'The Earl of Redbridge might be stubborn, but he is also still your father. His feelings for you are still there and his anger will pass in time. I know it will pass more quickly if you keep our little secret. Just for a little while. It might be just what is needed to heal the breach between you.'

Everything about what he was suggesting did not sit well with her—yet still she was seduced by the possibility. The idea that her father had enquired about her gave her some hope. He *would* see it as disloyal if she interfered and that could only serve to make the gulf between them wider. And she was desperate to see her mother again. Once her marriage was dissolved, her father might see his way to allowing her to visit from time to time if she could prove to be an asset to him while she was here. It was not as if she had any loyalty to the Wincantons. But Aaron had been noble in marrying her and he was kind. Did he deserve such duplicitousness?

Mr Thomas sensed her dilemma and regarded her solemnly. 'I give you my word, my lady, that nothing untoward is going on. I merely keep your father abreast of the Wincanton family and what they are doing.'

'If I have any doubt about that, be advised, Mr Thomas, that the first person I shall speak to is my husband.' Connie did not really believe the man. It was all too coincidental, but the prospect of seeing her mother and brother again was too tempting to risk offending her father further. For the time being she would maintain the status quo. If there was the slightest chance that she could heal the rift, then she had to give it a go. She would hold her tongue for as long as it took her to find proof that Mr Thomas was a liar and no longer. What difference did a few more weeks make?

Aaron arrived at the door of Connie's sitting room a respectable hour after they had endured another awkward dinner with his father. The fraught atmosphere was made worse by the fact that Aaron and the old man had been arguing about the state of the fields for most of the afternoon. But his father would not listen to reason and Aaron was hesitant to push him too far in case it overtaxed his fragile heart. For the time being, they agreed to disagree. A situation that was beyond frustrating because with every passing day things were becoming less salvageable.

Unfortunately, Connie was not in her nightdress when she bid him to enter. In fact, she was as formally dressed as she had been at the dinner table and was sitting primly on her sofa, embroidering something. He would have much preferred to see her drying her splendid hair by the fire, although this way was probably for the best.

'I brought port this time,' he said, waving the decanter in front of her and she smiled stiffly in response, barely lifting her eyes from her sewing. Her guard was up again, he could tell, and Aaron decided he was fonder of her when she was being true to herself.

'I have never tasted port.'

'Then you are in for a treat. This is one of my father's best bottles. I pilfered it from the cellar and he would be livid if he knew that I had taken it. He would be more livid if he knew that I was sharing it with a Stuart.'

'Then I shall enjoy the taste of it even more.'

He saw a brief flash of her humour then. Her green eyes had lit up with mischief and wiped away the mask for a moment. Aaron poured them both a glass and sat down on the armchair opposite. 'I am going to visit some of the tenants tomorrow if you would like to come with me? There are a lot of them so I will give you fair warning that you might be stuck in the saddle for a couple of hours.' Aaron also wanted to check up on Mr Thomas. The man had claimed that the seed would be delivered to all of the tenants on the morrow and Aaron wanted to catch him out on that blatant lie. Perhaps then his father would listen to reason and dismiss the wastrel. Of course, there was no real reason for dragging Connie around while he did this, except for the fact that he had found her presence today soothing.

Most mornings since his return, he rode around aimlessly for hours, trying to banish the horrifying images of his dreams from his mind. To his complete surprise, he had found that process much easier to do with Connie in tow. He had forgotten today's nightmare at almost the exact moment she had brazenly marched up to him in that magnificent riding habit. Lustful feelings aside, he had also thoroughly enjoyed her company. It had been nice to have somebody intelligent and witty to talk to rather than moping around on his own, stewing in his own pessimistic juices. Being with Connie made him feel more normal.

She positively beamed at him, forgetting to be haughty and uninterested, or regally benevolent. 'I would like that immensely! Do you think we might find the time to squeeze in another race? I thoroughly enjoyed thrashing you this morning.'

Aaron had enjoyed it, too, but for very different reasons. 'We can race from cottage to cottage if you want to.'

'Oh, I want to! I have not had so much fun in ages. My father forbade me from racing years ago. He said it was not ladylike.' She lowered her embroidery frame and the corners of her pink lips curved slightly, although her eyes clouded at the mention of her father. 'That has always been his most common criticism of me. Racing is not ladylike, arguing is not ladylike and having such strong opinions, and daring to voice them, are certainly not ladylike. Do you know he once told me that my red hair was not proper at all and that towering over everyone was not ladylike either? I think I have been a tremendous disappointment to him, aside from the fact that I went and got myself ruined, of course, because I have been quite unable to stop doing all of those things that he most dislikes about me. I do not think I have been a very good daughter.'

Bizarrely, she was smiling wistfully at the memory so Aaron held back what he wanted to say. He did not want to sour the mood by telling her that he thought her father was a nasty piece of work. He rather liked her height, her eyes and lips came level with his, and as for her hair? How the devil could hair be unladylike when it was quite the most beautiful head of hair he had ever seen? It was simply further proof to him that the Earl of Redbridge was a tyrant and a fool. Much like his own stubborn sire.

'Pay it no mind, Connie. As a fellow disappointment to a parent I can assure you that you will never truly be able to please him, no matter how hard you try.'

She lowered her embroidery again and gazed at him intently. 'How have you disappointed your father? Aside from marrying me, of course.'

Where to start? 'My father has always enjoyed hunting and I do not. When I was younger he used to force me to accompany him in the hope that it would toughen me up. He used to get very frustrated when I refused to kill anything.'

'Then I am to assume that you are not responsible for any of those ghastly stuffed heads?'

Aaron pulled a face that made her smile. 'They are awful, aren't they? But to answer your question, I am not responsible for even one of them. I could never understand what pleasure there was in chasing a frightened, senseless animal through the woods unless you needed to eat them. That disappointed my father a great deal. He was also dead against me joining the army. I had to wait until I reached the age of majority and then I had to purchase my own commission. My father thought he would stop me by reducing my allowance to such a paltry sum that I could barely afford to go out.'

'How did you manage to purchase a commission and a uniform? Those things are expensive.'

Now it was his turn to smile at a memory. 'I took all of the money I received religiously to a gaming hell and gambled until I had won enough to buy it all for myself. My father was livid when I came home in my new regimentals. He threatened to disinherit me.'

'But he did not?'

'This house, the estate and the title are all hereditary. The worst he could do was banish me until he died. The law states that it would still all come to me regardless of his wishes. Once I realised that, I knew all of his threats were empty ones. My father likes to control things. He could hardly attempt to control me if he had disowned me. It was all bluster and I called his bluff, the stubborn old fool.' She watched him take a sip of his port to cover his sudden agitation. 'He is still being stubborn. I tried to talk to him about the estate again today and refused to leave his study when he met with Mr Thomas.'

Inadvertently, he had given her an opening that she was not prepared to squander. Connie peered at Aaron over the top of her embroidery frame, suddenly nervous. Subtlety had never really been her strong suit and she would need to be very subtle now if she was going to find out what Mr Thomas was truly up to without tipping Aaron off. 'Did you find out why your estate manager has not yet planted the fields?' She pretended to focus on her sewing as if she were merely making polite conversation.

Connie could hear the frustration in his voice. 'That man is a weasel. He came up with some convoluted explanation about a new farming method he had been researching, that doubled the yield of a wheat crop by delaying it. It is apparently all the rage in Holland and the landowners there have seen a dramatic rise in their profits. My father was utterly convinced by it.'

'But you were not?'

He leaned forward in his chair, resting his forearms on his knees, and shook his dark head in exasperation. 'I just know that he is lying through his teeth. Unfortunately, I still do not know enough about farming to be able to argue back. I never paid attention growing up and now I am trying to cram in a lifetime's worth of knowledge in just a few weeks. I am beyond confused by it all. I just hope that it does not do more irreparable damage until I can take over.'

Connie jabbed her needle into the frame to cover up her own unease. 'Surely one bad harvest does not constitute irreparable damage?'

'One wouldn't—but this will be the fourth. The estate is not in a good way.'

She was certain, then, that her father had a hand in it and that Mr Thomas was up to much more than merely reporting back gossip. 'Exactly how bad are things?'

'They are not bad, Connie,' he said with resignation, 'they are dire. Many of the tenants cannot survive another poor harvest and, if things continue like they are, this estate could be bankrupt in two years. Why on earth do you think I was marrying Violet Garfield?'

Chapter Twelve

'You needed her dowry?'

'She came with twenty thousand pounds and a share in her father's businesses. Mr Garfield was quite desperate for his daughter to marry a title.'

For the first time Connie considered the implications that their marriage had had on him and it rendered her speechless. All this time she had been wallowing in her own self-pity and had not even spared a single thought to what it had cost him, apart from his freedom. 'I am *so* sorry, Aaron. I did not realise that you needed to marry Violet quite so desperately. Do you think that there is a chance that she might still marry you once our marriage is dissolved?'

He was silent for so long that Connie began to feel uncomfortable. When he finally spoke it was with resignation. 'I doubt it. I shall have to find myself another heiress to save the livelihoods of my tenants. With her riches, someone is bound to snap her up.'

Much like Connie had been by the Marquis of Deal. Ironically, her father had agreed to increase her dowry to twenty thousand pounds to convince the man to marry her. She suddenly felt a strange affinity with poor Violet Garfield. Both of them were apparently unappealing to any man without the lure of riches and Aaron was obviously disappointed to have been left with just her. Her needle slipped and pricked the top of her index finger. Pretending to try to save her embroidery rather than let him see how much his words had cut her, Connie hastily dropped it into her lap and examined the wound with irritation. She had to tell Aaron about Mr Thomas. Feud or no feud, her conscience would not let her keep such a dreadful secret. Not when innocent people were suffering. But the truth was likely going to cause a huge row, not only between the Wincantons and the Stuarts, but between her and Aaron. He would want to know why she did not tell him the moment that she had realised, but at least it was better late than never. Steeling herself for the inevitable, Connie turned to him.

Aaron's eyes were locked on her fingertip. More specifically, they were fixated on the small red globe of blood oozing out from the needle prick. His face was stricken and she watched all of the colour drain out of it until he was positively ashen. He suddenly stood with such force that the legs of the heavy chair scraped behind him in his haste to get away.

'Goodnight, Connie.'

He started to march towards the door as if his life depended on it. 'Aaron, wait, I need to talk to you…' The door slammed behind him and he was gone, leaving Connie completely at a loss as to what had just happened.

Aaron originally headed towards his bedchamber, but by then he could physically smell the blood. The rational part of his mind told him that was ridiculous, but there was nothing rational about his body's intense reaction. The metallic tang was burning his nostrils, making him gag, and his skin itched with the warm stickiness of it. Within seconds, the stench was so bad that he had to get some fresh air. Fearing that his dinner was about to make a sudden reappearance, Aaron bolted down the stairs, taking the steps two at a time. He ran through the hallway, ignoring the startled looks from the few servants he collided with, then through the morning room until he reached the large French doors at the far side of the room. Only when he threw them open, and felt the biting November air rush into the room, did he feel that he could breath.

Hastily, he tore the cravat from his throat and braced his arms on his knees while he sucked in the cold air like a starving man eating food at a banquet. It had just been a pinprick. Nothing more. Yet in that one simple accident he had immediately been transported to a different place. The place of his nightmares.

Ciudad Rodrigo.

Aaron forced himself to breathe slowly, hoping that by being calm he could chase away the blind panic that clawed at his gut. After several minutes he was still shaking, but able to stand up. He staggered towards the nearest chair and slumped into it, trying to make some sort of sense out of what had just happened.

His reaction to the blood had been so sudden and so violent, he had never experienced anything like it. He had fought battles where his uniform had been soaked with the stuff, retrieved the bloody remains of the bodies in the aftermath and even marched across fields so sodden with death that the mud itself had been almost bleeding as his boots had squelched across it. He had hated every second of it then, but he had coped. Why was the mere sight of a tiny droplet of it now enough to render him incapacitated? God only knew what Connie must be thinking.

Not that he had any intention of explaining it to her. How exactly did one go about telling someone that there was a distinct possibility that they were going slowly mad? That could be the only explanation for what had just happened. The nightmares had been getting worse. They were certainly happening more frequently. Last night he had awoken twice and each time he was reliving the same dreadful scene on the battlements of the fortress. But now, apparently, he could be transported back there whilst he was still awake, too. Alongside the awful smell of the blood had been the unmistakable cries and sounds from that battlefield in Spain. He could see the broken bodies of his men strewn out around him. He was in Connie's sitting room one minute and then that had faded away and he was all alone in the smoke and the chaos, stood amongst the carnage and wondering what the hell to do.

What would a gently bred young lady like Connie make of all that? At least his insanity would be good grounds for her annulment. That thought made him laugh bitterly without any trace of humour before he forced himself to make his way up to bed. At this rate, he would be carted off to Bedlam before he could fix the estate and that thought brought Aaron up short. He could not let that happen. There were people depending on him. No matter how many tricks his mind decided to play on him, he had to hide that from the world and get on with the task in hand. Once the estate was safe it would make no difference if he suddenly declined into complete insanity. If that happened, they could lock him in his bedchamber for all he cared. He just had to hold it all together until then. At least he had more of a plan now than he had had this morning. That was something positive to focus on. Now, once his father died he had to secure the annulment as quickly as possible so that he could find another heiress. It might not be the greatest plan in the world, and it hurt to even contemplate losing Connie, but it was all he had right now.

Connie woke early and, in the absence of any maid or any breakfast tray, dressed herself in a more forgiving habit and headed downstairs to find her husband. Yesterday he had offered to take her riding again and she needed to tell him about Mr Thomas. The first person she collided with was the housekeeper.

'Good morning, Mrs Poole. Have you seen my husband?'

The older woman shook her head apologetically. 'Sorry, Lady Constance, but we have not crossed paths this morning. Perhaps he has gone out for an early morning ride. He does that most mornings, usually before the sun is fully up. He is awake before the lark most days.' The smile on her face faltered and she looked down briefly, as if she were considering her next words carefully. 'On that subject, I am very worried about him.'

'You are?'

'If you would permit me to speak out of turn, Lady Constance, I have known Master Aaron since he was a boy and he is not the same man who went off to war. Something is very wrong, yet half the time he appears to pretend that those five years never happened and that he is exactly the same devil-may-care lad who went away. I am not convinced that he is. He disappears for hours on end some days, much like he has done this morning, or he locks himself away in the library. He never used to be so solitary or so preoccupied. He doesn't sleep well either. I hear him up at all hours of the night; sometimes I hear him screaming. Deaks went in to check on him one night and Master Aaron was furious.

He threatened to move out if anyone disturbed him like that again. He never sleeps past dawn. Wild horses would not have dragged him out of his bed before noon before he went away. I have asked him about it, but he will not confide in me. He just pretends that nothing is amiss and that I am imagining things. I thought that now he has a wife perhaps he might open up to you in time. I hope he does.'

The housekeeper's concerns reminded Connie of what she had witnessed last night. Aaron's behaviour had been odd in the extreme and Connie could not shake the feeling that it had something to do with seeing her blood. It made her wonder if he had deliberately gone out without her to avoid explaining it. Then there had been that brief flash of temper when he had let slip that he had witnessed the horror of men going to their deaths petrified and screaming, and she had seen for herself how deeply that still affected him. Something was definitely not right with Aaron. However, discussing it further with the housekeeper felt disloyal to him. He would hate that, she already knew, because he was so very proud.

'Thank you for telling me. I shall certainly keep an eye out for him.'

Mrs Poole looked relieved. 'Thank you, Lady Constance. That is a weight off my mind.'

Connie continued her search for her elusive husband to no avail, but she found his father in the breakfast room, reading the newspaper.

'Good morning, my lord,' she said politely from the doorway, 'I am looking for your son. Have you seen him?'

To her surprise the old man beckoned for her to join him. 'Deaks, bring Lady Constance some tea and set another place for breakfast.' Connie had no choice but to sit down. To do otherwise would be unforgivably rude and Viscount Ardleigh did appear to be making an effort. Whether that was truly the case, Connie supposed she was about to find out.

He offered her an approximation of a smile. The corners of his mouth turned up ever so slightly so she responded in kind, noticing that his did have a bit of a blue tinge to them. 'Aaron went out over an hour ago, I believe. Am I to guess, judging by your attire, that you expected to go with him?'

A cup of tea appeared miraculously at her right elbow, giving Connie a prop to hide behind if she needed it. She picked it up and used it to cover her disappointment. 'Perhaps he forgot. It is of no matter.'

'It is not like my son to be absent-minded. More likely he was avoiding trouble. He does that a great deal. Did the two of you have another fight?' It was obvious, by the knowing glint in his dark eyes, that he was regularly appraised about her and his son's relationship. The servants must have seen Aaron storm out of her rooms last night and assumed that he had done so because he was angry at her. But they had not fought and, since her illuminating conversation with Mrs Poole, Connie was even more convinced that it had been something more sinister that had sent him running away.

'Things were cordial between us last night.'

At the viscount's immediate smug smile, she realised that he had just misinterpreted what she had said. 'Well, that is splendid! I am glad to know that the pair of you are using your evenings properly.'

Connie gave him a brittle stare and took a sip of her tea. Aaron wanted the old man to think that they were going to provide him with a grandchild. She could hardly correct him in that belief, no matter how much she wanted to. The man was dying.

'With any luck you will have some news in the next few weeks.' She was not going to discuss their non-existent attempts to create a child. The very idea was as preposterous as it was improper. 'These things take time. It might even take many months. We all have to be patient.' She said the last quite pointedly in the hope that he would get the message. Unfortunately, the viscount simply laughed.

'Nonsense! We Wincanton males are very vigorous. Why, my wife was carrying Aaron within a month of our marriage.' He said this so proudly that Connie almost missed his eyes flick to a portrait of a woman over the fireplace.

'Is that Aaron's mother?' His good humour was suddenly a little subdued when he nodded. 'She was very beautiful.'

'Indeed she was. I think Aaron has also inherited a great deal of her personality. Elizabeth was always more affable. She died when he was a year old, but I think she would have been proud to know the man he has become.'

Something about the way he said this made Connie wonder if he was actually capable of something akin to genuine affection. He had never remarried, which was unusual for men with titles. It would have been expected that he produced another son in case the unthinkable had happened. Her own father would have, she knew. Had the roles been reversed, he would have got over the death of his wife quickly in order to cement the succession. Hadn't he repeatedly complained of his disappointment at having been given a daughter first? Especially such an outspoken and ungainly one. Perhaps, underneath all of that bluster, Viscount Ardleigh would soften towards her in time. Already, he had invited her to break her fast in his company. Surely that was something?

Connie stood and began to help herself to the covered breakfast dishes. If her father-in-law wished to have a convivial breakfast with her she might as well eat. It was not as if she had anywhere else to go, seeing as Aaron had disappeared without her. 'Aaron told me that you were unhappy with his decision to go into the army.'

'Of course I was. It was a reckless decision that could have killed him. But he is stubborn and went anyway. I am eternally grateful that he came back in one piece.'

'And by all accounts he came back a hero, although he is very closed lipped about it. What did he win his medals for?'

Connie had expected to see pride shining in the old man's face, but instead the viscount appeared irritated. 'He won them for putting himself at risk! Officers should lead from the rear, not the front. But, of course, Aaron has no regard for proper rules so he was always in the thick of it as far as I can tell. He won one of them at Badajoz, where he apparently went after a few of his men who had been taken by the French and took them back, single-handed. Like a blasted fool. He should have left them there. The second was at Ciudad Rodrigo, for another foolhardy act of selfless bravery. I cannot say how he came by it because he refuses to talk about it. Those damn medals do not seem to bring him any pleasure at all.'

Connie remembered his glib answer to her question, claiming that he had been commended simply for surviving. 'Maybe he is just being self-effacing and does not want a fuss.'

His father regarded her thoughtfully. 'Self-effacing? Aaron? I suppose there is a slim chance that might be the case.'

Good gracious! Had he just agreed with something she had said? Obviously the viscount wanted to improve relations between them and this conversation was a very positive step forward. Connie relaxed and took a bite of her breakfast. She had not swallowed when he spoke again. 'By the way, I have invited a few people over for dinner tomorrow. I thought you might enjoy the opportunity to play the hostess in your new home.'

She really did not, but tried to look enthusiastic. He was making a bit of an effort—besides, how hard could one small dinner be? 'That's nice. How many people should I inform the cook to expect?'

The viscount looked up as he mentally calculated, then pierced her with a gaze filled with mischief. 'Including the three of us—twenty.'

Constance almost choked on her food. That was in no way 'a few' and less than twenty-four hours' notice was outrageous. By the smug expression on his face the old goat knew it, too. 'Do you think you can manage, Constance?'

It was a test. Defiantly, she speared another piece of sausage with her fork, imagining that the meat was his face, and then gave him her most saccharine smile. 'I am looking forward to it, my lord. I do enjoy a challenge.'

One positive step forward, two huge strides backwards.

Chapter Thirteen

As he had suspected, no seed was delivered to any of the tenants that day. It was already getting dark and Aaron was completely at his wits' end—but the very last place he wanted to be was home. Home meant having to do battle with his father over the estate manager again. It also meant facing Connie after his spectacular emotional collapse last night. Even now, all these hours later, that peculiar reaction still left him more shaken than all of his previous nightmares combined. He had barely slept a wink all night because he was so terrified of the new tricks his mind was playing on him. Now he was so exhausted he could actually feel his body wilting in the saddle.

He should have gone home hours ago, but instead he had ridden aimlessly, desperately trying to sort out all of the problems that had started queueing up for him to have to deal with. The estate, his father's health, his own mental health and now Connie. Her reaction to seeing Redbridge House yesterday morning had bothered him, as did her confession that her letter had been heartlessly returned unanswered. It was obvious the girl was desperately worried about her family and understandably homesick. If he thought that it would make a difference, Aaron was quite prepared to ride over there and give her vindictive father a piece of his mind. At least that was a more constructive way of spending the day than avoiding going home. But such interference would only make things worse. If he spoke to the Earl of Redbridge or called him on his behaviour, the only person who would pay was Connie and she had paid enough already.

Feeling dissatisfied with everything, Aaron wearily made his way into the house, intent on spending at least an hour in the bath to soak away the aches of all the riding. He abandoned any hope of that luxury when he stepped into the hallway and met chaos.

Every servant was apparently engaged in something, whether that be fetching, carrying or generally rushing about in a purposeful manner, and all of them had a fraught look about them.

Deaks hastily put down the vase of winter

greenery he was carrying and relieved Aaron of his coat. 'Good evening, Mr Aaron. Lady Constance has asked me to tell you that a cold supper has been laid out in the family dining room and that you should help yourself to it at your convenience. I believe your father is already in there.'

'A cold supper? But it is freezing outside.' They never had a cold supper in winter. Not in living memory at least. Deaks offered him an awkward nod, then scurried back to his vase and disappeared down the hallway. At a loss, he went to see his father, who was indeed sat in the informal dining room behind a plate full of food and looking far too pleased with himself for Aaron's liking. 'What's going on?'

The viscount feigned innocence, but ruined it by grinning. 'I informed your wife that we were having one or two guests tomorrow for dinner and it has put her in a quite a tizzy.'

'Why did you invite guests when you know full well that Connie and I would prefer to avoid society at the moment? In case it has escaped your notice, we have been at the centre of a rather large scandal of late. I brought her here so that she could avoid public scrutiny for a while. There will be no dinner, Father. You *will* cancel the invitations immediately.'

'It is just one or two close friends, Aaron.

Merely a chance for her to cut her teeth as a hostess. The girl has responded to the challenge admirably thus far. Besides, it is far too late to cancel now. Many of them would have already set out from London, I'll wager, and will overnight at an inn en route. I doubt I would be able to get word to them this late in the day and the preparations are well under way. Your Constance has been very busy since this morning. She will be disappointed if you cancel.'

Aaron decide to hold on to his temper until he had spoken to Connie. If there was a slight chance that his father was correct, and that she was perfectly comfortable with the idea, then he would not interfere. If his father was lying, and he would put nothing past the wily old buzzard, then he would feel the full force of Aaron's temper. Poor Connie had suffered enough in such a short time already; Aaron was not going to let his father make it intentionally worse for her. He shot the old man a warning glance and then stalked from the room in search of her.

It did not take a great deal of effort to track her down. Aaron simply followed the line of panicked servants towards the rarely used formal dining room, a room that was far too large for *one or two close friends*. The long table had been extended to its full length and was already swathed in crisp white linen. Footmen were busy polishing the silverware and, by the looks of things, every knife fork and spoon that they possessed was being arranged in front of a plethora of chairs. At the furthest end of the room, her back turned to him as she stood issuing rapid orders to a stunned-looking maid, was Connie. Her hairstyle was well into the process of collapse—Aaron could see one thick coil of vibrant copper had already made a valiant escape and was currently bouncing next to her cheek as she moved. He felt the urge to take out all of her hairpins, one by one, and watch every curl bounce to her waist and then shook himself. Now was not the time for lustful thoughts. His wife was clearly in the midst of a crisis.

It was the maid who noticed him first, just before Connie spun around and gaped at him. Then her lovely eyes narrowed and her hands came up and planted themselves on her hips.

'There you are!' she spat accusingly, 'How *convenient* that you should disappear for the whole day and leave me with this!'

There was no other way to interpret her mood as other than livid. Her delicate, pointed chin was jutting outward and she was definitely looking down her nose at him. The servants closest to her began to back away, their heads bent but their ears, no doubt, wide open to hear him receive a thorough set down. Aaron immediately raised his hands in surrender and slowly began to walk towards her.

'I swear to you, this is as much of a surprise to me as I can see it is to you. I had no idea my father had invited guests and, judging by the sea of chairs around this table, he has also lied to me about the number. I take it we are not expecting one or two?'

'One or two!' She stalked towards him, her green eyes practically glowing with indignation, and prodded him in the centre of his chest with one angry, pointed finger. 'Try twenty!' Prod. 'And with barely any notice.' Prod. Prod. 'The wretch has done it on purpose to vex me!'

And had definitely succeeded if Aaron was any judge. Absently he rubbed his breastbone before she prodded him there again. 'We will cancel it, Connie. There is no way that I would allow you to go through all this because my father is making mischief. I shall go and put a stop to it immediately.'

This offer did not placate her in the slightest. Connie gripped the top of his sleeve with enough force to pull him back from whence he might have gone. 'Stay right where you are! *You* will not come to my rescue as if I am some pathetic dolt who needs a husband to fight her battles for her. I would not give *him* the satisfaction!' She let go of his sleeve and raised her pointed finger heavenward, her small bosom heaving with indignation. 'He *wants* me to fail. Your father would like nothing better than to have me cower away and hide from the world. He *wants* to beat me. It is a battle of wills in which *he* wants to emerge the victor. Well, I will not let him!' She had started to pace now, her expressive arms waving while she flounced around the room like an actress in a poorly acted Greek tragedy. 'I am a Stuart! And I will go to my grave before I allow that *vile* Wincanton to intimidate me! This—' she pointed at the table with a shaking finger '—will be the best dinner party this house has ever seen!'

Aaron wanted to clap his hands together in applause. It truly had been a magnificent performance and he was strangely proud of her stubbornness. In the face of adversity, Constance Stuart met the threat head on and looked every bit like an ancient warrior queen. She stood stock still, like a statue. Her copper hair was crackling in the candlelight and her plump lips were pushed out in the most delectable pout he had ever seen. A pout that he suddenly had the most all-encompassing, overwhelming urge to kiss.

For a moment, the surge of raw need left Aaron feeling off balance. His world was crashing down all around him, he might well be on the cusp of insanity and he still wanted to kiss her? And not just kiss her, he realised as his breeches began to feel a little uncomfortable. He wanted to take her upstairs and give her a very different outlet to divert all of that fire and passion towards. He might be half-mad, and well on the road to being penniless, but all of that apparently paled into insignificance when he thought about Connie. Or perhaps this unfamiliar sensation was further proof that he was going mad, because surely only a madman would want a woman so desperately when she had made it quite plain that she could never want him back. It was simply another way that his broken mind had found to torture him and send him plummeting into the abyss of total lunacy.

The silence between them hung until he realised she was expecting some form of response from him. A response that plainly did not involve him tossing her over his shoulder, running her upstairs and making love to her until neither of them could think straight. Automatically he tugged on his jacket to ensure that any evidence of his ardour was properly covered.

'Is there anything that you would like me to

do to help?' To his own ears, his voice sounded a trifle gravelly as he forced the words out. But really, she did look quite beautiful.

Something between a sniff and a snort escaped her and she flounced off again. 'You could look at my seating plan and let me know if I have put anybody next to somebody I shouldn't. They are Wincanton friends after all. Not *mine*.'

Clearly she expected him to follow so he did and found himself smiling in her wake. When she flounced, those hips of hers swayed in the most mesmerising fashion that, he was certain, she was blissfully unaware of. Connie stopped sharply at the sideboard and he almost went into the back of her because he was still staring at her delightful bottom. She snatched up a piece of paper impatiently and thrust in his direction. Typically, the print was too small for him to see properly.

Connie watched as Aaron reached inside his jacket and pulled out the wire-rimmed spectacles she had seen in his bedchamber. He spread the seating plan out on the sideboard and then carelessly put the glasses on as he studied it. Although Connie was, rightly, still furious at the man for disappearing for the entire day and driving her to complete distraction with worry for him, the sight of him in those glasses did funny things to her. Instantly, her body warmed in the most improper places and her heartbeat felt irregular. Damn him for being so effortlessly gorgeous! If she had been cursed with poor vision—alongside her ghastly carrot-coloured hair, extreme height and washboard figure—she had no doubt that spectacles would be the final nail in the coffin of her attractiveness. She would look like a pinched, pale spinster. Typically, the wire frames only served to enhance Aaron's strong features. His slightly magnified russet eyes were more hypnotic as he peered down his perfectly straight, perfectly proportioned nose at her handiwork. The fact that his dark hair was all windswept from a day's riding only added to his appeal. He smelled deliciously of fresh air and fresh man, making Connie wonder what it would feel like to bury her nose under the collar of his jacket and just inhale him. She would not mind sliding her hands beneath that jacket as well, so that she could learn the shape of his shoulders and arms.

His chest.

His back.

Good gracious, what had got into her?

'This is quite an eclectic bunch,' he said, scanning the names and startling her out of her unladylike and vastly improper musings, 'but most of them are all right when you get to know them. This arrangement appears to be in perfectly good order, but for your own sanity I would swap these two.' He pointed to Sir Gerald Pimm, whom she had purposely placed opposite her, and Sarah, the Countess of Erith. 'Sir Gerald can be a dreadful bore when he gets going and you might fall asleep, face down in your dinner. You will find Sarah amusing.'

Connie sincerely doubted it. 'I shall endure it. It is not done for ladies to sit opposite or next to each other as it ruins the balance of the table. If that is your only objection, Lady Erith can stay exactly where she is.' Which was as far away from Connie as she could get the awful woman—without seating her out on the terrace or bricking her up in an alcove. She and Sarah had come out at exactly the same time and Sarah had been one of the main protagonists in making Connie feel out of place that first Season. She had too many unhappy memories of pretending not to notice the beautiful, petite Sarah and her cronies laughing and criticising her behind their fans. To add insult to injury, spiteful Sarah had bagged herself a wealthy and titled husband that very first year and had since produced two sons while Connie had been left forgotten on the shelf, her own womb still as empty as Violet Garfield's head. It was bad enough having to sit at the same table with the woman. Connie certainly did not want to have to socialise with her as well.

'Where have you been?' she asked him sharply to change the subject and to hide the fact that she had been worried sick about him. Aaron's odd behaviour last night, combined with the revelations about his nightmares, had played on her mind all day. Even when she had been at her most stressed, trying to sort out this stupid dinner, Connie had continued to worry about the wretched man.

'I spent the day with the tenants.'

As he refused to meet her gaze she suspected he was not being completely truthful. If she were his real wife, rather than just a temporary one, she might have pushed him further. She might have also told him that he had made her worry and that he could talk to her about whatever ailed him, should he want to. But saying any of that made her sound needy and theirs was never going to be that sort of a relationship. 'You look tired. Perhaps you should have an early night?'

'I would not leave you with all this.'

Connie felt the sudden urge to look after him. He did look tired. In fact, he looked completely exhausted now that she was looking at him properly. There were faint shadows under his eyes and his features were quite drawn. To all intents and purposes he looked…troubled… and she wanted to fix that. Without thinking, and completely forgetting that she was in a bad temper, she reached up her palm and cupped his cheek. It felt a little rough where his whiskers were beginning to show, his skin lusciously warm beneath her fingers. Connie found herself drowning in the intensity of those hypnotic eyes while desperately wanting to chase away all of the ghosts that she suddenly saw there.

'You need some sleep, Aaron, and I am almost done here. I shall ask Deaks to have a hot bath drawn whilst you have something to eat. The warm water will help you to relax.' Of its own accord her thumb began to smooth away the tiny lines of fatigue next to his mouth. 'And then I want you to get some rest.'

He did not pull away from her tender touch. His eyes fluttered closed briefly and she saw him swallow before he opened them again. There was an emotion hidden in their depths that she could not identify. Perhaps despair? Perhaps need? Although why would he look at her with need? And then it was gone. 'If you insist, Connie, then I will.'

Connie's hand dropped away self-consciously until she clasped it with the other one, firmly, behind her back. 'I do.'

The strength of her physical attraction to him surprised her. Her emotional reaction to him had surprised her more. The concern she felt was almost wifely and totally at odds with the way she should be feeling for Aaron Wincanton.

'Then I will bid you goodnight.'

Chapter Fourteen

Connie could not sleep. There were too many things cluttering her mind. In an attempt to sort her thoughts into some form of manageable order she started to list them, a habit she had developed as a child in order to work through her worries. There was the dinner tomorrow. But all of the preparations, apart from the cooking and actual entertaining, were done so there was no point allowing that to occupy her thoughts now. There was also her natural concern for her family and the estrangement. Realistically, she could do absolutely nothing about that in the middle of the night so she would resume worrying about that problem tomorrow.

Then there was Mr Thomas and her suspicion that he was sabotaging the Wincanton harvest, especially after Aaron had stated that the financial situation was so dire that he had needed to marry an heiress to fix it all. She could not do anything to relieve his financial pressures but she could warn him about his traitorous estate manager. As she had already made up her mind to tell Aaron all, and would have already if he had not excused himself with such speed last night or disappeared for almost the entire duration of today, she could also tick that off of her list of things that were causing her insomnia. At some point tomorrow, she would tell him and then Mr Thomas would be given his marching orders. One problem solved.

Once Aaron's father was gone, they would hopefully get their annulment and he would be free to marry some other woman who could bring more to the marriage than trouble. In fact, Connie's insistence on an annulment was actually an act of charity on her part. One that allowed him to save his estate and the people who depended on it, she reasoned, even though picturing him married to another woman made her feel quite jealous. Not that she had any right to be jealous. He had merely been noble in marrying her and she was merely returning that kindness by being noble back and releasing him from the marriage. Any woman would be delighted to have Aaron Wincanton as her husband, so he would no doubt land on his feet. Connie would probably have to change her name and take work as a governess or lady's companion because an annulment would kill any future marriage prospects stone dead and her father would happily allow her to rot in hell before he helped her. But she was hopeful that her brother would take her in one day, so at least she would end her days in the bosom of her family even though she would be denied any prospect of having her own for ever. And she would not have to be married to a man who could never love her and had made his opinions on her physical attributes quite clear to all and sundry. That was another weighty problem almost solved.

The next problem was a tricky one. Connie wanted to be able to understand her unexpected feelings for Aaron. Despite all of the reasons why she probably shouldn't, she had to concede that she could not help liking the man. In fact, as the days wore on she found herself liking him more and more—which was worrying. He had a pleasant, easy way about him and she enjoyed his company. But was it more than that? Were her blossoming feelings growing out of friendship and concern or, heaven forbid, was she starting to think of him as a wife should think of her husband? That would not do at all in their unusual situation. He had happily agreed to annulment and without too much of a fight. Clearly he was as keen to be rid of her as she was him. Only now there was the tiniest chance that she was no longer quite as keen as she had been. She definitely found him attractive, but as he was a ridiculously attractive man, what woman wouldn't? And then there was that kiss that still popped into her thoughts and those thoughts made her body react in a completely improper way. But he could not know that she desired him. That would be mortifying and, as he had quite rightly pointed out, what sort of a man would willingly want to bed a shrew like her?

With a sigh of frustration Connie decided against analysing it all. Whatever was going on, she was not yet ready to face it. Everything was so new and so up in the air that it would be foolish to try to understand it just yet. The most probable explanation was that in this strange house, cut off from her family and friends, Aaron was the only ally she had. Therefore, it would make sense that she cared about him. It stood to reason that her sense of fealty towards him might then be misconstrued as affection. Perhaps in a few weeks, when everything was calm, she would lay out her feelings and examine them properly in private. Rationally.

Dispassionately.

That was definitely a more sensible course of action, she decided, so now would be a good time to finally go to sleep. Connie turned her pillow over, rearranged the bedcovers and settled down. Less than ten seconds later she sat bolt upright again. How could she sleep when she was now so worried about Aaron and his nightmares? She *had*, after all, promised Mrs Poole that she would keep an eye out for him. And Aaron had not been himself last night; hardly surprising when the poor man had so much on his plate. A dying father and a failing estate would be enough to keep the most hardened of souls from sleeping soundly. Perhaps her own sleep would come once she had reassured herself that Aaron was all right?

Decisively, she climbed out of bed and hurried out of her bedchamber towards his without bothering with a candle. The house was still and quiet, although the servants had left one or two lamps burning dimly near the stairs and they cast unfamiliar, eerie shadows up the walls. When she got to Aaron's door she pressed her ear against it, listening carefully. All was, thankfully, peaceful.

Reassured, she hovered outside for a few moments before turning back towards her own room.

'No!'

The single shout cut through the silence like a surgeon's scalpel and stopped Connie in her tracks instantly. She darted back to the door and put her ear against it again. There was no screaming or murmuring, but there was definitely movement. She could hear the sounds of the mattress shifting violently and bedcovers moving. Neither sounded anything like a person turning in contented sleep. For a second she debated whether or not to go in and check on him, mindful of how she had been told Aaron had reacted to Deaks's intrusion, until the sounds beyond became more agitated.

Connie cracked open the door and peered inside. The first thing that struck her was the cold. Every window and curtain in the room was open, allowing the bitter winter air to rush in unchecked. The only light came from the weak moon outside. It was enough to make out the shape of the bed until her eyes adjusted and she could see Aaron lying on his back atop it.

Although he appeared to be asleep, his body was twitching and flailing uncontrollably. Both arms were flung above his head, one gripping the pillow in his closed fist as if his very life depended on it. For some reason she seemed to remember being told that you should not wake a person up when they were in the grip of a nightmare, which left her standing impotently just inside the door, watching his distress. When he cried out pitifully once more, Connie decided that was nonsense. She had to wake him up and stop his torment. Leaving him to suffer through it was simply cruel.

Carefully, she tiptoed towards the bed. Up close, the pale moonlight revealed the blankets and sheets had been pushed away. They lay tangled around his straining hips and legs, effectively imprisoning his bottom half as he writhed. Above the waist he was quite naked. Aaron's eyes were clenched tightly closed, yet the expression on his face was of complete terror.

'Shh, Aaron. It is just a bad dream.'

Instinctively, Connie reached out her hand and lightly touched his shoulder. His smooth skin was covered in a sheen of sweat, but was icy to the touch. Instantly, his hands came down to his chest and he began to almost wipe himself down, flicking at some imaginary stain while his breathing became more erratic. More laboured. His voice was barely above a whisper, but she could hear him repeating the same name over and over like a mantra: Fletcher. Fletcher.

Connie bent her head and crooned close to his ear. 'Wake up, Aaron. It is just a dream. Just a dream.' She brushed her fingers softly over his damp hair and forehead. 'Please wake up.'

All at once, his body stilled and his eyes shot open. His breath came out in sharp, gasping pants and she watched him struggle to focus. Connie ran her hand gently through his hair in an attempt to bring him some comfort. 'Everything is all right, Aaron. You were just having a nightmare.'

'Connie?'

He blinked up at her and she smiled reassuringly down into his face. She saw the exact moment recognition dawned, then his strong arms wrapped around her and hugged her tight to his bare chest, dragging her shamelessly on top of his body, while he buried his face in her hair. Sensing that he needed the contact, Connie wrapped her arms around his shoulders and held him close, feeling the strangest wave of protectiveness. She could feel his heart beating frantically against his ribs, the chill of his body through the thin fabric of her nightgown. His hands felt like ice against her back.

'You are freezing cold!'

Without breaking the contact, Connie rummaged around for the edge of the bedcovers and hauled what she could over them both. Despite the intimacy of their position, she made no attempt to move away. She held him and whispered words of reassurance until she heard his breathing calm and felt his heartbeat slow to normal. His skin began to lose its chill, absorbing her body heat slowly, as they huddled beneath the covers. Soon, his arm about her waist began to feel heavy and she realised that he had fallen back into sleep.

With infinite care, Connie disentangled herself from Aaron's arms and gently rolled off his chest. No sooner had her body touched the mattress beside him, he turned on to his side, curling his arm possessively around her waist again and snuggling around the curve of her back.

'Don't go, Connie,' he mumbled sleepily against her neck. 'Not yet.'

Unsure of what to do under the odd circumstances, Connie stayed exactly where she was. In a minute or two, once he was back in the arms of Morpheus, she would move. But his arm remained locked around her while his body warmed hers under the covers. It felt solid, and so lovely, that without thinking she allowed herself to adjust her own body so that she was more comfortable, curling her knees up into her favourite sleeping position. His own legs immediately followed suit and she was cocooned by him. The steady rise and fall of his chest, and the feel of his warm breath against her hair, was more soothing than a lullaby. For the first time in her life, Connie felt dainty and protected, wrapped in those strong arms. Was it so wrong to allow herself a minute or two more to revel in the feeling, allowing herself to drift momentarily in the safety of his embrace?

The next thing that she realised, from her nest under the cosy blankets, it was light. Straight after that came the awkward realisation that her head was nestled against a very warm, very solid male shoulder and her hand was resting intimately on the bare skin directly over his heart. Connie stiffened instantly. At some point in the night they had changed positions and she was completely, shamelessly, draped over him. Her nightgown had risen up slightly, so now her bare leg was hooked over his equally bare calf. Even more shocking was the feel of something very large and very firm pressing insistently against her hip. With both of his arms and legs accounted for there could only be one other explanation for what that thing was. Judging by the deep sound of his breathing, Aaron was fortunately still asleep. Unfortunately, his arm was wrapped loosely around her waist, his palm rested possessively on her hip. Escaping without him waking was not going to be particularly easy.

She twisted her hips slightly, carefully lifting the weight of her wayward leg off him, until his hand slid off her hip. She waited a beat and then gingerly raised herself up on to one elbow. The movement caused her heavy hair to brush his shoulder and Aaron shifted slightly, flinging his free arm over his head and out of the covers. Frightened even to breathe in case it disturbed him, Connie froze.

His face looked so peaceful in sleep, all signs of the anguish he had displayed last night banished. His features were relaxed, his dark lashes forming sooty crescents against his skin, all evidence of the tightness she had seen about his mouth yesterday had completely vanished. Her heart clenched at the sight.

As unwelcome as the situation was, it was also most enlightening. Connie had never seen a man quite so…natural before. This close, she could clearly see every tiny whisker beginning to sprout from his chin and the tiny pulse that beat at the base of his thick neck. She was tempted to touch it, out of blatant curiosity, and then feel the shape of the intriguing muscles now visible on the one arm that was uncovered. Those same muscles did not appear to be confined to just his arm. They ran across his shoulder and down over the very top of his chest. Connie could just make out the way they curved in towards the flat plane of his breastbone before her view was hampered by the top of the blankets. The sight threw up more questions about the male anatomy than it answered.

The light dusting of hair she could just see on his chest, for example. Did it go all the way down his body? Were those interesting muscles something that only appeared on the arms and shoulders? She could definitely feel them under the palm of her hand where it still rested above his heart, so perhaps there were more there to discover? And what exactly did that proud bulge under the bedcovers look like? She had seen statues of male nudes—but on those that particular part of their anatomy had been presumably at rest. Aaron's was apparently at the ready and she had no idea what that really meant at all.

Frustratingly Connie did not know the answer to any of her questions but, scandalously, she was desperate to find out. Her fingers positively itched to explore him. Feeling very naughty and a little bit daring, Connie slowly lifted her hand from his chest, raising the blankets as she did so, and allowed herself to take a guilty peak.

The dark dusting of hair fanned out across his pectoral muscles in a very pleasing fashion, two flat male nipples suddenly pebbled as the cold air whispered over them and drew Connie's eyes lower. The hair tapered then, feathering across his flat stomach, down past his ribs where it arrowed through his navel and disappeared into the darkness. His skin was so much darker than hers. She was almost a ghost in comparison, although she liked the contrast they created together. Dark and fair. Solid and soft. Female and male. Definitely male. That hot hardness briefly grazed against her hip again.

Mortified and ashamed of her burning desire to see what went on below his navel, Connie still risked raising the covers a little higher to have a look. Aaron murmured something incomprehensible and adjusted his position. Terrified of the prospect of being caught, Connie whipped her hand away and then deftly slipped out of the bed with the minimum amount of fuss and the maximum amount of speed.

For one dreadful moment, his eyelids fluttered and she feared that he would open them. Being caught like this, when it would be quite obvious to him that she had spent the night in his bed, was too awful a prospect to have to consider. What would she say to him? How would he react? How would *she* react? Already she could feel the embarrassed blush branding her skin, like an angry red confession of her carnal desires. Decisively, she turned and bolted for the door, opening and closing it with as much stealth as she could muster, before she fled to the sanctuary of her own bedchamber. Once there, she covered her burning face with her hands and cringed at her unashamedly wanton behaviour. Thank goodness he did not know.

Chapter Fifteen

Aaron's eyes drifted open slowly. Only then did he realise that something was amiss. For once, apparently, he had woken up naturally. It was broad daylight and he was completely rested. He was not sweating or breathing heavily or shouting in a blind panic. Instead his thoughts were completely dominated by much more pleasing thoughts, like long legs, round bottoms and magnificent red hair. He was curled up on his side, completely content.

He had forgotten how good it felt to wake like this. He felt invigorated, energised and, to his utter surprise, completely aroused. He must have been dreaming about his new wife again, he thought with a sigh. She had begun to crop up in them quite a bit in the last few days. Usually, in those welcome dreams, they were back in that library and she was kissing him—except in those dreams they were not interrupted by an audience so he was able to properly ruin her. That must be the reason why his first waking thoughts had strayed to her. So far this week he had already dreamed about ruining her in every room in Ardleigh Manor, once in the stables and, most spectacularly, out in the open where his mind had conjured up a truly wonderful image of Connie, that tight green riding habit rucked up around her waist and his body buried deep inside her.

He allowed himself the rare luxury of enjoying the whole miraculous experience of this glorious morning by plumping his pillow, closing his eyes and burrowing further under the blankets. They smelled deliciously of summer roses. The heavy, cabbage type of roses that draw all of the bees and can barely hold the weight of their fragrant red petals on their delicate stalks. Aaron loved that smell. It reminded him of Connie. She always smelled of roses, too.

At that thought, Aaron cracked open one eye. Was his mind able to conjure up smells now, too? The scent was too vivid to be merely a memory, no matter how erotic the dream might have been. To make sure he buried his nose in his pillow and took a healthy sniff. His bed definitely smelled of Connie. It was then that he saw the solitary strand of long copper hair lying on the empty pillow next to him. He raised himself up on to his elbow and stared at it. There was definitely a head-shaped indent in that pillow, too, as if she had been there.

Aaron tried to sort through his hazy memories of his dream. She had definitely been in it. In his imagination he could still here her voice. *Everything is all right, Aaron. You were just having a bad dream.* Except he now had the distinct feeling that he had not imagined it. She had been there. That was why he could smell her perfume in his bed and on his skin. He had not imagined the feel of her spooned against him in the night. He had slept with her in his arms and she had chased his nightmares away.

Connie could chase his nightmares away? That thought was as humbling as it was terrifying. Humbling because he realised that she must have seen him in the throes of one, comforted him and brought him back from the brink. Terrifying because he had never, ever wanted another soul to know about them or to see him like that. Terrified. Lost. Inconsolable. Mad.

What if he had said things to her? Whispered his deepest, darkest secret? Confessed the truth about himself and what he had done?

Suddenly, his morning did not feel quite so perfect and he sat up, feeling more vulnerable than he was comfortable with. There was no point in putting it off, he realised. If she had seen him like that then she would expect some answers. Feeling suddenly queasy, Aaron rang the bell for his valet. The only way he could know how to answer her questions was if he found out what he had inadvertently told her, then try to limit the damage that he might have done. There was no point in trying to avoid her—even though he desperately wanted to.

As soon as he was dressed he headed downstairs in search of her. As she had been yesterday, he found her in the dining room.

'Good morning, Connie. Might I have a word?'

As soon as her head whipped around to look at him, she blushed as red as a tomato and struggled to meet his eye.

'Certainly, Aaron.'

She excused herself from the battalion of servants and scooted past him back into the hallway beyond. Aaron was more than a little confused as he followed her at some pace towards the morning room. He had expected disgust or disappointment to be her first reaction, not acute embarrassment. It was almost as if he had just caught *her* doing something wrong rather than the other way around.

Once they were alone, she sat stiffly on one of the chairs and peaked up at him. Her neck was all blotchy, she was blinking rapidly and she looked as guilty as it was physically possible for a person to look. She waited for him to speak like a condemned man waiting for the axe to fall. 'Is everything all right, Connie?' he asked out of sudden concern.

She smiled a brittle smile back at him. 'Of course. Why wouldn't it be?'

Aaron decided to take the bull by the horns and broach the subject. Clearly she was rubbing off on him as his usual response would be to go for a ride and hope that it all went away.

'I know that you came to visit me last night.'

He watched her face closely for her reaction to see if he had disgraced himself. Her eyes widened, her jaw dropped a little and then she positively combusted with a blush so ferocious Aaron could almost feel the heat of it. All at once she buried her face in her hands and moaned.

'You were having a nightmare. I came in to wake you from it. I didn't mean for anything else to happen!'

'And did anything else happen?'

Aaron held his breath and waited for her to condemn him. She was still covering her face so all he could see were the tips of her red ears and the top of her copper head. It was difficult to gauge her reaction like that.

'Nothing untoward,' she said after a pause. 'I woke you up and settled you back down.'

'Did I say anything?' Because that was the crux of the matter.

Connie shook her head, which was still covered by her hands. The relief he felt was so intense that it took him a moment to realise that her face was still covered and the skin he could see was all pink and blotchy. It really was the most extreme behaviour for a person who had simply awoken someone from a nightmare and then toddled off to their own bed.

'Did I do anything untoward?' Perhaps he had enacted part of the shadowy dream that lingered in his mind and ravished her. If he had, then she was certainly not furious with him and that thought buoyed him. If Connie was open to a good ravishing, then he would be only too happy to comply. She dashed those hopes immediately.

'Of course not. You were asleep, silly.'

'Then I have to ask, Connie, what has got you all flustered and flushing with mortification—if I neither said nor did anything that I oughtn't?'

She lowered her fingers just enough for him

to see her mortified green eyes. 'I was not expecting you to be…um…naked.'

'Did you see my…?'

'No!' she practically shrieked. 'Fortunately that part of your anatomy remained covered.'

He had not thought she could get any redder, but apparently he was wrong. Aaron's laughter escaped in a bark. It was both relief at not having to explain about his past and amusement at her lovely and completely innocent reaction to a little bit of bare skin.

'Stop laughing at me, you wretch!' She stood up then, her delicate hands clenched into fists that appeared ready to pummel him at any given moment.

'I'm sorry,' he managed between guffaws, 'I don't mean to laugh.' But he couldn't help it. The more annoyed she became at his reaction the more he chuckled. 'If this is the way you react to the sight of a man's bare chest, I would love to see what happens when you get an eyeful of the rest of him.'

Connie swatted at him then. It was all so unfair. Once again she was being made to look a complete dimwit in front of Aaron Wincanton. Charming, handsome, *eligible* Aaron Wincanton!

'Yes, I am sure that you would find my discomfort hilarious. I'm sure you've seen more naked women than most. I'm sure that you have seduced hundreds with your charming words and silly flirting. Well, it is different for ladies. We are not allowed to indulge in such vices. We have to stay pure and chaste for our stupid future husbands and are declared ruined the first time that we even kiss a man!'

His laughter stopped abruptly and he stared at her agog. Connie barged past him. She did not want to see his pity at her ill-conceived confession. Why on earth had she told him that pertinent detail? It would only make her seem even more pathetic and unattractive in his eyes. Poor Constance Stuart. So ugly nobody had ever tried to kiss her.

'I was the first man to kiss you?'

Connie did not stop walking. She was too ashamed, fearing that she would burst into tears if she stayed. She grabbed the door handle and wrenched it open. Once in the hallway, she mustered the strength to issue one parting salvo.

'Go to hell, Aaron!'

Then she broke into a run.

Chapter Sixteen

It was no mean feat to avoid Aaron for the rest of the day. As the evening fell, the enormity of facing a table full of guests, alongside her irritating and irresistible husband, was almost too much to bear. Connie considered crying off, but knew that she had too much pride to allow anyone to think that it was too much for her. Now she was sat at her dressing table, staring at her own disappointing reflection, wondering how she was supposed to compete with the other ladies attending the dinner—or, more specifically, her beautiful nemesis Lady Erith.

Mrs Poole, the housekeeper, bustled back into her bedchamber. Connie had asked her if any of the maids were any good at dressing unruly red hair and the older woman had smiled kindly and offered to do it herself. Having been the lady's maid of the deceased Viscountess of Ardleigh, she had claimed that it would be her pleasure to help. The older woman was wielding a comb and an enormous box of hair pins.

'Before we start, Lady Constance, have you decided on a gown first? I always think that the hair should complement the cut of the dress.'

Connie shrugged despondently and gestured to the bed. 'I have narrowed it down to those two.' Neither one would suddenly make her more attractive. As lovely as the dresses were, her washboard figure and ghastly hair would ruin them.

Mrs Poole studied the two gowns and frowned. 'If I may be so bold, Lady Constance, why don't you wear that lovely red dress that I have seen in your closet? I should imagine that you would look magnificent in that.'

'It's too bold, Mrs Poole. I am not feeling particularly bold this evening.' She was terrified and ashamed and felt totally ridiculous. Too vulnerable for crimson.

'Nonsense! If ever you needed to feel bold, it is tonight. I don't know what his lordship was playing at, foisting on to you such a task so soon after your arrival. That dress will make a statement.' There was a sparkle of mischief in the housekeeper's eyes as she grinned at Connie in the mirror's reflection. 'It will let his lordship, and all of those silly guests of his, know that you are not a lady to be trifled with.'

Mrs Poole was apparently an ally and Connie was suddenly hugely grateful. 'Are you sure?'

'I am.'

Mrs Poole marched to the wardrobe and retrieved the dress. After eyeing it critically she smiled. 'I shall just give this to one of the maids to press and then we will do something magnificent with your hair.'

'Please do not pile it on top of my head. I am quite tall enough and do not need the extra inches.'

Aaron waited impatiently in the drawing room. Connie had deftly avoided him all day, seemingly too busy with the preparations for tonight's dinner to even spare him as much as a glance. But he knew he had upset her even though it had certainly not been his intention to do so. The knowledge that he had not only ruined her, but had also been the very first man to kiss her, was all too fresh in his mind. And probably for all of the wrong reasons. He supposed he should feel some shame. But he didn't. Instead he felt privileged to have been the only man who had known her in that way, possessive even, although he had no right to feel that either. Connie had made it plain enough that she did not want to be married to him and he definitely needed to find a new bride who came with a huge heap of money because he could not think of another way to fill the gaping hole in his finances. Nevertheless, for now she was his and he did not want her to feel sad.

Beside him, his father looked at his pocket watch impatiently. 'Our guests will be here in a moment and our hostess is still not here to greet them. I bet she will claim a headache or some other sort of malady in order to keep to her rooms. I knew she was not up to the task.'

Aaron turned the old man angrily, ready to tell him off, but Connie sailed into the room, looking lovelier than he could have imagined. The crimson evening gown was simply styled, but no less daring as a result. The gently puffed sleeves were set to sit off her elegant shoulders, the neckline cut so that it swooped low at the front and even lower at the back. Acres of perfect alabaster skin was on display, enhanced by the candlelight, and a stark contrast to the rich colour of the silk. The bodice hugged her body to follow the willowy shape of her figure, whilst the plain skirts were nipped in at the waist before falling in a graceful soft folds. Her glorious hair had been coiled into a smooth and exuberant knot at the base of her neck. Only a few wispy copper tendrils were allowed to hang free, framing her face and emphasising her emerald eyes and plump red mouth. The overall effect was so stunning it rendered him temporarily speechless.

'Good evening, gentlemen,' she said with an air of disdain and Aaron realised that haughty Constance had come to dinner. That meant that she was nervous. Already, in such a short time, he knew her moods. Understood them.

'You look stunning, Connie,' he said, meaning it. She gave him a polite smile in acknowledgement and he realised that she did not think that he meant it. Was it possible that Constance Stuart lacked confidence in herself? How curious.

She had timed her entrance to perfection because the first carriage was already arriving. She did not want to talk about what had happened this morning. Whilst Aaron understood this, he still would have like the opportunity to make her feel better about what had transpired. Instead he offered her his arm and escorted her to the hall to greet their guests.

To begin with Connie did a splendid job as a hostess. As the drawing room began to fill up with his father's friends, she was polite and charming, chatting with the guests with the ease of a diplomat. It was only when the Earl and Countess of Erith arrived that he saw a chink in her carefully constructed armour.

His father did the honour of introducing them to her. Connie smiled graciously at the earl as he bent to kiss her hand, but her eyes narrowed, and her polite expression froze, the moment she greeted Lady Erith. Lady Erith inclined her head somewhat coldly towards Connie in response. At that exact moment, Aaron realised that there was no love lost between these two women. In fact, if he was any judge of character, he was almost certain they positively loathed one another. As was expected, Connie ensured that they were both given drinks before she turned away. Sarah, on the other hand, made a beeline for Aaron and draped herself on his arm.

'I suppose I should congratulate you, Aaron, on your hasty marriage.'

'Thank you.' To say anything else would have been unforgivably rude, although the woman clearly had her claws out. 'I trust you are well, Sarah. How are your delightful children?' Aaron politely changed the subject.

'They are thriving, thank you. But how are you? We were all *so* surprised when you married in such a hurry. And married dear Constance to boot. I never would have put the two of you together.'

Out of the corner of his eye, Aaron saw Connie stiffen at the barb although she pretended not to hear it. She had already been claimed by Sir Gerald, who was no doubt priming himself to bore her to death. His hesitation in answering allowed Sarah to sink her claws further into Connie.

'What was it that you used to call her again? Oh, I remember—the Ginger Amazonian! And now you are married to her. Isn't that ironic?'

The patently false tinkling laugh combined with the unnecessary volume of her voice drew the attention of everyone else. Because Sir Gerald had even turned to look, poor Connie was forced to face them and await his response. He saw the brief flash of pain in her eyes whilst Sarah's danced in malicious triumph. Enough was enough. It was time to put this cat back into her bag. Calmly, he took a sip of his drink.

'Surely you were not fooled by my petty remarks all those years ago, Sarah? Surely you realised that I was in love with Connie even then?'

Connie gripped her glass so tightly that she was surprised that it did not shatter into a thousand pieces. Of all of the lame excuses or apologies she had expected Aaron to make, that one caught her off guard. In front of all of their guests his eyes lazily sought hers out and locked on her with such heat that she felt a blush stain her cheeks. It was a very clever way of putting Spiteful Sarah in her place, she had to give him that. Fortunately, the blush and the way she automatically looked away made the whole exchange appear believable to everyone else. A few of the guests were smiling at the apparent romance of it all. But the easy lie made Connie yearn for it to be true.

Sarah, of course, snorted her disbelief. Immediately, Aaron turned to her, looking completely sincere and completely gorgeous. 'I remember seeing her for the first time at Almack's. I thought she was the most beautiful creature I had ever seen. But, as you all know, we Wincantons have always been at war with the Stuarts so I feigned indifference, even though my heart was already lost. I thought our situation was hopeless. It was only after I returned from the war and heard that she was betrothed that I decided to do something about it. I could not stand the thought of her married to another man.'

Connie thought he was laying it on a bit thick now, but the other guests, with the notable exception of Lady Erith, all appeared to be quite enthralled by the tale.

'What did you do?' asked Sir Gerald's plump wife.

Her question was rewarded by the most wicked smile Connie had ever seen. Aaron turned towards the woman conspiratorially.

'You all know what I did.' Scandalised laughter erupted from almost everyone while Aaron sauntered towards Connie and threaded his arm through hers, staking a claim on her in front of everyone. 'And I am not the slightest bit sorry for it.'

Chapter Seventeen

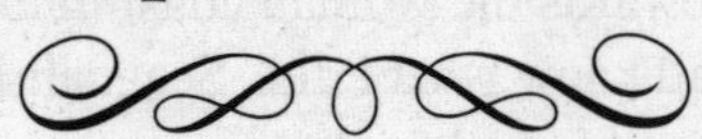

Crisis averted, the rest of the evening was almost a resounding success. It would have been a complete success in Connie's eyes had it not been for the fact that Aaron had been completely correct in his summation of Sir Gerald Pimm. The man really was the most crushing of bores. With the final course still to go, he was waffling on about his lime kilns, of all things. Pasting an interested expression on her face, and purposefully ignoring her smug husband's knowing looks every time their eyes met down the long table, Connie prepared herself for the next never-ending lecture from her dinner companion on a subject she could not care less about.

'I spent years trying to turn a profit from growing crops. Then I realised I didn't need to. My land is all chalk, you see, and chalk is a commodity.' Sir Gerald said this with such an air of authority that Connie instinctively nodded sagely although she was slowly losing the will to live. 'If it is burned you get quicklime and quicklime is one of the best fertilisers around. My tenants now quarry the chalk and we burn it all in my kilns. I have ten now and plans for at least ten more. It has become a most profitable venture. There is far more profit in chalk than there is in wheat. Chalk is the crop that keeps on giving.' He laughed at his own joke so Connie did the same. She could feel Aaron's obvious amusement at her predicament so she purposefully did not look at the wretch. 'The biggest problem is I cannot get my workers to dig enough of it for the demand. If I had twice as much land, I could make twice as much profit. Except nobody wants to sell their land because they are all so wedded to growing wheat.'

'Yes, indeed. What a fortuitous situation you have found yourself in, Sir Gerald. This conversation has been most enlightening.'

Connie had meant that comment as a signal to talk about something else, but Sir Gerald was only just warming up to the topic. 'Of course, sometimes we find hidden jewels in the chalk.'

'Like diamonds or rubies, sir?' Please let it be something interesting. Anything to relieve the interminable boredom of his words.

'Better! Flint!' His pale eyes were positively glowing with what could best be described as religious fervour and her spirit was instantly crushed again. 'Flint is highly sought after at the moment because it is used in guns, you see. No rifle or pistol can fire without a piece of flint to first make the spark.'

How Connie wished she had a pistol now. She was not entirely sure whether she would use it on herself or Sir Gerald. If she chose herself, it would put an end to her current misery—but if she used it on Sir Gerald she would be saving all future dinner party guests from of the misery of being left with him. It would almost be a public service. If she had a pair of pistols she could shoot Spiteful Sarah as well. The woman was still sulking and had barely said a thing since Aaron had put her, so wonderfully, in her place.

Instinctively, she flicked her eyes in his direction. He was being his usual charming self, telling some tall tale that had his own dinner partners squealing with laughter. When he was like this, all easy smiles and affability and looking far more handsome than any man had a right to, if was difficult to imagine the terrified and troubled man she had held last night. There was much more to Aaron than all of these people could possibly realise. Beneath that social façade was a man who carried a great deal on his magnificently broad shoulders.

He must have sensed her watching him because his eyes suddenly found hers and locked. He winked at her—not in a cheeky way—telling her in that tiny gesture that she had done well tonight and that he was proud of her. In that instant, the rest of the noisy table disappeared and for the briefest of moments it was just the two of them. Connie looked away, secretly pleased that he had noticed, and slightly discomfited by the cosy intimacy they had just shared in one simple, wordless gaze.

'Of course, chalk is also used in whiting…' Reluctantly Connie allowed Sir Gerald's monotone to permeate her thoughts and felt her eyes glaze over almost instantly.

Aaron joined the gentleman for their after-dinner port, but still found himself thinking about his wife. She had been a confident and charming hostess so far, even though she did not really have to be. His father had set her up to disappoint and it would have been completely natural for her to live up to his low expectation. But Constance being Constance, she hadn't. Even his father had begrudgingly admitted as much by acknowledging her efforts to the guests who had complimented him so far. She really was a remarkable woman.

Formidable.

And then again not. There were so many layers to Connie, so many conflicting and contrasting elements to her personality that she reminded him of a rainbow. At one end of the spectrum she was indomitable, sharp-tongued and aloof. He had been on the receiving end of that with alarming frequency and they had only been together for such a short time. But then she was kind-hearted. Hadn't she insisted that he go to bed yesterday because he looked tired and had to come him in the night to soothe his nightmares? Finally, buried beneath all of that, was a seam of vulnerability that she worked hard to hide—but he knew that it was there. Her reaction to hearing that awful nickname he had saddled her with, all those years ago, was testament to that. She had been braced for the censure and vitriol of Lady Erith as if she had expected it, and had been so obviously grateful to him for saving her that he had wanted to drag her outside, hug her close and kiss away the distress swirling in her lovely eyes.

By the time they re-joined the ladies he was looking forward to seeing her again. Odd that he had missed her reassuring presence in such a short space of time, but a fact regardless. Her eyes flicked to his briefly and they were filled with warmth and mirth. Connie was obviously enjoying herself. Aaron wandered to the brandy decanter to fill his glass, although really he was using it as an excuse to watch her more, enjoy the languid way she moved and the way that the chandelier picked out all of the many shades of copper in her hair.

After a moment, something about her did not ring true and for a little while Aaron's brain scrambled to work out what it was. Then she glanced at him again and all at once it struck him. For some inexplicable reason, although clearly standing, Connie was several inches shorter than usual.

Curious, and more than a little amused by this strange phenomenon, Aaron positioned himself closer so that he could see what she was about. After a few minutes, it became obvious to him that she was standing in a crouch which the long crimson skirt disguised perfectly. The silly woman's legs must be aching by now, he thought as he edged alongside, and as soon as the conversation was briefly diverted away from her he reached out his arm and hoisted her upwards. She gazed at him a little startled, then coloured slightly at being caught out, but did not say anything because Lady Erith and her husband were coming towards them. Aaron could feel Connie tense next to him although her face was a serene mask of conviviality.

'My, my. It always staggers me how very tall you are, Constance, when we are stood so close. I do not think I have ever come across another lady who is quite as statuesque as you. Or as thin. In places there is nothing of you.'

Another spiteful barb from Lady Erith that Aaron was not going to let slide. He opened his mouth to speak.

'Yes, indeed,' his wife said politely before he could intercede. 'One can only hope that I will follow in your footsteps, Sarah, and put on some weight now that I am married.'

Aaron barely managed to stifle the laughter that threatened. Sarah smiled tightly, looking every inch the brittle, nasty piece of work that he now knew her to be. 'It has been a pleasant evening, but, alas, my husband and I must now bid you goodnight.'

The exit of the Earl and Countess of Erith signalled the end of the evening, and soon all of the guests were departing. Aaron's father, looking very grey around the gills, excused himself to go to bed, leaving Connie and Aaron to see people safely into their carriages. Sir Gerald and his wife were the last two to go and he could not have been more effusive in his praise.

'My dear Lady Constance, it has been quite lovely to meet you. I thoroughly enjoyed our long chat over dinner and I hope that I shall be fortuitous enough be seated next to you when we next meet.'

She accepted his compliment graciously and stood waving next to Aaron as their carriage finally pulled out of the drive.

'I told you he was a crushing bore,' he whispered out of the side of his mouth. 'Perhaps next time you will listen to me.' The very idea of a next time, and of playing the role of his wife, made her feel all warm inside. The evening had been a triumph and she had enjoyed playing the mistress of the house for once, instead of the disappointing daughter or the aloof wallflower.

'If I had listened to you, I would have been stuck next to Lady Erith. I think I would take Sir Gerald over her any day.'

'You might have a valid point there. I had not realised that she was so vindictive before tonight. She used to be much more agreeable company.'

Connie snorted her disbelief. 'I have always found her to be completely obnoxious and malicious. The woman has never liked me. Thank you for sticking up for me before. Your convenient lie saved me from a great deal of embarrassment.'

He looked at her oddly, then smiled. 'Would you like to take a little stroll before we go back inside? I need a little fresh air before bedtime.'

Connie snuggled inside her heavy shawl and gazed up at the sky. Despite the cold, it was a perfect winter's night. Clear black skies, an almost full moon and a smattering of twinkling stars. 'I should like that.' Aaron had spent the entire evening in the company of others and he still wished to spend some time with her alone. The prospect made Connie feel special. And excited.

The pair of them walked in companionable silence along the drive for a little way, his hand resting warm on hers, as her arm was threaded through his.

'It wasn't a complete lie,' he suddenly said, staring out into the darkness.

A tiny bubble of something—hope or anticipation—bloomed in her chest, but she still groped for her mask of indifference. 'Do enlighten me.'

They were still strolling slowly down the drive, the only sound was the gravel crunching under their feet and he was still looking out towards the stars with an odd expression on his face. Nerves?

Surely not.

Then he let out a sigh. His breathe wafted in the frigid air like a white cloud and she realised that he must have been holding that breath in while he decided how to answer her.

'I remember the very first time that I saw you. It was at Almack's. There was a sea of debutantes that night, all decked out in frothy white dresses with their ringlets bouncing and you were all being introduced together. I was with a group of friends and we were exchanging comments about the new crop of young ladies, as young men are prone to do. We were all looking at one girl, she was very pretty, I recall, and daring each other to ask her to dance. Then I saw you. You were stood alone at the edge of the ballroom, all dressed in white, with your hair done in a similar style as it is tonight, except there were more curls about your face. But I do remember thinking that you were quite the loveliest thing I had ever seen. I had no idea who you were, but I kept staring at you as you walked across the floor. You were so graceful. So unique. You stood out from all of the others. I smiled at you, I'm not sure if you remember? You did not smile back. In fact, you looked at me as if I were some kind of snake or insect or something.'

Connie could not quite believe her ears. Was he trying to charm her in the same way that he tried to charm everybody? Maybe he was trying to make up for the way Sarah had behaved tonight. Or he was simply being kind. Although she dimly recalled him smiling at her that night. At the time, she had been well aware of who he was. Her mother had pointed him out straight away. She had thought that the smile was to goad her, or make her feel uncomfortable, because he was Aaron Wincanton. If he was telling the truth, which Connie sincerely doubted, and he had not been aware of who she was, then that smile had been genuine. And maybe he had thought her lovely. Her throat began to tighten at the thought.

'Of course, my friends saw the exchange,' he continued a little shyly, 'and teased me mercilessly. It was only then that I learnt your identity. So being young—and feeling very foolish—I lied to them. I claimed that I had been staring at another girl, not you, and that I would never, ever find anything appealing in a Stuart, especially one who looked like a ginger Amazonian.'

He stopped walking then and turned towards her. She saw genuine regret and shame on his handsome face. 'I wish I had never said that, Connie. It was a silly, flippant remark and I never meant for you to ever hear it. It galls me to think that my crass stupidity that night gave a catty, vindictive woman like Sarah a weapon to use against you.'

Out of habit she dismissed it breezily. 'It is of no matter. That silly nickname has never bothered me.'

'Don't lie, Connie. I saw the way you stiffened when she said it. I also saw you attempting to be shorter with my own eyes tonight.'

Oh, good gracious! The man always managed to make her feel like an idiot. Even in this chilly air she could feel the start of the blush begin to burn. 'I loom over people!' she said defensively, turning her head back towards the house to hint that it was time to return.

'You don't loom over me.'

His hand touched her cheek and turned her face back towards him. Where Connie was sure she would see amusement, she saw something she could not quite decipher. His eyes were even darker than usual and they were looking directly at hers in a way no man had ever looked at her eyes. It was intense and intimate, almost as if he could see past all of the barricades she used to protect her wounded heart, and it set her pulse racing. There was desire there, she was almost certain, and the sight of it made her heart rejoice even though everything sensible in her mind told her not to believe it could be true. An attractive man like Aaron surely did not really find her appealing—did he? Yet he had just said that she was the loveliest thing that he had ever seen. He had appeared sincere, almost shy, when he had said it, too. Would it be foolhardy and impetuous to want to believe him? Or was she being pathetic and needy, so desperate for it all to be real that she would ignore the nagging doubts and throw caution to the wind?

She wanted to look away—but couldn't.

Something about him was so mesmerising that all she could do was gaze back at him longingly. When his eyes slowly drifted down to her lips and lingered there, Connie's heart began to race. His palm was still cupping her cheek, making her skin prickle with an awareness that was both quite alien and intoxicating at the same time. Her lips began to tingle and she licked them nervously, regretting it instantly as his own began to curve upwards in a knowing smile. He probably thought she wanted him to kiss her.

Which, of course, she did.

More than anything.

He let his body tilt forward until his face was

inches away from hers, then closer still until their foreheads were touching. The hand on her cheek brushed over her skin in search of her hair. He let his fingers trail the entire length of one of the tendrils that framed her face and Connie forgot to breathe.

The moment was so magical, so unexpected and so perfect that she lost herself in it. Time stood still. She had no idea how long they stood there like that, skin touching skin and mouths a whisper apart, his warm fingers twining in her hair. But she could feel that his breathing was as erratic as hers; sensed the trepidation that he was also feeling at that exact same moment.

The air crackled with promise; carnal need warred with common sense. Connie was suddenly desperate for that need to win the battle. She wanted his lips on hers, wanted to feel his hands on her body again and lose herself in the glorious sensations of passion—but she was too frightened to make the first move. His body shifted slightly, and with wonderful impatience, so that he could be closer still until not only their heads were touching. She could feel his shoulders, hips and thighs so close to her own, his nose gently rested against hers, his warm breath heating her lips. He was gauging her reaction to his intrusion to see if his advances were welcome and Connie was not inclined to either push him away or close the distance between them. She would not be the first one to retreat or the first one to surrender to her desires. To do either would be to sacrifice her pride.

'Mr Aaron!'

They broke apart at the panicked shout, just in time to see a footman skid to halt before them on the gravel, his eyes wide with alarm.

'You need to come quickly, sir. It's your father…'

Chapter Eighteen

Aaron took the stairs two at a time, conscious that Connie was close behind him, then ran to his father's bedchamber. Inside the room he saw Deaks stood awkwardly next to his father's valet. The valet was kneeling on the floor, bent over his father's body. Both men respectfully moved to the side as he rushed in.

'He heard him fall,' Deaks hurriedly explained, gesturing to the valet. 'We think he is still alive, sir. I think I felt a pulse. I cannot be sure.'

Aaron stared in panic at his father's prone body. He was lying on his side, eyes closed and not moving. He dropped to the floor and pressed his fingers on the base of the old man's neck. There was a pulse. Barely. 'Help me to get him on to the bed!'

The valet and Deaks sprang to his assistance.

The valet carefully cradled his master's head while Aaron and the butler gently lifted him on to the mattress. It was only then he saw the cut on the side of his father's head. Fresh blood oozed from the wound, trickling on to the pillow and staining the pristine white cotton red.

Everything suddenly blurred, his head spun and the room evaporated. The roar of battle filled his ears and he wanted to clasp his hands over them to block out the sounds of the screaming. The metallic tang of death and blood was everywhere. It filled his nostrils and his lungs, so thick and acrid it threatened to suffocate him.

It was so overpowering he could taste it. His stomach lurched in rebellion. He could even feel it on his skin. Warm. Sticky.

Abhorrent.

Aaron did not need to see the carnage. He was stood in it. His comrades now formed a swamp of death. They were no longer men, instead needlessly reduced to the gruesome constituent parts that had once made them whole. Unidentifiable.

Frantically he searched for Fletcher, calling out to him, until he realised that the stickiness on his uniform *was* Fletcher. It was all Aaron's fault. It should be his face lying lifeless in the mud.

'Aaron!'

Someone was calling him and he turned towards the voice desperately, hoping that they could save him. Connie's face was inches from his. She was staring intently into his eyes. He had no idea how she had got to Spain, or why she was at the fortress, but his relief at seeing her was almost his undoing. He became aware of her gripping his shoulders and turning him around, away from the slaughter. The battlefield floated away, leaving the lifeless eyes of his father's hunting trophies stared down at him in utter disgust at what he had done.

'Aaron!'

Then he remembered that his father was dying. His father was dying! But the madness had chosen that exact moment to show itself again and had rendered him useless. Ashamed and shaken, Aaron stared at his feet. Everyone had seen it. They all knew now.

Connie knew. Her hands cupped his face and angled it up to look at hers again. Her eyes were filled with pity. Connie had found a way to get to him on that battlefield and drag him back. 'I need you to go and fetch the physician. Can you do that, Aaron?'

He saw the desperation and fear in her lovely green eyes and nodded gratefully. It did not matter that his father lay dying, he had to get away and she was giving him an excuse to do so.

'I will be back as soon as I can.' His voice was still trembling, his knees still unsteady, but at least he was back where he was meant to be. Aaron did not turn around to look at his father, fearing the worst if he did, instead he dashed from the room towards the fresh air. He did not stop running until he reached the stable.

Connie made the viscount as comfortable as possible and tended to the open wound on his head herself. It was just a flesh wound, but judging by the angry swelling that was appearing behind it, he must have hit his head on the nightstand as he fell. The viscount remained unconscious throughout. Now he looked weak and grey against the freshly changed pillowcase, one side of his face pulling awkwardly downwards as if the muscles on that side no longer worked.

She dismissed all of the servants and sat nervously, waiting for Aaron to return with the doctor, silently praying that she had made the right decision in sending him. She had no doubt that he would come back. Aaron's sense of responsibility was unquestionable, but to send him away like that, when she had seen first-hand the sheer terror on his face troubled her. At the time, she knew he was on the cusp of losing control.

It had been the strangest thing to witness. Aaron had rushed in and immediately taken command of the situation—but then he had frozen. Although in actuality all this happened in a split second, Connie had known that something was desperately wrong. He had seen his father's blood and then his eyes had glazed over as if he was no longer there, his hands fisted at his sides so tightly that she had seen every pronounced vein, his body so rigid it might have been chiselled out of marble. She had rushed to him then, turning him away from the sight of the blood, and had called his name. To begin with it was as if he had not heard her, then she saw him focus and saw the same terror reflected in his eyes that she had witnessed the previous evening when he was in the full grip of his nightmare. Whatever haunted his dreams obviously tormented his waking thoughts, too.

The bedchamber door burst open and the physician came in, closely followed by her husband. She saw his gaze dart quickly to his father. She watched him take in the clean bandage on the wound and then she saw him almost slump in relief—even though he was obviously still gravely concerned for his father. The sight of blood bothered him. It had triggered the odd episode, Connie was now certain. How she knew this, she could not say, except that she did know it. She also knew that hell would freeze over before he was likely to ever admit to it.

They both stepped outside to allow the physician to do his job. Aaron purposefully stood a little away from her, his hands gripped tightly behind his back and his posture once again stiff as he paced around the hallway like a caged animal. His usually fluid and graceful movements were jerky and stilted. He did not look at her or speak, giving Connie the distinct impression that he would much rather she wasn't there at all. Only an hour or so before, she was convinced he had been about to kiss her, yet now a vast chasm of awkwardness had opened between them that neither knew quite how to bridge.

That was not strictly true, Connie reasoned. The chasm was of his making, not hers. He was in pain, worried sick and embarrassed. To cover that maelstrom of perfectly natural emotions it was Aaron who was creating the distance between them. She needed to be the one to close it.

'Lots of people are frightened the sight of blood, Aaron. I do not think any less of you for it.'

He stopped pacing instantly and she could practically feel him strapping layer upon layer of imaginary armour over himself before he responded. 'It is not that I am frightened of it. I have merely seen too much of it.'

In his hasty defence he had inadvertently given her a window into his past. The war had left an indelible mark on him. He had seen things that he could not forget. 'I am sure that you have.'

That was apparently also the wrong thing to say because he became immediately defensive. 'I know that I reacted badly, but you have to understand that even though I have been expecting this and had prepared for the worst, seeing my father like that was still a shock.'

Connie wanted to go to him and wrap her arms around him, but everything about his stance and his expression warned her against it. She could see that he was holding his emotions together tightly.

'Of course it was. Please do not think that I am criticising you. Your reaction was completely understandable.' Connie inched towards him. Whether he wanted her comfort or not she wanted to give it.

Instantly he backed away. 'Please don't, Connie,' he managed stiffly, then stared unseeingly down the brightly lit landing, his back presented to her like the battlements around a castle, a signal for her to keep away. Several painful minutes ticked by until Aaron broke the deafening silence, although resolutely still turned away from her gaze. 'Did I do anything untoward, Connie?'

'You don't remember?'

He shook his head stiffly, still staring off into the distance. This insight into the man she had married broke Connie's heart. He had asked a similar question the morning after his nightmare, suggesting that when he was in the grip of whatever it was that tormented him he was not in control of himself. He was not only mortified by his reaction, she now saw, it terrified him.

'It was all over in the blink of an eye,' she soothed, coming up behind him and laying her hand upon his shoulder. The corded muscle beneath her palm tensed further so she gently ran her hand back and forth over it. 'You did nothing untoward, Aaron. You just stood there, a little stunned, but perfectly still. That's all. You did not scream or wince or do anything that would have given the servants cause to gossip.'

He let out a shuddering breath. 'But you knew something was wrong, didn't you, Connie? That's why you sent me away.'

'I could see that you were not yourself, but that has nothing to do with why I sent you away.

I did that because I knew that nobody else could ride faster to the physician than you. And I was right.'

And Aaron was also right. Sometimes it was kinder to lie to a person when you knew that they would find the truth too painful to bear. Connie had sent him away because she feared that Aaron was in grave danger of losing his tightly held control in front of the servants. She had tried to protect his pride and his dignity for his sake, not hers. She was still doing that.

The doctor came out then, saving her from having to embellish her lie, and Aaron finally whipped around so that she could see him. His face was drawn and etched in worry.

'Is it very bad?'

'He has had a stroke, I am in no doubt about that, and he has still not regained consciousness. I have no idea if he will. Occasionally, patients make a partial recovery. More often than not they do not. Your father's health was in a poor state before this happened so I fear that this episode might signal the beginning of the end. Only time will tell. I'm afraid I cannot give you any more hope than that. I have left some laudanum on the nightstand in case he wakes. A few drops of that will ensure that he is not in any pain. I will come back in the morning and check on him again. I am dreadfully sorry, Mr Wincanton, that I cannot do any more than that. You should prepare yourself for the worst.'

Chapter Nineteen

There was no change in Viscount Ardleigh's condition for several days. Once or twice, they feared that he was hovering on the brink of death and each time he rallied. Then again, they had been equally as convinced that he might regain consciousness, too. The unharmed side of his face would become mobile and his eyelids would tremble as if he was fighting to wake up. They were in a state of perpetual limbo. Aaron could neither fully grieve nor fully hope, which left him feeling more useless and ineffectual than ever.

They took it in turns to sit with him. That meant that their paths rarely collided. If he was being completely honest with himself, he had orchestrated it to be that way, making himself scarce to avoid having to spend any time with her. Aaron was grateful for the distance. Aside from the fact that he needed time to get his jumbled thoughts together, he could not shake the feeling that she saw through him and that frightened him. Inadvertently, Connie was becoming too close and keeping his guard up around her was becoming increasingly difficult.

Every time he saw her, he would see the questions in her expression alongside the sympathy and he knew that Connie understood exactly what was going on behind his eyes. To the rest of outside world, he was bearing up stoically, as would be expected of a man who was about to take on the mantle of viscount, but inside he was slowly falling apart. All of the feelings of uselessness and inadequacy that he had fought so hard to bury for so long were boiling up within, demanding release, and sometimes he felt as if they might all burst out at once, leaving him completely broken. Each time he felt like this, he desperately wanted to go to her so that she could make him feel better, as if she could. As if anybody could. Connie would recoil in horror if she knew what he had done and that was a far more daunting prospect than dealing with his own demons alone. Although he deserved it, the thought of losing her to the truth was too painful to bear.

He barely slept. He did not want to. When he

did, Aaron was soon transported back to Ciudad Rodrigo, covered in blood and wishing he was lying dead alongside his comrades so that his nightmare would finally be at an end. He woke up terrified, dripping in sweat and desperately hoping that Connie would come and save him. She didn't, of course, because he had taken to barricading his door with a heavy chest to prevent her from venturing into his bedchamber and seeing him so unmanned. Again.

In the last few days she had certainly witnessed him at his lowest. First there had been the nightmare and then there were the awful two instances where he had lost himself at the first sight of blood. Goodness only knew what the woman thought of all that. But then his mind kept thinking about the moment that they had shared after that fateful dinner, where he had desperately wanted to kiss her and had been convinced that she had wanted him to. He almost had. Aaron supposed that he should be relieved that the kiss had never happened because he would have hated to witness the inevitable regret on her lovely face now that she definitely knew that he was not right in the head. Except he wasn't relieved. Every time he spotted her he wanted to kiss her, then lose himself in her arms and pretend that all was going to be well.

When he wasn't with his father or descending into the pit of madness, Aaron holed himself up in his father's study and tried to make sense of all of the ledgers and papers that he had never been allowed to see before. The baffling array of costs and demands on the estate's money threatened to bamboozle him—but he was determined to make some sense of that at least. This afternoon, he had demanded a meeting with Mr Thomas to explain them—and with his father so gravely ill, this time the sneaky fellow would have no one to hide behind. He had also summoned the family solicitor. As his father was incapacitated, and was unlikely to be otherwise, it seemed like the sensible thing to do.

There was a light tap on the study door and, to Aaron's relief and horror, Connie walked in. Behind her was a maid carrying a laden tray. She quickly deposited it on a table and hurried out, closing the door behind her and leaving him alone with his tempting, intuitive wife.

'You did not eat breakfast,' she stated in a matter-of-fact tone, 'so I have brought you some luncheon.'

He thanked her and bent his head back to the ledger, hoping she would assume he was inordinately busy and leave. Being Connie, she did not. Instead she made herself comfortable in one of his father's ugly wingback chairs and began to arrange two place settings from the piled crockery on the tray.

'In case you are in any doubt, I will be eating with you. I am tired of worrying about your health as well as your father's, therefore I have decided that we will take all of our meals together so that I can make sure that you are properly fed.'

'There really is no need.'

She pinned him with her obstinate glare, the one that brooked no arguments and terrified lesser men. 'There is every need. You *will* come and sit down with me right this minute, Aaron Wincanton, or you will *feel* the full force of my temper.' To emphasise her words, she stared pointed at the pile of leather-bound ledgers on his desk. 'I should imagine one of those is much heavier than *The Complete Farmer*.'

Aaron felt the muscles in his cheeks pull upwards and, despite everything that was dire and sombre and hopeless about his current situation, he felt himself smile. She did have a point. There was so much to do. In the next few weeks there was a veritable mountain to climb and, to do it, he had to keep his strength up. He pushed himself up from the desk and drifted over to the matching wingback chair opposite hers. Connie did not ask him what he wanted, she simply piled a plate up with slices of ham, cheese and bread which she handed to him unceremoniously with a single instruction.

'Eat.'

His lack of enthusiasm for the task soon changed when the first morsel hit his stomach. All at once he was starving. It was a tremendous effort not to shovel the rest of the food into his face like a savage while she poured him tea and plonked that in front of him decisively. 'I am tired of watching you run yourself into the ground from the wings, Aaron. I am well aware of the fact that you have been avoiding me and, frankly, I am sick of it. This is a dreadful time and I will not be made to sit around and be made useless. I want to help you.'

But if she helped him he would have to spend time with her. 'There really is nothing you can do.'

Her own teacup suddenly clattered into its saucer, sending a waterfall of liquid over the rim. 'Perhaps I did not make myself clear. When I said that I wanted to help I meant that I *am* going to help you, whether you like it or not. I am not some ornamental woman and I will not let you treat me like one. You have already admitted to me that you have no idea how to run an estate, therefore I fail to understand your objections to me assisting you. Surely two heads are better than one?'

Two heads would be better, much as it pained him to admit it, because he was completely out of his depth. Maybe Connie had more of a head for figures than he did. All the numbers started to swim before his eyes after a while.

'It's all such a mess, Connie. My father has been spending above our means for years. The costs of running this house and the one in Berkeley Square are staggering.'

'My mother gave me a great deal of instruction on how to run a household. Let me look at the accounts. I am sure that I can find fat to trim. For example, if things are so dire, do you actually need the house in London?'

'I will need somewhere to stay when I go hunting for my next heiress.' Aaron had intended it to be a flippant statement that would make her smile. It did quite the opposite. Her green eyes darkened and she appeared almost wounded by the comment.

'Of course. I had not considered that.' Her slim shoulders straightened and he wondered if he had just hurt her feelings. But then she smiled slightly, all business again. 'Maybe costs could be cut by paring down the size of the household in your town house. You could always take servants from here back with you to town when you needed them. That would reduce your wage bill.'

It was a solution that Aaron had not even thought of and a sensible one. There was a chance that Connie might be better at all of this than he was. Aaron conceded he would be a fool not to utilise her practicality even if he was loathe to spend time with her.

'Come,' he said, making an instant decision that he hoped he would not live to regret. 'Let me show you the mess.'

For the next hour, the pair of them scrutinised the complicated ledgers. Working alongside her was actually very pleasant. Connie seemed to understand all of the columns of numbers much quicker than he did, a blessing indeed because she was also able to explain it to him in a way that he could understand. By tacit agreement, neither mentioned anything that made the situation awkward and Aaron found that having her with him made him less likely to descend into the melancholy that constantly threatened to suffocated him. They were so engrossed in the task that both of them were startled when Deaks knocked on the door.

'Mr Thomas is here, sir. Shall I send him in?'

'Yes, please.' It was going to be a very brief meeting so there was no point in uprooting Connie when they were making such headway.

Mr Thomas slid in with his usual disingenuous smile fixed on his face. 'How is your father, Mr Wincanton? I have been so very worried about him.'

'He is dying, Mr Thomas.' Aaron felt slightly sick saying that out loud, but he stared levelly at the estate manager. 'The physician is not optimistic that he will ever recover, which means that I am now going to be taking full control over the estate.'

Mr Thomas bowed his head like a true toad. 'Then I am at your service, Mr Wincanton.'

In the army, Aaron had learnt to discipline his troops effectively. Swift, sharp justice was a better way to administer it than procrastination. 'Actually, Mr Thomas, you are not. I have decided to terminate your employment.'

He heard Connie's sharp intake of breath, but did not look at her. Perhaps he did appear callous, but he was not going to feel bad about it. Thomas was an appalling estate manager and Aaron did not trust him. Instead of appearing shocked or upset by the news, Mr Thomas positively snarled as he pointed accusingly.

'She has made vile accusations, hasn't she?'

His wife's face had paled considerably and her eyes were quite wide. At first he had assumed that she was as outraged by the outburst as Aaron was, then her eyes darted to his and quickly went to the tightly clasped hands in her lap. There was something going on here that Aaron was not aware of. Going with his gut instinct, he decided to challenge her in private. Whatever it was had no bearing on his decision.

'The *she* you are referring to, Mr Thomas, is my wife, so I will insist that you defer to her with respect.'

'You would trust a Stuart over a man who has been in your employ for over four years, when she has been here less than five minutes? I have given years of loyal service!'

'To be frank, Mr Thomas, I would sooner trust Napoleon himself than I would you. You have neglected your duties for too long. The estate has barely made any profit under your stewardship, you do not keep your word and you are frequently impossible to track down. I have no faith in you, Mr Thomas. So to answer your impertinent question, my wife has not influenced my decision in any way. She really did not need to.' He bent his head back to the ledger, his mind brimming with questions for his suddenly anxious and guilty-looking wife. 'We are done, Mr

Thomas. Get out now or I will enjoy personally throwing you out.'

Mr Thomas stood quaking with unsuppressed anger before he spun on his heel and stalked to the door. For several seconds he hovered in the doorway, then he turned and practically spat at Connie.

'Your father will hear of your treachery, Lady Constance; you mark my words.'

She visibly balked at the threat and continued to stare wide-eyed at the door long after the estate manager had gone.

'Would you care to tell me what all that was about?' Aaron was experiencing an enormous sense of foreboding. Connie was worrying her plump bottom lip with her teeth and wringing her hands in her lap. Whatever she had to say was not likely to be good.

'When I saw Mr Thomas the other day, I recognised him.' The pink blotches had already begun to bloom on her cheeks and neck and she could not meet his eyes. 'I confronted him last week and he assured me that my assumptions were false, but you see, I have seen Mr Thomas many times before. I am certain the man works for my father.'

Aaron digested this for several moments, experiencing the foul taste of betrayal and the anger that it inevitably left in its wake. *I am certain the man works for my father.* In a sudden rush he considered all of the ramifications of that damning, simple sentence. It all made perfect sense to him now. The late sowing of the harvest, the declining profits, the dissatisfaction of the tenants, not to mention Mr Thomas's elusiveness—it was all part of another grand scheme by the Stuarts to destroy the Wincantons. Except this time, it had possibly done irreparable damage. Connie's father was not just destroying the Wincantons, he was also dragging the innocent farmers who depended on the estate into the battle and potentially ruining all of their lives, too. And his father had fallen for the ruse because he was too consumed with the silly feud to pay proper attention to his own holdings. The Earl of Redbridge must have been congratulating himself for years at the success of his duplicity.

And Connie knew all of this.

'Why did you not tell me all that a week ago?' He sounded hurt and he wished that he didn't. Suddenly he did not want her to know that her betrayal cut much deeper than Thomas's or her father's. He had expected that of them. Aaron had come to expect so much more from Connie. Her betrayal was uniquely personal to him.

Her whole face turned red as she stared mournfully down. Dispassionately, he noted the slight tremor in her bottom lip and hardened himself against any sympathy. He should have expected this.

'In my defence, recent events have rather got in the way.'

Aaron shot to his feet and stalked across the study, raking a furious hand through his hair to try to cool his simmering temper. As if there was any excuse that would justify her dishonesty. When given the opportunity to rise above the historic, and petty, quarrel between their two families, she had chosen to keep her father's perfidy a secret. And he had been as stupid as his father because he had trusted her. Mt Thomas had put it quite aptly, he now realised, Aaron had known her less than five minutes yet he had still believed that she had been capable of rising above three hundred years of bad blood—to see him as he really was. What an idiot he had been.

He embraced his anger then, allowing the heat of it to wash over him and consume him. It was far better to be furious at her than disappointed in his own naivety. 'Pray, enlighten me, madam. How can you defend the indefensible?'

'I was waiting for an opportune moment.' Her

voice had risen several octaves in response to his sarcastic tone and he could see she had the audacity to begin to bristle with indignation.

'An opportune moment? And when would that be? When I am declared bankrupt? Or perhaps when I have been thrown into debtors' prison?'

Connie launched to her feet and looked outraged at the suggestion. 'I had a dinner party to arrange. For twenty people! And then your father had a stroke. What was I supposed to do? Sidle up to you whilst he is lying on his deathbed and you were sick with worry and say, by the way, your estate manager is not what he seems? He assured me that his association with my father was merely a coincidence…'

'Which, of course, you believed, because you are such a trusting soul, Constance! You are always so willing to think the best of everyone.'

'I didn't believe him, but—'

'Oh! Now we get to the heart of the matter. You didn't believe him, but you did not feel the need to tell me—a vile Wincanton!'

'It was not like—'

'Yes, it was!'

Her delicate nostrils flared and her chin lifted. 'If you would stop interrupting me, then perhaps I could—'

'What? Spout a pack of lies to justify your treachery?'

'Argh!'

Her arms flew up in the air and she curled her hands into fists. 'You are the most insufferable man I have ever met!' Her long legs tore up the distance to the door and she stomped out of it, slamming it loudly behind her as she left. Aaron marched to it and promptly opened it.

'This is my house!' he shouted to her retreating back petulantly. 'And this is my door! And if anybody is going to slam it, it is going to be me!'

The hinges screeched in protest as it swung closed again, with an impressive thud, and Aaron was left staring at it in utter disgust. The woman was impossible. He had bent over backwards to make her stay here more bearable and she still resorted to histrionics when he had the nerve to challenge her shoddy behaviour. Aaron stalked to his desk and slumped in the chair. Now he was so riled he would not be able to make any sense of any of these numbers and that was all her fault, too.

His head snapped up at the knock on the door and he primed himself to continue the battle, recognising that his anger was nowhere near spent and he still had plenty to say to the woman. But it was not Connie at the door, it was Deaks.

'The solicitor is here, Mr Wincanton, shall I send him in or do you need a few minutes more?'

Chapter Twenty

Connie was still pacing her sitting room, half an hour later, when remorse descended like an April shower, dousing her temper like a cold bucket of water. He had every right to be angry at her. Losing her temper had been a mistake. She should have allowed him to vent for a few minutes before she had tried to explain herself. She could understand why he had misinterpreted her silence as something more sinister than it was. Initially, in the wake of the viscount's stroke, it had not crossed her mind. As the days passed by and Aaron had done everything in his power to avoid her, there had been little opportunity and she had been more concerned with the way he had suddenly withdrawn into himself than she had been about her suspicions regarding the estate manager. She should have found a way to tell him about Mr Thomas by now. It had been quite wrong of her to keep it a secret, even though a small part of her had hoped that, in doing so, her father might be more benevolent towards her and that he might consent for her to have some contact with her mother and brother again.

Stewing up here all alone while he was doing the same thing in his study was not a particularly sensible way of dealing with things, she now realised. It was merely avoiding the inevitable conversation in which she would have to explain her reasoning and hope that he understood. Without thinking, Connie moved towards the mirror and adjusted her hair. If she was about to eat a slice of humble pie, there was no need to do it looking in disarray. She was certainly not checking her appearance for Aaron. The wretch.

A maid burst in without knocking, causing Connie to jump. 'Lady Constance! His lordship is waking up.'

Instantly, Connie picked up her skirts and hurried after the maid. Once in the viscount's bedchamber, she could see for herself that he was moving much more than he had in recent days. His left hand was clearly twitching against the bedcovers and his breathing was more erratic, yet stronger than it had been. Automatically she went to him and took the hand to comfort him. It must be frightening to wake up and not to be able to move as you expected and further distress might worsen his condition.

'Good afternoon, your lordship,' she whispered softly close to his ear. 'You have had a bit of a turn. Try not to panic. Everything will be all right in a little while.'

Her words seemed to placate him a little. His breathing slowed and the fingers of his left hand closed around hers.

'Shall I fetch the doctor?' the maid hissed in a facsimile of a stage whisper that could only serve to create panic. Connie nodded impatiently while still stroking the back of the viscount's cold hand. She did not want him to know that he was so gravely ill that it would necessitate the immediate summoning of the physician.

'Tell Aaron his father is awake. I know that his lordship would much prefer to see his son.'

Almost as soon as she was left alone with him, the viscount cracked open his left eye and she watched him struggle to focus on her face. His left eyebrow and that side of his mouth were drawn down in an expression of pure terror. The other side of his face hung immobile.

'You have had a small stroke,' she said softly by way of an acceptable explanation, as if minimising what had happened to him might make him feel less anxious, 'You are lying in your own bed because you need to have a few days' rest.'

The viscount's mouth moved as he tried to speak, but no discernible noise came out. 'Try not to talk yet. Your throat is probably very dry. Let me get you a drink.' Connie had been trying to spoon water past his parched lips for days with limited success. Carefully, she lifted his head a little and pressed the spout of the invalid cup to the good side of his mouth. Even though she poured only the tiniest trickle, most of the liquid bubbled out of his mouth and dribbled down his cheek. Taking a towel, Connie dabbed the water away, trying not to notice how grey his skin was, how blue his lips had become and how much weight he had already lost in such a small amount of time. The deterioration had been frighteningly rapid. The man in the bed was only a shell of the man whom she had argued with a week ago.

Regardless, Connie smiled cheerfully. 'You did give us a quite a scare—but at least you are on the mend now.' He was still watching her warily, his dark eyes watery and filled with fear, but the brightness in them had dimmed. He might well be conscious now, but she could see the life was slowly ebbing out of his body.

'Aaron will be pleased you are awake. He has been doing a splendid job of overseeing things while you have been resting. I am sure that you will be up and about and keen to take back the reins in a few days.'

She heard a rustle behind her and saw that Aaron had entered the room. 'Here he is now,' she said breezily, backing away, 'No doubt he will be able to tell you himself how smoothly things are running.' Connie could not help giving her husband's arm a reassuring squeeze as she walked past him and when she got to the hallway she quietly closed the bedchamber door behind herself to give them some privacy.

The doctor had been and gone and Connie was quietly reading when she next saw Aaron several hours later. Saw was really the wrong word to describe it though, sensed was a better one. She had sensed his presence before she had lifted her head and saw him leaning against her doorway. His arms were folded and his dark head was tilted against the doorframe and she got the distinct impression he was assessing her.

'How is he?'

'Asleep again. The doctor gave him a draught because he was becoming a little agitated. He is not hopeful that there will be any physical improvement, especially as my father is struggling to swallow anything. I think it is only a matter of time now.' There was a bleakness in his russet eyes that confirmed that there was no hope.

'I am sorry to hear that.' Although she had no affiliation or affection for the viscount, she did not wish to see Aaron suffer, but knew that there really was no way of her preventing him from doing so nevertheless.

'It was kind of you to let him believe that he would recover. I think he found some comfort in your words.' He sounded so sad that Connie wanted to go to him and simply hold him. As if he sensed her thoughts, he jerked away from the doorframe and wandered towards the window. 'I suppose we need to talk about what happened earlier.'

Connie stared at his back and waited for him to start. After a moment she realised he wanted her to speak first. Perhaps he was prepared to listen to her now that his anger had dissipated?

'I did have every intention of telling you about my suspicions, Aaron. I had made up my mind to tell you on our ride—but that never happened. Then I was so consumed with the preparations for that awful dinner party that it slipped my mind. Then your father fell ill.' All of those things were plausible excuses, but he deserved the truth. 'And I suppose, deep down, I wanted to believe that if I held my tongue my father might look upon me a little more favourably. Mr Thomas suggested that he might relent and let me see my mother and brother again. He said that my father had specifically asked about my health and that my mother was grieving the loss of me. Mr Thomas swore that he was not trying to sabotage the estate and I desperately wanted to believe him. I know that is selfish, but…'

Her voice trailed off and when he turned she looked completely desolate. It shamed him. With all of his own troubles, he had forgotten how difficult this all must be for her. Only a few weeks ago she had been wrenched from the bosom of her family and left to flounder in a house of strangers, estranged from everyone and everything that she knew. Despite it all, she had endured it all stoically. The flashes of temper and outrage were always quickly replaced with contrition. She had risen to each new challenge better than he would have under the same circumstances, and he was barely coping with it all, and had shown herself to have an indomitable, yet forgiving, spirit. Hadn't she spent hours at his father's bedside despite their unpleasant relationship? She had certainly been the rock when Aaron had almost fallen apart. Even now she was thinking more of his comfort than he probably deserved. Not only nursing his father, but helping Aaron with the accounts and feeding him. Caring for him. Was it so unforgivable that she had tried to keep her own, vindictive, father happy as well as his?

Without thinking he sat next to her on the sofa, draped his arm around her shoulders and pulled her close. 'It doesn't matter, Connie,' he whispered against her hair. 'The damage had already been done long before you realised what he was up to.' She was still clinging to him, still obviously upset by their argument and Aaron wanted, more than anything, to tell her something to chase that sadness away. 'I spoke to the solicitor about the annulment.'

He felt her tense slightly in his arms. 'You did?' She sniffed and pulled away from him then, creating some distance between them and sitting proudly staring off to the side so that he would not see her tears. She hastily wiped her eyes and turned back to him with a smile. 'What did he say?'

'He said that under the circumstance he believes that there is a chance that the annulment will be granted. The fact that we married in such haste and that you only agreed to it under duress are points in our favour. I am sure that the vicar who married us will confirm that you were quite a reluctant bride. Then, of course, the feud between our two families is well documented. The case will have to be heard in this diocese, so I am sure that the bishop will have some sympathy for our plight. The fact that we have only been married for such a short period of time is also a positive factor. It will show the ecclesiastical court that we both recognised that we had made a mistake quickly and that we want to rectify it.'

Saying it out loud was more upsetting than he had thought it would be. A few hours ago he had railed at the poor solicitor, declaring his own desire to be well shot of their inconvenient marriage and the blasted woman that he had been saddled with. But Aaron had still been furious at her then, his feelings had been hurt and he had been in a fit of temper. Now he was not convinced that he did want to be rid of Connie. Her perceptiveness terrified him, but he was becoming inordinately fond of her presence, despite the occasional fireworks. But he even enjoyed those.

'That is good news.'

Her voice sounded flat and Aaron wondered if perhaps she was also having second thoughts, too. The solicitor had also cautioned him to have a plan in case things did not go as they hoped and had reminded him that Connie would have nothing if the marriage was dissolved. That thought plagued him more than he wanted to consider. If she wanted shot of him, why should he care what happened to her? Except he did.

'Of course, an annulment is not guaranteed. There is still a strong chance that the petition will be dismissed and we will be stuck with one another. If that is the case, there is a perfectly good Dower House on the far edge of the estate that you can set up your own household in.' He hoped that would give her some peace of mind.

Connie tried to appear buoyed at the thought even though she had suddenly developed an uncomfortable, empty feeling in the pit of her stomach. He clearly wanted the annulment else why would he have spoken to his solicitor about it so soon after his father's stroke? 'Surely it will not come to that, especially as we have not… you know…' She felt the colour fill her face and frantically tried to think of a delicate way of putting it. In the end, abject mortification won out and she simply flapped a hand ineffectually in the air until he finished the awkward sentence for her.

'Done the deed?'

She could not look at him and suspected he

was grinning at her utter and total mortification. When she heard him exhale abruptly she risked a peek. He had slumped fully on to the couch, his head resting on the back, and was staring vacantly up at the ceiling. When he spoke, he did not look at her. 'I did mention that to the solicitor as well and apparently it really does not make that much difference to the judgement at all. It might have been a pertinent detail in Henry the Eighth's time, but not any more. The existence of, or lack of, your virginity is irrelevant. In fact, bringing it up at all might turn out to be horrible for both of us.' He turned his head then and smiled sheepishly. 'The only way that it is relevant to a case is if one of the parties is incapable of the act—and that has to be corroborated with medical testimony. We would both have to undergo quite intrusive physical examinations. Aside from the fact that I would not wish to put you through that, I have to admit that selfishly I would rather not have to submit to the tests myself. They are apparently quite thorough.'

It took several moments for Connie to realise that he was also blushing profusely. The sight was so unexpected and so totally out of character for him that she giggled. The tests must be quite intrusive indeed for him to react that way and his reaction made her burn with curiosity.

He shot her withering glance, rolled his eyes and then chuckled, too. 'Do not ask, Connie, for the answer would shock you and I am not sure that I could get through the telling without cringing with embarrassment.'

Looking delightfully and completely flustered, he decisively stood and stared at the fireplace. 'Why don't I rustle up some tea for us both? And then, if you are still up for it, we can continue trying to make head and tail of all of those ledgers.' She was grateful for the fact that he was desperate to change the subject.

'I should like that a great deal. It will be nice to be able to do something constructive. I shall be down in a minute.' Just as soon as she had splashed enough ice water on her face to calm the intense burning and resemble less of a beetroot. Just talking about those intimacies had made her all flustered. And curious.

'Excellent.' He bounced from foot to foot, his own cheeks still glowing a little bit. It made him look quite adorable. 'You will probably rue the day that you agreed to help me.' His eyes scanned her from top to bottom and she could have sworn that his colour deepened. 'Well, I shall see you momentarily then.'

It was a tactical retreat, Aaron thought as he bounded down the stairs. Discussing marital relations with Connie had made him think about them. Now that he knew that they could have been having them for all this time without ruining her chances for an annulment, well, frankly, he did not quite know what to think.

His body, on the other hand, was not having that problem. It seemed to be in no doubt as to what it wanted to do. The first stirrings had occurred shortly after he had wrapped his arm around her in consolation—but once she had started glowing pink he was done for. There was something quite erotic about Connie's vibrant blushes and that particular one had been particularly vivid. Her graceful neck had heated and the blush had disappeared behind the pristine white lace that topped the bodice of her exceptionally well-fitting gown. It had left him wondering if her breasts blushed, too. Once he started thinking about her breasts he remembered how they had felt squashed against his chest, how smooth the skin above her garters had been and then, to torture himself further, he began to consider if she was a proper redhead in every sense of the word.

What had possessed him to invite her to help him with those blasted ledgers again today? He might actually spontaneously combust with lust if he had to sit with her again so soon, inhaling that intoxicating perfume of hers. He simply had to think of more sobering things.

Fortunately, that proved to be a very simple thing to do. The estate was still in peril because he was rapidly running out of money, his father was still hovering between life and death and, thanks to his curt dismissal of his estate manager, the Earl of Redbridge was bound to view this as evidence of his daughter's betrayal.

By the time he was sat back at his desk in the study, Aaron was even more troubled. Poor Connie. She had done nothing wrong and yet now her family would be even more lost to her. If only there was something Aaron could do to make it all better. Deaks popped his head around the door.

'I have today's post for you, sir.'

It was the sight of those letters on the silver tray that gave Aaron an interesting idea.

Chapter Twenty-One

At Connie's insistence, all of the account ledgers were moved up to her small sitting room the very next day. Not only was the light much better than in the dark panelled study, but she could not stand the cloying, musty smell of the viscount's tobacco or work particularly comfortably with all those dead animal heads glaring down at her. Aaron clearly did not like the environment either because he had barely put up any sort of a fight when she had put the suggestion to him.

For two days the pair of them had spent every free moment, when not sat with the ailing viscount, poring over the books and had created a much simpler summary of the state of things. The situation was indeed grim. There was no way of pretending otherwise. Aaron's father had squandered a lot of money on unnecessary things, worse, his outgoings in the last three years had been significantly more than his yearly income. The income generated by the estate had dwindled considerably under Mr Thomas's stewardship. This year's harvest was not even in the ground and, as Aaron had feared, with December knocking on their door it was now much too late to put it there and expect it to grow.

Then there had been the viscount's ill-conceived purchase of the one hundred acres of barren land on the other side of her father's estate. He had paid seven thousand pounds for that land, double what good arable land in this part of the country should be worth, and it was plainly not good arable land. In actual fact, it had not earned him so much as a farthing in return and, if Aaron was to be believed, it was unlikely to earn any more than that in the future either.

As Connie had suspected, the London town house, even though it had been rarely used in the years Aaron was off to war, still maintained a full complement of staff. In reality, those staff had effectively been paid handsomely to stand idle while hundreds of pounds had been wasted on heating and feeding them all. Fortunately, Mrs Poole and Deaks ran a much tighter ship here at Ardleigh Manor and Connie could find little trimming that would make any tangible difference to the finances.

All in all, the deficit was close to ten thousand pounds. It was a substantial amount of money and at the moment they had no clear plan on how to replace it. In desperation, Aaron was currently scouring through the weighty pages of *The Complete Farmer* for inspiration.

'What about barley?' He was peering at a particular page most intently through his spectacles, his hair in complete disarray from the numerous times he had already ran his hand through it and looking like an adorable cross between a rogue and a scholar.

'What about barley?' she asked, parroting his question with a smile. 'Can it be sown in the winter?'

'Not exactly. I can find no crop that appears to be sown in England in December. But we can plant barley in February if it is reasonably mild and it is ready to harvest much quicker than wheat.' He was looking delightfully pleased with himself, an expression that reminded her of the way he had looked at her the other evening when she thought he had been about to kiss her. Just thinking about it set her pulse aflutter.

'Is there a good market for barley?' Connie

asked dubiously to cover that errant thought. She had only ever had it in soups and stews. Barley, that was, not kisses.

'It is apparently one of the primary ingredients for beer, so I assume so. It also grows almost anywhere. Perhaps it is worth a try?' With that he sat back, tossed his spectacles down on to the table and sat back, rubbing the bridge of his nose. 'I need some fresh air. Let's go for a ride.'

'You go. One of us needs to be here for your father.'

'The doctor was here less than an hour ago and declared there to be no change. If we tell the servants which direction we are headed, then someone can fetch us easily enough if we are needed.' He stood up and held out his hand. 'Come riding with me, Connie. We have both been cooped up inside for too many days.'

She was sorely tempted. 'I shall need to change first.'

'Excellent. You do that and I will get us some horses saddled.'

Less than twenty minutes later they were both headed across the parkland at a fair old pace and Connie got the distinct impression that they were not merely riding aimlessly. Aaron definitely appeared to have some purpose. 'I shall race you to that hill over there.' He pointed towards a rise in the distance. 'Unless that is too challenging a course for you?'

'Do you need a head start, *husband*?'

He just grinned at that and it warmed her. When Aaron smiled one of his genuine smiles she felt it all the way down to her toes. 'After three. One. Two…'

On three they both flew and for a substantial portion of the race he was alongside her, bent low of the saddle and a look of pure enjoyment on his face. At some point she must have taken the lead because he was well behind her when they reached the hill. He accepted her gloating with a good-natured shrug, then led his horse to the crest of the rise where he stopped. Connie followed him and felt her breath hitch at the sight beyond. This insignificant hillock was in fact part of the border between the Wincanton estate and her father's. Beyond were Stuart fields, gently sloping and undulating towards Redbridge House.

The sight of it still pained her and Connie was about to turn away when she spotted two figures emerging out of a small copse of trees. She shot Aaron a look, unsure of how to react to such an unbelievable coincidence, but she could tell by the expression on his face that he had orchestrated it.

'Go,' he said, taking the reins of her horse loosely in his gloved hand. 'I will keep a lookout.'

Connie did not need to be told twice. Within moments she was running down the other side of the hill to the waiting open arms of her mother.

Watching them seemed unnecessarily obtrusive, so Aaron tried to look out over the land ahead. But he saw the way the two women hugged each other and cried. The reconciliation with her brother was equally as boisterous before the three of them disappeared into the cover of the trees. His throat felt tight with emotion. For the first time he truly saw all of her grief and sadness at the loss of her family until she had realised that they had come to see her, then the relief and desperation on her lovely face had moved him and he was glad that he had been able to do this one tiny thing for her. She really was a brave little thing and she deserved better than to be shackled to a man who was so unworthy because she had been given no choice in the matter.

She also deserved to have a happy life in the future, although that was unlikely to happen after the scandal of the annulment. That bothered him a great deal, too. His solicitor had explained how these things were always blamed on the woman much more than on the man. In time, society might well forgive him. He was titled and male and therefore a commodity. But Connie would have to live with the stain. It was highly unlikely that any decent man would marry her and he did not want her to be alone.

Even though Connie was dead against it, remaining married to him but having her own household in the Dower House would offer her protection from public censure, yet give her freedom. Many unhappily married couples lived apart and such arrangements were accepted. Connie could take a lover and live her life exactly how she wanted. Aaron would not stop her.

Except just thinking about her living within arm's reach, yet so far away, made him angry. Already he could feel his teeth hurt from the way his jaw had clenched at the mere thought of her in another man's arms. Or in another man's bed. Which led Aaron to the conclusion that neither solution to their marriage was acceptable to him. If only he deserved her, he would tell her so. If he had not been going mad from all of the guilt and shame he carried in his heart, he would impress upon her his desire for them to give their fledgling relationship a chance so that he could prove that he could be a worthy husband and that he would make it his life's work to make her happy. But he did not deserve her or the happiness that having her would undoubtedly bring.

When she emerged from the trees she was smiling. Her eyes were swollen from crying, her cheeks were rosy and yet he had never seen anything quite as beautiful in his life. She rushed to where he stood and engulfed him in a spontaneous hug. He could feel the intensity of her emotion in her trembling body as she held him tight.

'Thank you, Aaron.'

The choked whisper was so close to his ear that he was sure that he felt her soft lips brush his skin. Instinctively, his own arms came around her and found the curve of her waist while he tried to ignore the surge of wanting that coursed through his body. It was more than lust, he realised with a jolt. Somewhere along the line he had developed an affection for Connie that was separate from, and yet inextricably linked to, his fierce attraction for her. When this was all over he would mourn her absence, a rogue thought that had his arms tightening around her. He allowed himself the luxury of burying his face into her hair before he broke the contact and stepped back. There was no point in torturing himself further even though he was certain the damage to his unworthy heart was already done.

'We have agreed to meet again next week. I hope you don't mind?' She was worrying her luscious bottom lip with her teeth, drawing his eyes them and tempting him like forbidden fruit.

'Of course I don't mind. I do not want you to be miserable, Connie. I know how much they mean to you.' Awkwardly he fiddled with the reins to hide the wave of longing that he knew must be visible in his eyes. 'They looked to me to be as happy to see you as you were them.' Another emotion rippled through him then. Envy. He had no memory of his mother and he had never had that sort of a relationship with his father. There had always been distance between them caused by the differences in their characters. He knew his father cared about him, but they had always clashed more than they agreed on anything. Now it was too late to change that. Soon his father would be dead and Connie would be gone and Aaron would be left all alone again.

'My father has forbidden them from even mentioning my name at home.' There was sadness in her voice, 'So I doubt that I will ever be reconciled with him.'

'That is his doing and his loss. At least you know that your mother and brother still care for you.'

'My mother told me that you passed a letter to her through the vicar's wife. She asked me to thank you for that. She has been so worried about me so it was a great comfort to her to know that I am comfortable.

Comfortable. Hardly a glowing compliment, but perhaps a clear indictment of the state of their marriage. 'My brother has assured me that he will allow me to come home when he is the earl. Redbridge House is not lost to me for ever so my future is secure.'

A childless, husbandless, Aaron-less future that left a bad taste in his mouth, but he smiled for her sake because she appeared pleased with the outcome. 'Then I am glad for that at least and I am glad that you are able to continue your relationship with your mother and brother, even if it has to be done in secret.'

They rode home in virtual silence, although Connie kept glancing at him through her lashes when he was not looking. As always, Aaron appeared to be quite calm and content about the state of things, if she ignored the tight lines of worry about his eyes and the complete look of exhaustion about his features.

He was probably relieved to know that she had a home to go to in the future because she knew that he felt responsible for her. He had already proved himself to be a decent and honourable man. He had married her and given her his name when nobody would have expected him to, sacrificing his own future plans in the process. He had also been an understanding and gentlemanly husband. Not once had he tried to force his attentions on her, although she would probably welcome them if he did, or treated her with a lack of respect. And his selfless behaviour today, whilst he was dealing with so much, had touched her deeply. Each time she gazed at him she experienced a rush of affection, so intense that she wondered if she had deeper feelings for him after all. There was certainly something lurking in the deep recesses of her heart that transcended the obvious physical attraction she had for him. Before, when she had held him close, she had definitely felt more than just gratitude. Her body had practically melted against his with need and she had wanted to kiss him so badly, that for a moment she almost bared her hand and did so.

What would he have done then? Would he

have pulled back in disgust, but disguised it as politeness? Or would he have kissed her back? At times, Connie got the feeling that he might be as tempted by her as she was by him. Once or twice in the last two days she had caught him staring at her with such intensity that it had made the tiny hairs on her arms stand on end with awareness. But those moments were always so fleeting that afterwards she was not entirely sure whether he had actually done it or if she was simply wishing that he would. She also knew that the face he presented to the world was not entirely genuine. Underneath it all, he was troubled and Connie wanted to ease all of those burdens for him, so that his real smiles, the ones that made his dark eyes sparkle and her heart melt, were more frequent.

At the stable, he helped her down from her horse, his hands spanned her waist as he gently lowered her to the ground and she saw it again briefly. That intense look that spoke volumes that she didn't fully understand or dare to believe. But then he excused briskly himself to go sit with his father, leaving Connie to wonder if she was merely trying to project her own need and desire on to him. Was it possible that she was falling just a little bit in love with Aaron Wincanton?

As she watched him disappear back into the house, Connie had to accept that there was the distinct possibility that she was.

Chapter Twenty-Two

Connie felt the strain of too much study pull at her eyes. She pushed the ledger away and glanced at Aaron on the sofa. He had been poring over a book on soil cultivation, but clearly it had proved to be too boring to hold his concentration. The book lay open on his tummy, his charming spectacles were askew and he was lost in the land of nod.

Asleep, his face was free of all of the worries that had clouded it this past week and he looked perfectly content to be snoozing in her little sitting room. Connie considered whether or not she should wake him and decided against it. She was well aware of the fact that he had not been sleeping. She had checked on him several times and had heard the fevered sounds of his nightmares through his heavy bedchamber door, but he had taken to barricading himself in so that she could not enter. Whether he had done that because he did not want to have her anywhere near his bed again, or whether he was too humiliated by his nocturnal rantings, she did not know. But for now he was peacefully asleep so she was reluctant to deny him that.

Connie went into her bedchamber and retrieved a warm blanket. She carefully removed his spectacles and the book and then covered his semi-reclining body as best she could. After blowing out the candles she took herself off to bed, leaving her bedchamber door open a sliver in case he awoke.

Several hours later, she heard him murmur quietly but the sound was enough to drag her out of a deep sleep and into the here and now. Quickly, she padded back into the sitting room in time to witness Aaron pull violently on his clothes in obvious distress.

'Fletcher,' he cried, 'I'm so sorry!'

Connie knelt beside him and lightly ran her hand over his hair. 'Wake up, Aaron—you are having a bad dream.'

But he did not hear her. Whatever scenario was playing out in his mind, it was also physical. He clawed at his waistcoat, ripping several buttons off as he tried to yank it open, all the while muttering to the mysterious Fletcher as if Fletcher were in his chest. Connie tried to stay his hands, but he would have none of it. Fearing for the garment and commiserating with his pain, Connie undid the surviving buttons and spread the waistcoat wide, all the while whispering soothing words to no avail.

'He's all over me! I have to take it off. I can smell it!' It was a curious jumble of sentences that she had no understanding of, except that the clothing was apparently the root cause of his distress.

'Let me help you then. Can you sit up for me, Aaron?'

Miraculously he did, his eyes suddenly open wide although still gripped by the terror of his dream, and Connie pulled the waistcoat off his arms and then dragged the damp linen shirt over his head. Fortunately, that did appear to calm him a little although his breathing still sawed in and out. After a few moments she watched his eyes focus just before he dropped his head in his hands.

'I'm sorry, Connie.'

His words sounded so desolate that her heart broke for him. She rose up on her knees and curled her arms around his neck, pulling his head to her chest and kissing the top of it.

'They are just nightmares, Aaron, and nothing to be sorry about.'

He allowed her to comfort him, nestling against her sorry excuse for a bosom and wrapping his own arms around her possessively. Connie combed her fingers leisurely through his thick hair, marvelling in the silky texture and enjoying the intimacy of being able to touch him. For several minutes he seemed quite content with this, then his hands moved. Slowly they roamed over her back, his fingers trailing a lazy path down her spine before his palms traced the twin curves of her hips.

'You seem to be able to make me forget, Connie. It is never as bad when I am with you.'

He sighed against her ribs. Just that made her skin heat. A prickle of something, she suspected it was desire, made her more conscious of her body. Connie tried not to read anything into it. He was upset and in need of human contact, the motions of his warm hands meant no more to him than that. Did they? With aching slowness, his head nuzzled upwards into the crook of her neck and she felt her pulse begin to race with misguided anticipation. She was definitely mapping her desires on to his innocent actions—wasn't she?

When she felt his lips press against the beating pulse at her throat she shivered. That had definitely not been innocent, nor was the way his hands were snaking up the sides of her rib-cage, or the feel of his teeth tenderly nipping their way towards her sensitive ear lobe. Hoping that he would see it as an invitation, Connie arched her neck to give him better access and the whisper of a sigh escaped her lips when he placed a soft, open-mouthed kiss on her cheek.

When his lips finally touched hers she was practically vibrating with need. Every nerve in her body was tingling. As his hands brushed the side of her breasts, her nipples puckered against the thin cotton of her nightgown, aching to be touched. Connie shamelessly pushed them against the solid wall of his chest, while her hands began exploring the muscles of his shoulders and chest of their own accord. Oh, how she needed this. It didn't matter if it was only temporary. Right now, right this minute, this just felt right. Beneath her palms she could feel his own heart racing, felt the force of his own desire and sensed that he was holding it back for her benefit. Under his skin, she felt the tension in his abdomen as she touched him.

It was Connie who deepened the kiss, but he followed her lead, hoisting her off the floor and into his lap so that he could plunder her mouth with his own. One big hand cradled her head while the other ran down her leg until he found the hem of her nightgown and burrowed under it, sliding his palm over her knee, her bare thigh, her naked hip until it found her needy breast.

The sensation of his thumb stroking the taut bud of her nipple was almost too intense, and she made a sound deep in her throat that she had never heard herself make. It spurred him on further, so that he relinquished her mouth and used his lips and tongue to torture her breast through the fabric of her nightgown until she was certain she could stand no more.

'If you want me to stop then you had better tell me now,' he growled, rolling on to the floor and dragging her on top of him. She ran her hands over the flat plane of his chest and stomach then, enjoying the feel of the crisp hair under her fingers and the way he trembled when she touched him.

'I don't want you to stop.' Her voice sounded breathy. It quivered slightly from both the hot passion that consumed her and at the fear of the unknown.

He pushed her back then, so that she sat straddled his hips. She could feel his hardness straining beneath his breeches and undulated against it because that is what her body told her to do.

His eyes closed in response and his own body tensed. Connie could see the veins in his neck and arms protrude slightly. His dark nipples had hardened to points and she ran her thumbs over them as he had done to her. A growl rumbled deep in his throat as he gripped the hem of her nightgown and yanked it off her body in one swift, fluid motion that she had not expected. All at once she felt exposed and inadequate, covering her small breasts with her arms, conscious that her figure was lacklustre at best, downright disappointing at worst.

His hands came up to circle her wrists and he gently prised them away. Connie watched him stare at her and hoped that he would not be too horrified by her lack of womanliness. She was not entirely sure what she expected him to do next, but it was certainly not reaching up and slowly unbraiding the heavy plait that fell down her back and then spreading her wild hair all over her shoulders.

Wordlessly, he sat up and kissed her with such tenderness that it took her breath away. She did not notice at what point he reversed their positions so that he was leaning over her, but she definitely noticed his lips and hands drifting all over her body—kissing, nibbling, touching every part of her until her limbs were quivering and an intoxicating heat had spread up her thighs and now burned between her legs.

And Aaron was looking directly at that most secret part of her, a slight smile on his face that was all that was male and potent, before he brushed the dark auburn curls with his fingers. 'I did wonder if you were a true redhead,' he whispered, lowering his mouth on to hers again. She tensed instinctively when she felt his fingers dip between her legs, but soon forgot about the intrusion when he found a part of her that felt glorious when he caressed it, his fingers mirroring the motions of his clever tongue until she was arching against his hand wantonly. Connie did not care that her legs had fallen open and that he could see every part of her as nature had made her. All that mattered was that he didn't stop.

But he did stop. He sat back on his heels and hurriedly tried to undo his breeches with slightly shaking hands. Was he nervous, too?

Connie rose up to help him and together they finally got all of the buttons undone. He allowed her to push the fabric down from his hips and she found herself licking her lips in anticipation of seeing that part of him. It sprang free of the restraining material, much bigger than she had imagined, and she stared at it while Aaron shimmied out of his breeches, unaware that his eyes never left her face.

She wanted to touch it, but was not sure if she should. All male arrogance, he lay back on the floor with both of his arms hooked behind his head, giving her the first true glimpse of what a completely naked man should look like. Aaron was all golden skin, dark hypnotic eyes and a lazy smile that looked like sin. It was almost as if he were daring her to touch him as he had her, so she reached out her hand and lay it on the taut plane of his abdomen.

'I thought you were fearless, Connie.'

Another dare and one that emboldened her. She would not be fearful and meek. Not now. This might well be her only opportunity to experience these intimacies. She slid her palm slowly up his body, across his shoulders and then, even slower, she dragged it back down again. When it passed his navel she felt the muscles in his abdomen constrict and heard the subtle change in his breathing. He might be lying there passive, but he was not unaffected by what she was doing. To torture him, she allowed her fingers to rest in the soft hair at the base of his manhood. She could see it straining towards her hand, saw the tension in Aaron's wonderful body as his eyes pleaded with her to touch him.

His eyes narrowed. 'You are doing that on purpose. Bear in mind that I will pay you back in kind.'

He made the threat through a pained smile, but it was a delicious threat and one that her body reacted to. Her womb ached. It was the strangest and most overwhelming sensation. Her body instinctively wanted him to be inside her.

Brazenly, Connie's palm drifted towards his arousal and gingerly brushed it. It was warm, and smooth as silk, but beneath it was so hard. Aaron sucked in a breath so she did it again and he growled.

'I am not made of glass, Connie.'

His hand came down and grabbed hers, wrapping it around his hardness tightly and squeezing his eyes firmly shut while she learnt the feel and shape of him properly. When he could stand it no more he flipped her on to her back.

'I want you so much it frightens me.'

His words made her feel beautiful. That was a heady feeling indeed. 'Then have me.'

He kissed her deeply then, his tongue dancing with hers as his hands parted her legs. He positioned himself between them, again she felt his arousal straining against her, but still he held back, his breathing laboured, his dark eyes intense, almost pained.

'I have never made love to a virgin before. I am told that it can hurt the first time.'

Connie wrapped her arms tightly about his body in reassurance, 'And I am told that passes quickly. I want you, Aaron. Nothing else matters.'

With a groan he positioned himself at her entrance and softly kissed her as he nudged inside. To begin with it was not unpleasant, but as he edged further and further into her body she felt overstretched. He sensed her discomfort and stopped. His whole body stiffened with the effort and then she felt him slowly begin to withdraw. Connie wrapped her long legs around his hips and dragged him back.

'Just do it, Aaron. Then make it better.'

He closed his eyes and slid into her in one fluid stroke and kissed her when she winced. For several moments they simply lay there locked together as he allowed her the time to get used to the intrusion, then carefully, and with aching tenderness, he began to move inside her. It did not take her body long to accept what was happening and soon she was anticipating each thrust, arching her hips towards it and revelling in the feel of him so intimately close that he had become an intrinsic part of her.

His eyes were open as he kissed her, letting

her see that he was as absorbed and overcome by what they were doing as she was. Connie felt his heart beating next to hers and even their heartbeats seemed to be in tandem with each other. As the sensations in her body built she realised that this was more than a joining of flesh, but a joining of hearts and minds as well. The only thing that mattered was Aaron and that she loved him.

When he tilted her hips slightly, so that his movements could also caress that wonderful place he had shown her, Connie forgot to think and surrendered herself to simply feeling. She cried out when her body began to pulse around him. He did, too, burying his face in her neck and collapsing against her while Connie locked her legs tightly around his hips, glorying in the last of the tremors that still rippled through them. She wanted desperately to tell him that she loved him, but held back, knowing that such an admission would only make him feel beholden to her. So she repeated the words silently, over and over in her head until they were both completely spent. Aaron curled his big body around her, engulfing her in his solid warmth, and moments later he was sound asleep. Connie remained still, but her insides were churning.

She loved Aaron Wincanton.

It was a revelation that rocked her to her very core. Connie was not entirely sure when it had happened, but it was not something that could be undone. Not like a marriage could be. Soon they would go their separate ways. Even if they could not get an annulment, Aaron had already made plans to give her own household in the Dower House. Why else would he have done that other than to be rid of her? Although it was what she had asked for, now the thought of it broke her heart.

Chapter Twenty-Three

Aaron woke with a start and took in his surroundings. He was in an unfamiliar bed and the weak winter sun was filtering through the window. His arm was draped over the soft, warm skin of an unmistakable female hip. Connie's hip. It took a moment or two to orientate himself until it all came back to him in a rush. They had made love. Twice. Once on her sitting-room floor and then, when he had stirred in the small hours, he had carried her into her bed and she had welcomed him into her sleepy body once again.

Now he felt rested, a peculiar sensation that he had last experienced the last time she had visited him in the night and chased away a nightmare. Clearly she had some sort of power to make them go away. She stirred and shifted on to her back, one hand resting lightly on the arm he still had around her, the other carelessly flung over her head. There was a contented expression on her face, her lips turned up in the corners ever so slightly and still pink and slightly swollen from his kisses. Because he enjoyed looking at her, Aaron propped himself up on to his elbow and looked his fill, searing the image of her on to his memory so that he could revisit it often when she was gone. She was so beautiful and dear, and so much better than his own fevered imagination had constructed her, that she dazzled him.

One lovely long leg had found its way out of the bedclothes, which were pooled just below her ribs. Her red hair was fanned out over the pillow, a few tangled tendrils fell artlessly over her delicate shoulders and partially covering the acres of satin-smooth, pale skin of her upper body. Her small pert breasts, capped with delectable pink nipples that he now knew were wonderfully sensitive, beckoned to him. Just looking at her made him hard and aching all over again, except the aching was not just in his groin, but in his heart, too.

Connie had taken hold there. There was no point pretending otherwise. Last night he had been so overwhelmed with affection and tenderness for her that he had had to stop himself from saying things to her that he knew she would not particularly want to hear. Not that he was in a particularly fit state to be making declarations like that, not when his mind was deteriorating so rapidly that he could not close his eyes for more than an hour before his demons came back to haunt him. Except when he was with Connie, of course. Connie the demon slayer.

She sighed and stretched before opening just one eye. Seeing him looking down at her, she opened the other eye and smiled shyly up at him. 'Good morning.'

All at once, Aaron's throat tightened, strangling any sort of response, and he felt the overwhelming urge to weep, to confess everything to her once and for all and beg her for forgiveness for what he had done. Ask her to love him, the way he loved her, because with her he was a better man, not a broken one. Then make love to her until everything was all better and all of his problems were gone. Lose himself in her so that she could save him. Beg her to stay with him despite his crimes.

Frustrated by and ashamed of his own vulnerability and his selfish need for her, the only option left to him was to put some distance between them immediately in case he rashly acted on all of those emotions. He could feel them all fighting for release, but knew that she would be horrified by what he had done. He was nothing but a filthy coward and he did not deserve her. It would be best if he remembered that.

Connie watched the pained expression pass across his features and was instantly uneasy. After last night, she was not entirely sure what she expected of the morning, but she had hoped that it might include a repeat of some of the wonderful things that they had done together during the night. She had hoped that things might change between them. That her feelings might be reciprocated. Now she realised that those hopes had been nothing but besotted foolishness. Aaron certainly did not look like a man enamoured. In fact, she was certain he was as far removed from that as it was possible to be.

He suddenly turned away from her and sat up stiffly. Because it seemed the right thing to do, Connie sat up, too. 'Is everything all right, Aaron?' She dreaded his answer because it was obviously not all right.

He turned to her, his eyes dropping briefly to her naked breasts. He grabbed the sheet and covered them with it as if he could not bear to look at them in the unforgiving daylight. Connie gripped the sheet to her chest, instinctively covering her bare leg with the bedclothes lest the sight of that offend him further. Clearly her figure displeased him, hardly a surprise when it had always displeased her, too, but the reality of it was like a knife in her back it hurt so much.

'I should go and see my father.' His tone was flat, almost callous, and he rose quickly from the bed without a backward glance. He scanned the room for his clothes, then, realising that he had left them in the adjacent sitting room, he stalked purposefully towards the door. He hovered there momentarily until he finally spun around, looking completely agonised and filled with remorse.

Before he could say the inevitable words, Connie did.

'What happened between us last night was a mistake. It changes nothing, Aaron. I still want an annulment.'

He nodded then closed the door behind him, leaving her feeling stunned and completely humiliated. His cold revulsion was almost too awful to bear—and yet she had to. She had no choice. She had disgusted him. In the cold light of day, she did not tempt him at all—worse, he had clearly regretted that it had happened in the first place. All those things that he had told her about her being the loveliest thing he had ever seen had all been lies to soothe her and like a desperate, needy fool she had wanted to believe them—just as last night she had wanted him to feel the same love for her as she did him.

No doubt her pride would come to the rescue eventually. She was, or had been, Lady Constance Stuart, so she would cover the hurt with disdain and uninterest as she always did and dare him to believe that she was not unaffected in the slightest by his rejection. But right now, when the wound was so fresh and her fragile heart was completely broken, all Connie could do was wrap her arms around her knees and cry.

Aaron had completely detached himself from her. In the week since they had shared a bed, he had managed to avoid her unless it was absolutely necessary that their paths crossed. The separation suited Connie perfectly. The last thing that she needed was to be reminded of how much she disgusted him. If they did collide, he could barely look at her. Their conversation, if one could call the awkward exchanges they shared that, was stilted and limited to essential information that one or other of them had to impart.

'Your father is asleep. The physician is here. I am going out for a ride.'

There were no quips or smiles or arguments. No shared looks or companionable silences.

Their relationship had been reduced to a cold shell of indifference and a great deal of disappointment on his part and hurt on hers.

Connie had no idea if he still barricaded himself into his bedchamber at night. She had not allowed herself to check on him and he certainly never attempted to venture into her rooms. Now that he had been there and done that, and had found her so wanting, he had completely lost all interest in her and withdrawn into himself. She did not want to care either way.

The trouble was, Connie did care. Not a minute went past when she did not want to seek him out, shake and scream at him for being so distant and so cold. She was sick and tired of missing him. Her day now consisted of endless, pointless embroidery, solitary walks and rides and countless hours sitting with the viscount and reading to him. It was a very sad state of affairs that she had grown to enjoy reading to a frail, unresponsive invalid because it was the only thing that she did that made her feel useful. The only sunshine in this depressing week had been her second clandestine meeting with her mother and brother. She had ridden to meet them alone, but unlike their last fraught reconciliation, this time the three of them talked for almost an hour. Had it not been in the middle of a wood in the chill winter air, it had been just the way it had always had between them. When they parted, after promising to meet at the same time every week, her brother had stated that he intended to ride every morning while he was at home and that if she happened to be in this vicinity, then he might well see her. It was a lifeline she intended to grasp with both hands.

A quick glance at her father-in-law told her that he was asleep again. In the last few days he had spent more time in that state than he did awake, which was a blessing. His incapacity frightened him, she could see it sometimes in his eyes when he looked at her. The most awful thing was that he was incapable of swallowing anything more fortifying than weak broth, so he was literally wasting away in the bed that had become his prison. The physician still came every day and declared it a miracle that he had lasted this long. Everyone expected him to go at any minute, except as time went on Connie was certain that he was clinging on for something and would not give himself over to the peace of death until he was satisfied that it was safe to do so. And she was coming to think that he was waiting for news of a grandchild, that hoping that there might one day be one was not quite enough for him.

Connie sensed Aaron enter the room quietly. Pride kept her from turning around and looking at him. Looking at him hurt too much. 'He is asleep.' She marked her place in her book and stood up, ready to leave. 'You might use this as an opportunity to get some sleep yourself. You look tired.' What had made her say that? Connie did not want him thinking that she cared. He needed to know that she was indifferent to him. 'I have been meaning to talk to you about the Dower House. It needs to be made ready for me to move into, because I should like to do so as soon as…' Finishing the sentence with his father lying just a few feet away from her seemed unnecessarily cold.

Aaron appeared to be completely unaffected by the request. He merely nodded and stared at his father. 'I shall have Deaks and Mrs Poole make the arrangements immediately.'

As there was apparently nothing else to be said, Connie left him alone, feeling a little unsteady and unexpectedly bilious. At least she would be reunited with her brother, Henry, again in less than two hours. Not everything was lost to her. Just him. Yet he was now the only thing that truly mattered.

Aaron waited until she was safely out of the room before he slumped into the chair next to his father's bed. She probably hated him now and rightly so. And probably that was for the best. He was a mess. His life was a mess. And he had already made enough of a mess of her life already without further complicating matters with his own selfish desire to keep her near—even if he could not summon the courage to tell her how he felt. How exactly did one go about telling a woman that he loved her, but that he was unworthy of her? Or telling her that he needed her but had nothing whatsoever to offer her in return? Under the circumstances, and for the sake of his tenuous sanity, it would be kinder all around if she did move out sooner rather than later. Except just thinking about it made him sick to his stomach.

His father made a strange choking sound that made Aaron turn. His pallor was ashen, his lips a ghostly blue while his breathing sounded shallower than it had been. The fingers on his right hand were curled slightly, the knuckles so white and tense that Aaron knew that something was dreadfully wrong. He ran to the door and called to a footman, 'Get the doctor!' Before he could think better of it, Aaron gripped the servant's arm. 'And get my wife!'

If the worst was about to happen, and he had another episode, he would need her strength, he reasoned, although in truth he just needed her beside him.

By the time he rushed back to the bed his father's eyes were struggling to open. Aaron held his hand. He had no idea what else to do. His father was apparently fighting for every breath now; the exertion necessary was reflected in the pain in his panicked eyes. Fortunately, Connie burst through the door and took stock of the scene quickly.

'Oh, you are awake,' she said cheerfully, laying her hand on the old man's fevered brow. 'But you must try to calm down. There is nothing wrong. You have just got yourself into a bit of a state.'

Aaron watched his father's gaze settle on Connie and saw him calm at her soothing tone.

'I have sent for some more broth—I know how much you hate it, but you have to keep your strength up—and when it comes we will sit you up and I shall read to you whilst you eat.' She was behaving as if nothing was amiss, as if his father was not on the very cusp of dying, and it was working. The ragged breaths became shallower, his eyes less terrified, but the light in them was dimming. Aaron knew in his gut that his father's time was imminent and that he should perhaps find the right words to say goodbye. But his mind was blank. All he could think of was all the similar situations he had found himself in, watching good men die on the battlefield. There could be nothing positive about death.

Feeling impotent, Aaron watched Connie smile knowingly at his father. 'Whilst I am loathe to admit that you were right, and you have no idea how much saying that sentence to a Wincanton galls me, but apparently your bold claim that you Wincantons are very virile was quite correct…' she had his father's full attention, but Aaron had no idea what she was talking about until he saw his father's eyes flick to Connie's belly '… I am with child.'

For a moment the room spun until he realised that she could not know that yet. Not in a week. She was simply lying to ease his father's passing. It was an unbelievably generous and thoughtful act that humbled him. To compound the lie, she grabbed Aaron's free hand and placed it on her flat tummy and smiled, trying to convince his father that there was love between them and this was not merely her upholding her side of their bargain. Except the love he felt was quite real and he suddenly wanted there to be a child beneath his fingers because a child would bind her to him. For ever.

A strange peace settled over his father's face and Aaron felt the faintest flex of his fingers in his hand. When the old man sighed, his eyes fluttered closed, but there was a faint smile on his lips. They stood there silently for several minutes, neither looking at the other, neither moving, one hand still holding his father's and the other still rested on Connie's belly. All the while Aaron waited for his mind to fail him and drag him back to that battlefield in Spain. But it didn't happen.

His father had died content.

There had been no screaming or terror. Connie had seen to that. Aaron let his hands drop, feeling strangely empty. Before he could stand, Connie wrapped her arms about his shoulders and hugged him close. She offered him no words of comfort. What was there to say? Nor did she mutter any of those meaningless platitudes that people uttered in times like these and he respected her for that. All she offered him was her strength and the warmth of her embrace, and strangely, that was all he needed.

Chapter Twenty-Four

The next few days whipped by in a blur, taken up by the expected formalities of a funeral. So many people came to pay their respects that Connie felt as though gallons of tea was constantly swishing around in her stomach, while her throat was hoarse from thanking them for their condolences. The viscount had been laid out in one of the formal receiving rooms and practically every visitor expected to see him. Constantly being confronted with his father's dead body obviously bothered Aaron—each time he came out of the room he was beginning to look more and more like a startled fox—so to shield him from the ordeal Connie had taken on that role under the pretence that Aaron had enough to do writing his father's eulogy, receiving the guests and sorting out the estate.

In keeping with the viscount's status and social expectations, his funeral took place after dark. Connie had to watch Aaron walk alone at the head of the torchlit procession while she stayed at Ardleigh Manor with the other wives, nervously worrying about him. He had withdrawn to his father's study immediately after the wake and was still there now, hours afterwards, even though it was well past midnight and he must be exhausted. Connie had sent the worried-looking servants to bed just after eleven and then had taken herself to her own bed shortly afterwards, but trying to sleep was futile. She was too worried about him. So worried, that she had temporarily discarded her mask of indifference and did not care if he knew it.

Ignoring the cowardly nagging voice in her head, Connie padded downstairs to find him. As she approached the study door she saw the thin strip of light bleeding from the bottom, illuminated proof that he was still up and not resting as he should be. The silly man was apparently incapable of taking care of himself and this was merely a charitable favour and hardly evidence of her unwelcome feelings for him. She dawdled outside for a moment, unsure whether to just barge in or knock and then decided she was being ridiculous. For the time being, she was his wife and she did not need to scratch at his door like a servant. Raising herself up to her full height, Connie opened the door and marched in.

Aaron was sat in one of the ugly wingback chairs, staring into the dying fire. He had discarded his jacket, waistcoat and cravat, allowing the fine linen shirt to billow loose about his throat. Both sleeves had been pushed up his arms as he lounged, a little haphazardly, in the chair, cradling a barely filled brandy glass in one hand. Connie took one look at the almost empty decanter near his elbow and decided that he was very probably drunk—a state that she had never seen him in despite all of his woes.

'It is past midnight,' she snipped in her best Lady Constance Stuart tone that brooked no argument, 'and you need to go to bed.'

Far from being intoxicated, two very lucid russet eyes turned towards her. Their handsome owner smiled without any humour. 'There is no point. I cannot sleep any more.'

'Go to bed, Aaron. It has been a long and trying day and you look exhausted.' There were now dark shadows on top of dark shadows and in the dim light his face was looking gaunt.

'I have often heard people claim that some take solace in drink when life gets difficult. I thought I might give it a go. See if it made any of my problems go away.' He poured the last dregs from his glass into his mouth and reached for the decanter again.

'Has it worked?'

'Not yet,' he said, tipping more of the brandy over his fingers than in the glass, evidence that he was perhaps not quite as sober as she had first thought, 'They are all still there. But I am hopeful. If I could just stop thinking about them all, then I know I would be able to sleep and if I could sleep, then perhaps there is a chance that I won't go completely insane.'

Connie carefully prised the decanter from his hand and placed it on the desk out of his reach. 'Perhaps the solution cannot be found at the bottom of a glass. Perhaps you should unburden yourself by telling me all that ails you. Apparently a problem shared is a problem halved.'

'You can't solve these, Connie. Nobody can.'

She sat down primly on the opposite chair, pulling her dressing gown tightly around her in case she inadvertently displayed anything that he would not want to see—even though he had already seen it all. 'Try me. When I have problems, I put them all in a list and then approach them one at time rather than try to solve them all at once. When you break down your worries one at a time they are less daunting and therefore easier to find solutions to. Let's list them.'

'We will be here all night.'

'As that was your original plan for the evening, indulge me.' Although she sincerely hoped that it would not take all night because the taxidermy heads were much more sinister in the dim lamplight and this room still smelled of his father.

Aaron took another slug of his brandy and then stared at the empty glass in disgust when he realised that he had not poured much into it. 'Unless a miracle happens, I shall be completely bankrupt in a year.' He stared back at her defiantly. 'Can you stop that, Connie?'

'It will not come to that. I thought we had agreed that you should plant barley so that you can have two crops this year. Two crops means twice the profit. And I found some significant savings by reducing the staff at your townhouse.'

'A few thousand pounds will barely make a dent in what is missing. Not that I don't appreciate your efforts. It all made much more sense when we worked on it together. I can't make head nor tail of it all on my own.'

They would still be working on it together if he had not cruelly shut her out. Silly man! 'You could also sell that land your father purchased to spite my father. That has to be worth something.'

'Just shows what you know, Connie. Mr Thomas arranged that purchase, no doubt upon your father's express instruction, because he knew something that my father didn't. That land is useless. I doubt I could give it away.'

'All land has a use, Aaron. I am sure that someone will buy it.'

He shook his dark head and gave her a lopsided attempt at a smug grin. 'It is solid chalk—like the White Cliffs of Dover—except not as useful. The soil is too thin for anything apart from weeds to grow on it and the ground is too hard to build on.'

'If things get too dire, then you could still sell that town house. It is not entailed and properties on Berkeley Square are always quite highly sought after. It would raise a good price.'

'I suppose so,' he slurred begrudgingly, but then leaned forward, his black brows drawn together in consternation. 'But the state of my finances is the least of my worries, Connie. I also have a wife who would rather not be my wife. In fact, she would rather live out her days completely ruined by the scandal of an annulment than stay with me. How's that for a problem?'

That was definitely not a topic that she was

prepared to be drawn on. It was too raw and too personal, so she sidestepped it. 'Come on—let me help you up to bed.' She reached out and took his arm and tried to make him stand, but he would have none of it. He snatched his arm away angrily.

'I don't want to go to bed. I have nightmares. Every time I close my eyes I am back in Spain.' But he stood shakily and let her take his arm anyway, leaning heavily on her and then looking a little bewildered. 'I feel dizzy.'

Hardly a surprise when he had consumed such a vast amount of liquor. 'Come on. Let's get you upstairs while you can still stand.'

Connie led him away from the study towards the stairs. She had scarcely managed to get him up more than two steps when he stopped abruptly and turned towards her conspiratorially. 'The only time that I don't have the nightmares is when I sleep with you.' He pointed his index finger into her breastbone and spoke directly into her face. 'Perhaps you should take me to bed again so that I can sleep. I shall be a perfect gentleman, Connie. I promise. Let me sleep with you. You're my demon slayer.'

Heaven forbid he would ever want to do anything else, he had made his thoughts on that quite clear already, and she could not bear the thought of lying so close to him when she knew that she repulsed him. 'I don't think so, Aaron.'

'Then I am going back downstairs!' he announced dramatically. He was swaying a little now and was starting to list quite substantially to the left. He really did need to lie down. Perhaps, if she put him to bed in her room while she slept in his that would suffice?

'I shall take you to my bed. Just please put your arm around my shoulder. I am frightened that you might fall down the stairs.'

Obligingly, he swung his heavy arm around her shoulders while Connie gripped him firmly about the waist. Despite his acquiescence, getting him up the stairs proved to be more challenging than she had originally anticipated. Once or twice he almost toppled backwards and it took all of her strength, and a great deal of her patience, to get him to the top. By the time she had manoeuvred him to her door he was practically unconscious and almost a dead weight.

He lent sluggishly against the door while she wrestled with the handle, so when it opened he fell to the floor and dragged her on top of him, cushioning her from the impact with his floppy, brandy-pickled limbs.

'The last time we were on the floor together you were naked.'

Connie did not need to be reminded of that fact and she definitely did not want to witness the soppy grin he had on his face.

'If you wanted to get naked again, Wife, then I am sure that I could oblige you.' He tried to wink at her. Instead of closing one eye saucily, he scrunched both together and them appeared to be quite confused by the fact that he could not get his eyelids to work independently of each other. The effect would have been quite comical if she had not been so mortified by what he was suggesting.

Enough was enough. She did not care how drunk he was, suggesting that he would perform his husbandly duty because he was now suitably numb with drink was just plain insulting. Connie scrambled to her feet and then grabbed both of his hands. There were times when it was quite handy to have the body of an Amazonian because, after one enormous, unladylike grunt, she heaved him back to his feet and dragged him unceremoniously to the bedchamber beyond. How typical of Aaron Wincanton to be the one man of her acquaintance who was bigger than her.

Aaron sat heavily on the bed, causing the bedstead to creak ominously, looking more delightfully rumpled than he had a right to and completely foxed. The brandy had clearly worked its way around his entire body and he was now experiencing the full effect. He could barely keep his head up on top of his slumped shoulders. Connie knelt and pulled off his boots while he watched her sleepily. He really was practically dead on his feet, the poor man, and it was tragic that he was so terrified of closing his eyes. She might hate him still for hurting her, but that did not mean that she was devoid of sympathy for him. Or feelings. 'Lie down, Aaron.'

He shook his head. 'Can't. Need to take my clothes off first or they will get covered in blood again. Hate that.'

Lord only knew what that meant, but she was too tired to argue. It was not as if she had not already seen his magnificent body. Or touched every inch of it.

Or kissed it.

She only had to close her eyes and she could easily picture it. All of that firm muscle, golden skin and sinful, delicious hardness… Shaking herself out of her sudden carnal thoughts, Connie quickly went about the process of undressing him as dispassionately as possible. She made quick work of the shirt, but his breeches were more problematic, especially as he just kept grinning down at her as she fought with the buttons. Once he was fully displayed in all of his naked glory he allowed her to tuck him into bed, but even then he refused to close his eyes. 'You have to get in, too, Wife. If you are not next to me, then Fletcher will come again and I don't want to see him. I want him to leave me alone.'

The panic was back in his eyes again so she relented. Ensuring that her dressing gown was tightly knotted over her nightgown, she lay stiffly on top of the blanket beside him. 'Who is Fletcher?'

It was a reasonable question. Aaron called the man's name every time he had a bad dream and was still frightened of him when roaring drunk.

'He was my lieutenant.' That did not sound particularly terrifying. 'But I can't tell you what happened to him, Connie, because it is my deepest and darkest secret.'

Aaron rolled on to his side so that he could nuzzle his face against her neck, wrapping his free arm snuggly around her waist while he burrowed into the mattress and made himself comfortable. When he threw one leg proprietorially over her hip, and his breathing became deep and rhythmic, she realised he was fast asleep already.

The poor dear was obviously quite spent, which was quite understandable. On top of his many burdens, real or imagined, he had buried his father today. It did not matter that Connie was now burning with curiosity, he needed to sleep. Perhaps the brandy would help him to do so. It had certainly helped to loosen his tongue. Instinctively she wrapped her arm around him, just to comfort him in his hour of need—she certainly did not need the reassuring contact.

And then again, this might be her only opportunity to find out what lay behind Aaron's tortured nightmares and understand why he was becoming increasingly more withdrawn. Surely, in the quest to help him, prising the truth out of him would not constitute taking advantage of his inebriated state?

Connie gently shook his arm to no avail. Aaron was so sozzled and so tired that he probably could have slept through a full military marching band traipsing over his bed. Gripping his shoulder firmly, she rocked his big body from side to side until he groaned in sullen protest.

'Go away!'

His ribs were rising and falling in a steady rhythm, but he shifted his position slightly, sliding his hand up to cup her breast, through the layers of clothing she was still wearing, and reminding her that her body was still a traitor where he was concerned. Even in this state she still wanted him. How pathetic and needy was that?

Connie continued to shake him with determination. 'What happened to Lieutenant Fletcher?'

Finally, he mumbled words that chilled her to the bone.

'I killed him.'

Chapter Twenty-Five

Connie sealed the note with a blob of wax and gave it to the waiting messenger. After spending an entire sleepless night next to Aaron, worrying about everything he had told her, it felt good to be able to do something constructive.

His drunken admission had left her reeling. Whatever had happened now weighed on her mind so heavily that she knew that she would not rest until she had properly talked to him about it. After dropping his bombshell, she had not been able to get another word out of Aaron. He had slept so soundly he had not even moved until just after dawn, which meant that she was held captive in his arms for several long, agonising hours, with only her own racing thoughts to keep her company.

However, the more she thought about it, the less likely it felt that Aaron was capable of kill-ing someone without a justifiable explanation. She knew him too well. Underneath all of that charm and stubbornness was a man who took his responsibility to others very, very seriously. He had married her when he had not needed to simply because it was the right thing to do. He was desperate to save his estate—not for himself, but for the tenants who depended on it. Whatever had happened to Lieutenant Fletcher had not been done maliciously. Connie was sure of that. She was too good a judge of character to have fallen in love with a cold-blooded murderer.

Driving herself mad thinking about it, Connie had desperately tried to take her own advice and categorise each of Aaron's problems to try to find solutions to them. Only then did Sir Gerald's dinner-party conversation come back to her—he quarried chalk and he desperately wanted more chalky land to quarry more!

As soon as she was able, Connie had escaped the bedchamber and written the letter. Even if Sir Gerald did not wish to purchase the land, she had asked him to call on them and explain how they could go about making a profit from the chalk themselves. Either way, it opened another financial avenue that they had not known existed.

After instructing Deaks to send up a cup of

hot, sweet tea and some toast to settle Aaron's stomach, Connie headed for the stable. Since the viscount's death she had ridden with her brother every day, and although she had kept the most damning and pertinent details of her mockery for a marriage to herself, she had found Henry to be an excellent listener with an astute head on his young shoulders.

When Aaron woke, the first thing that struck him was that the bed appeared to be moving. As soon as he prised open one unwilling eye, several other things struck him simultaneously. The daylight was painful, his head felt as if elephants were tramping over it and it wasn't just the bed that was spinning. The walls and ceiling were, too.

Instantly, he squeezed his eyes shut in protest and waited for the bed to stop rotating and dipping with such ferociousness. It was like being seasick—only a hundred times worse—and it was all self-inflicted. There was only one thing that had the power to make him feel this ill and that was brandy. Or whisky. Or even port. In vast quantities. He had ridden a spinning bed before, usually after a particularly raucous regimental dinner, and it never ended well. Already he could feel his stomach begin to lurch in protest and through it all, he had the distinct feeling that he had done something that he oughtn't—although he could not quite put his finger on what that was.

It was late into the afternoon by the time Aaron felt able to leave Connie's bed and stumble downstairs. As the fog in his head had begun to clear he began to feel more and more uneasy about what had transpired the night before. The gaps in his memory bothered him. The snippets he did remember were sketchy, to say the least, and did not fill him with much confidence. He remembered talking to Connie about the estate—nothing harmful there—but he had a very clear memory of confessing that he could not sleep unless he was with her and he must have been persistent because he had woken up in her bed.

Alone.

But completely naked.

He had found his clothes neatly folded on a chair—and as that was not something he ever did, even when stone-cold sober, then it was highly likely that Connie had undressed him. He also had a vague recollection of suggesting that they might engage in more than just sleep. Had he been unguarded enough to tell her how he truly felt about her? And had she allowed more liberties than merely sharing a bed? Not remembering that would be the greatest irony of all. Aaron had wanted her almost constantly since that one, life-changing night they had shared. Or did he owe her a grovelling apology? The simple fact was Aaron did not know.

Unfortunately, a servant informed him that his wife had gone out riding so he was unable to ask her to fill in the gaps for him, however humiliating that conversation was bound to be. Out of habit he wandered into his father's study and sat in one of the chairs facing the fireplace. There was no point sitting at the desk. He could barely function, thanks to his ridiculous decision to consume an entire bottle of brandy. Aaron simply sat and stared at the walls.

After a few minutes he noticed something that had never occurred to him before. The glassy, lifeless eyes of the numerous hunting trophies lining the walls reminded him a great deal of the dead bodies lying still on a battlefield. The mere thought sent a shiver through him. What had possessed his father to decorate his study with something so macabre? They were enough to give anyone nightmares. They really had to go. The last thing he needed was more reminders of the war and death.

'You are feeling better, then?'

His wife breezed into the study looking all windswept and wanton in his favourite tight, green riding habit, her glorious copper hair already escaping its pins. Good grief, she was stunning. Even with the last remnants of his drunken debauchery still lingering in his system he instantly felt a surge of raw lust, so strong that his chest tightened as well as his groin. But this was not the time or the place for such thoughts. There were things that needed to be said. Questions that needed to be asked.

'If that is your polite way of asking me if the effects of the brandy have worn off, you do not need to dance around it. I am not completely sure what possessed me to over-imbibe—but as I am still suffering from the after-effects, you can rest assured I have no desire to repeat the experience. Also, I have come here to offer you a blanket apology for whatever I said or did last night that might have offended you.'

'There is nothing to apologise for. You had just buried your father.'

A sudden blush stained her cheeks and she was fiddling with the ribbons of her bonnet rather than look at him, he noticed. That was not a good sign. Unless…?

'Did we engage in…um…did we make love?' The seams of his breeches strained at the prospect. Even talking about the act roused his ardour for her. It really was a good thing that he was sitting down or he would have a great deal more to apologise for.

Her face instantly suffused with vivid colour. 'You will be pleased to know that you were spared that ordeal.'

Ordeal? What an odd—and worrying—turn of phrase. Had she not enjoyed what he had done to her that night? He was sure that they had both been quite satisfied.

'You merely insisted that you would not be able to sleep unless you slept with me. Because of your nightmares.'

Oh, dear. He had been talkative. Please God he had spared her the details. 'And then what did I do?'

'You slept, of course, you silly man!' But she could not quite meet his eyes as she said it and that fact left him feeling decidedly off kilter. If she was not reluctant to tell him what he had done, he would have to coax it out of her gently.

'Did you enjoy your ride?'

Her shoulders relaxed slightly at the change of subject and she balanced primly on the edge of one of the chairs. 'I did. I met my brother again and we chatted for over an hour.'

'I did not know that you had started riding with your brother. That is good to hear.'

She stared down at her lap and worried her bottom lip with her teeth anxiously. 'There is something I need to talk to you about, Aaron.' Connie risked a peek at him through her lashes. 'You told me some things last night.'

'Did I?'

His response sounded innocuous enough, but Connie was not fooled by his casualness. He visibly paled and she watched his jaw tighten. There were so many things that she wanted to ask him about, most predominantly what had happened to the mysterious Fletcher, but such things needed to be approached delicately and at the right time. Aaron certainly did not appear to be ready to discuss *those* things. Even his hands had begun to grip the arms of the chair as if he were braced to bolt at any moment. There were easier things to talk about first.

'You told me that the land your father purchased was made of chalk.'

His fingers unfurled and his Adam's apple bobbed in relief. 'What of it?'

Connie grinned at him. 'Chalk is a valuable commodity. Perhaps more valuable that wheat or barley.'

'No, it isn't—whoever gave you that ridiculous idea?' he scoffed, shaking his head in denial of what she knew to be fact.

'It *is*, Aaron. Do you remember I sat next to Sir Gerald Pimm at the dinner party and you warned me that he would bore me senseless? Well, he did. He waffled on for close to an hour on the many uses of chalk. To quote him: "Chalk is the crop that keeps on giving." He is desperate to buy more land to quarry.'

Aaron sat forward, suddenly interested, his dark brows drawn together, making him look even more appealing than usual.

'My brother says that there is a growing market for all manner of quarried stone nowadays and that there is considerable profit in it. He thinks that selling the land to Sir Gerald might well be the answer to all of your financial worries and that—'

'You discussed this with your brother!' His interested expression had been replaced by a thunderous one.

'Henry has a very good head for business and I trust—'

'You have no right to discuss my finances, or anything else about my sorry situation, with your brother!'

'I trust my brother implicitly.' She had intended to placate him but was irritated at the implication. 'He would not do me wrong.'

Aaron shot out of his seat as if he had been fired by a cannon and loomed over her. 'He's a blasted Stuart, Connie! Everything you tell him will go straight back to your father. I can almost hear him gloating and crowing about it all from here. How dare you discuss my private affairs behind my back?'

Now he was just being plain unreasonable, the insufferable man, and he knew full well that it was hurting her neck to have to crane up to look at him. He was not the only one who could loom menacingly. Pulling herself up to her full height, Connie looked him straight in his stubborn eyes. 'Who else could I confide in?'

'You might have tried confiding in me! I am your husband after all.'

'How convenient.' She started to pace around the floor to stop herself from wanting to throw something at him. 'However, it is difficult to confide in a person who hides away from his wife whenever things get a little difficult. You are my husband when you are in the mood to be and a brooding recluse the rest of the time! Well, seeing as we are confiding in each other, you might as well know that I also took it upon myself to write to Sir Gerald this morning to offer him the land on your behalf.'

'Does your impertinence know no bounds at all, Connie? You had no right to do that either. Not without asking me first!'

'I would have asked you, but you were too busy feeling sorry for yourself and lying in a drunken stupor!'

'Once! I got drunk once, damn you, and under the circumstances, who could blame me? Stop flouncing around as if you are the one who has been wronged, Constance.'

'Flouncing!' That made it sound as if she was merely being dramatic rather than genuinely aggrieved by what he was saying. And he never called her Constance.

'Yes—flouncing.' He started to prance around the room, waving his arms. 'My name is Constance Stuart and I am a spoiled brat!'

'How dare you!'

He didn't stop. 'Look at me flounce! I'm so dramatic. And innocent. I would never go behind my husband's back so that I can stab him in it. But I am a Stuart, after all, so I suppose I couldn't help it.'

He thought she had stabbed him in the back. That hurt. 'I have had enough of this. I try to help and you behave like this?' She turned towards the door.

'How typical. I suppose now you are going to leave in a sulk?'

Now he had gone too far. 'No. I am leaving you, Aaron! Permanently.'

Connie stalked out of the study, slamming the heavy oak door as hard as she could, and marched to her private sitting room. The man was an idiot! A stubborn fool who she would be well rid of. It was long past time she put an end to this travesty of a marriage. She stomped to her closet and pulled out her trunk. She did not care if the Dower House was ready or not. She was going to move out today and stop caring about Aaron Wincanton if it killed her.

Chapter Twenty-Six

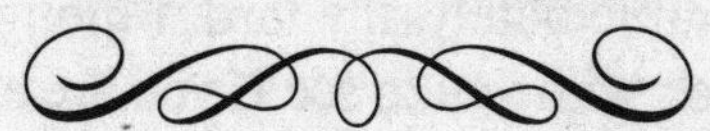

Aaron watched her fly out of the room and fought to bring his temper under control. She was in the wrong. How could she not see it? His financial situation was humiliating. It had taken a great deal of trust to confide in her, yet now it was as good as public knowledge. Once her brother told her spiteful father, the sorry truth would be bandied about and, aside from making him a laughing stock, the implications of that were horrifying. Redbridge could pull in favours and make life extremely difficult for him. What if he was refused credit? Opportunists would circle like vultures ready to pick his carcase clean.

Yet above all of those worries was the awful possibility that Connie might have done it deliberately. Even if she had not meant to ruin him, she had chosen her family above him and that thought physically hurt. Aaron might well be unworthy, and he definitely did not deserve it, but he had wanted her to choose him. Only him.

Deaks scratched on the door and looked embarrassed. 'Her ladyship has ordered a conveyance to transport her belongings to the Dower House immediately, my lord. I thought I had best check with you to see if you are agreeable to her request.'

Aaron's lungs suddenly felt constricted and it became an effort to breath. Obviously, she thought that she was going somewhere. The fear was as instant as it was unwelcome. He wanted to hate her, he had every reason to hate her, but he was terrified that she might actually leave him. He barged passed the butler and tore up the stairs two at a time. She had betrayed his trust and he was damned if he would allow her to have the last word this time. Or leave him.

Her bedchamber door crashed open with a satisfying thud and he watched her eyes widen as he strode towards her. His volatile wife was obviously shocked by his sudden intrusion, but she recovered quickly. She stood unrepentant, clothing clutched in her hands and an open trunk stood at her feet.

'Go away, Aaron.'

A maelstrom of emotion was boiling violently

in the pit of his stomach and needed to be vented or else he would combust. Aaron snatched the limp garments from her fingers and tossed them to the floor before firmly kicking the trunk at the wall. 'You will leave this house when I say and not before. Do. I. Make. Myself. Clear?'

He watched her swallow nervously before her green eyes hardened to flint. But, for once, she said nothing. It was just as well; Aaron was so furious he could barely see straight. He sucked in a shuddering breathe as she continued to glare at him, trying to stem the painful wound of her betrayal and failing. 'How dare you go behind my back like that?'

'I did not go behind your back, you fool. I was merely trying to help you.'

'By informing my enemies that I am broke? By giving your father the satisfaction of knowing that he has finally beaten the Wincantons? What a *great* help you are, Connie!'

'Do not use sarcasm with me!'

Oh, that was rich! She had the audacity to be affronted. 'Does it irritate you, Constance? How ironic. The queen of sarcasm doesn't like it back. It makes me feel sick to think that I trusted you!' And that he had allowed himself to fall in love with her. That he had almost told her of those epic feelings. He had been on the very cusp of laying himself bare at her feet and in return, she had now trampled all over him as if he did not matter to her at all. What a complete and utter fool! And now she wanted to abandon him. Incensed, humiliated and in danger of letting her witness how deeply she had wounded his heart, Aaron marched to her wardrobe and grabbed an armful of gowns and ceremoniously dumped them into the trunk.

'I want you out of my house and my life today, Constance!' No, he didn't. But still the hateful words spilled forth. 'I am sorry that I married you.'

'Not as sorry as I am that I married you!' Was that a catch he just heard in her voice? 'But at least now you can go and get yourself a beautiful wife who is more to your liking! One that you do not need to cover over with a sheet r-rather than l-look at!' He definitely heard her falter then, as if she was actually upset. As if he had actually upset her when she had destroyed him.

'What are you talking about?' He grabbed her arm and spun her around to face him. There were tears shimmering in her stormy green eyes. 'I have never covered you with a sheet!' What a truly preposterous thing to say. Could she not see that she was the one that had betrayed him? He had trusted her. Confided in her. She should be grovelling for his forgiveness and promising to stay, not accusing him of covering her in a blasted sheet, of all things.

'How dare you?' She pushed him away. 'How dare you feign ignorance when you know full well that you could not bear the sight of me? You jumped out of the bed so quickly I thought that the blankets must be on fire! And then you covered me with the sheet so that you would not have to look at my disappointing body in the daylight. Admit it—I d-d-disgust you!'

For a moment he thought she had actually gone quite mad as he replayed their interactions since last night step by step. Had he missed something? As far as he was concerned it had been the most spectacular night of passion of his life. He was certain that she had enjoyed the whole experience as much as he had. In fact, he had been completely broad-sided by it. Damn it all, he had very nearly told her that he loved her that morning. How could she have taken that as disgust?

Fat tears of sheer misery began to roll down her lovely cheeks just like they had that first, fateful evening in that library and everything suddenly became clear. Aaron had covered her over that morning, he remembered with a jolt, and Connie had misinterpreted it. Remorse at his clumsiness swamped him. Time and time again she had left him clues about her insecurities, but yet he had not put them all together. Ghastly hair, washboard figure, looming, plain and, God help him, the Ginger Amazonian. The silly woman believed herself to be ugly and it was, unforgivably, all his fault. And he had just ordered her to leave. All of his anger dissolved under the weight of his new guilt, but Connie was already halfway to the door. Aaron was not going to let her leave on those dreadful last words. Even if it meant admitting how he felt.

'I never meant you to think that.' He caught her about the waist with one arm and dragged her rigid body backwards into his embrace. 'I can understand why you thought it. Truly I can.' She squirmed in his arms. All the while, silent tears still dripped from her eyes. One fell on to the back of his hand, humbling him, and he knew that he owed her the truth. 'I panicked. I was so overwhelmed by what had happened between us, and by the intensity of my feelings, that I had to escape. Seeing you like that, Connie, all naked and lovely, was too much of a temptation. I almost told you that I loved you and wanted to beg for your love in return.' His heart began to race at the confession. As if he stood any hope of her returning his feelings? Once he told her the truth about himself he would kill that hope just as surely as he had poor Fletcher.

His heartfelt declaration fell on deaf ears. Her body stiffened as she tried and failed to wriggle out of his hold. 'Oh, please! Do you seriously expect me to believe that? I do not need your pity or your flowery words. I am well aware of what I am and why you married me...'

'I think you are the most beautiful creature I have ever set eyes on. Right from that first moment in Almack's I desired you.'

'Liar! There is nothing about me that you find attractive!'

Her strength was impressive. She was wriggling free, her fingers were already closing around the door handle. Aaron was going to have to show her how wrong she was; the stubborn wench was never going to believe him otherwise. He pressed his hips insistently against her bottom, using his weight to push her against the door.

'Do you feel that, Connie?'

It was difficult not to. He planted his hands on her hips and turned her to face him, letting his hard body rest intimately against hers while it imprisoned her. 'I am not sure what you know about a man's body—but I can assure you *that* only happens when we find a woman attractive. Every time I look at you, you take my breath away. I have never wanted a woman as much as I want you.'

He took hold of her hand and pressed her open palm against the impressive bulge in his breeches, holding it there sandwiched between them, his lips so close to her ear.

'A moment ago we were shouting at each other—and yet still I wanted you. I might find you exasperating, and God knows you fire my temper more than anyone ever has, but I always want you. This is evidence of that. It is not pity. Nor is it a lie. You have done this to me. You are the most beautiful woman I have ever seen.'

'I don't believe you!'

Connie wanted to drag her hand away and cover her ears. But it felt so good to touch him and be held so firmly in his arms. When his mouth came down on hers with a ragged sigh he kissed her urgently, plunging his fingers into her hair and pulling out the pins.

'I love your hair, Connie. Especially when it is all loose and spread over my pillow.' His lips found her ear, making her shudder as his teeth scraped over the sensitive flesh there.

'My hair is too red, you idiot, and does not do as it is told.' He loved her hair? How marvellous.

His clever hands were now working on the laces at the back of her dress while his mouth never left hers. When he had loosened it enough, he pushed it down her shoulders roughly, exposing her unimpressive breasts to his greedy touch.

'I have no curves!'

'Then why do I let you win every horse race? Unless I do it on purpose so that I can watch your lovely bottom bounce in the saddle and imagine that it is me that you are riding with such skill?'

His shocking words thrilled her, but still she goaded him. Still needed more proof of his desire.

'I am flat-chested.'

'I beg to differ. If you were, I would not be able to do this so easily.' He sucked her nipple into his mouth, swirling his tongue around the tip and making her arch against him wantonly. Connie found herself clawing at the buttons on his falls desperately, needing to feel skin on skin. When he finally sprang free she wrapped her hand around him, caressing his hardness until he groaned and hoisted her skirts up her legs.

'I am unladylike. I speak my mind. And I am difficult.' Her voice sounded ragged to her own ears, her throat tight with need and passion. She had never felt so desired or as alive as she did right as this moment. 'You think that I have betrayed you!'

'Perhaps not intentionally.' If she would stay he would forgive her anything. 'You really are the most vexing woman I have ever met, Constance Wincanton. And I love your legs. I have never seen legs as long and shapely as yours.'

'I am too tall,' she blurted defiantly, daring him to deny that at least.

He gripped one of her thighs and hooked it around his hips. 'And thank God for it,' he growled as he plunged into her wet heat and took her against the wall, his russet eyes burning with lust.

Their coupling was fast and urgent and glorious, leaving them both panting and stunned afterwards. When it was finished he stepped back a little to let his gaze rake possessively over her semi-clothed body, lingering on her bared breasts and the damp auburn curls between her legs before he spoke. 'If ever you are in any doubt about your attractiveness to me, I am more than happy to prove you wrong, Connie.'

Afterwards, she had shyly led him by the hand to her bed and let him undress her in the daylight, allowing him to spend the rest of the afternoon showing her just how lovely she was.

Now they were lying together drowsily, her head resting on his chest, his fingers idling twining in her hair, both lost in their own thoughts. She had no idea what Aaron was thinking, but Connie was considering the best possible way to broach the spectre that tortured him. It stood between them more impassable than any feud or silly misunderstanding could.

'Tell me about your nightmares, Aaron.'

She felt his ribs rise as he inhaled slowly and fall as he sighed it out. Almost in resignation. 'What do you want to know?'

He was obviously not going to volunteer anything unless she pushed him. 'How long have you had them?'

'Three years now. They came infrequently at first, but since I came home I have them every night.' His fingers twirled around one lock of hair intently as he lapsed back into silence.

'What are they about?'

'The war. Battle. Death.'

Beneath her fingers she felt the muscles on his abdomen tense. His explanation might be superficial, but his memories were not. Connie let her palms rub his chest in lazy, soothing circles but she could sense his growing discomfort. Every limb was rigid with tension—as if he feared even speaking of it. But she knew instinctively that he had to. It was eating him from the inside.

'Explain one of them to me. I want to understand what happens in your dreams.'

'They are all the same, Connie,' he said impatiently, shifting his body so that he could sit up and put some distance between them. 'Every night I have to see the same things again and relive the horror of that night. Please don't ask me to talk about it.'

She had to. He had to verbalise it so that he could face his demons. 'Is it the night that Fletcher died?'

Aaron stilled instantly. His eyes were ravaged with pain and disgust and shame. 'What do you know about Fletcher?'

'I know that you think you killed him. I know that the mere thought of that is tearing you apart.'

'I did kill him, Connie!' All the fight went out of him as he buried his face in his hands. 'He was my responsibility and I put him in harm's way. In fact, it was worse than that. I used him to save myself.'

Aaron waited for her censure or her disgust, but instead she wrapped her arms around him and pulled him close. 'Tell me what happened.'

'Wellington ordered us to take Ciudad

Rodrigo—one of the most heavily fortified and impenetrable fortresses on the northern border. My regiment was in the thick of the assault, under the command of Major-General Mackinnon. He was a good man. A great soldier. Fletcher joined my regiment shortly before we arrived in Spain. He was not a good soldier. In fact, he was one of the worst soldiers I have ever had to command. He was lazy and kept shirking his duties. This got worse once we surrounded the castle. For days we were under constant fire from the enemy soldiers as we dug trenches for cover. Fletcher kept disappearing from the front. While the other men dug and risked their lives, he hid himself away. As his commanding officer, it was my job to keep him in line and I suppose I became frustrated with his lack of effort or solidarity with the rest of the men. After five days under constant cannon fire, we managed to get close enough to begin to attack the main walls, and finally we made a huge breach in one of the corners. Mackinnon decided to storm the fortress. We filled the ditch with sandbags so that we could get across it and then began to scramble up the wreckage of the walls. I kept Fletcher close to me, convinced that he would run or do something equally as stupid in a pathetic attempt to save his own skin, but at the wall he just froze. I knew he was terrified—but we all were. There were two big cannons above our heads and the enemy were poised ready to fire them. We were sitting ducks. The French were firing musket balls down on us—each time they reloaded they fell like hail. Speed was of the essence and Fletcher was putting us all in danger with his dithering. I tried to reason with him, to no avail, so in the end I grabbed the collar of his uniform and called him a coward. I pushed him up the wall in front of me, dragging him up against his will. He was crying and pleading with me to let him go.'

Aaron's skin was now deathly pale and his voice became strangled with emotion. 'The next thing I knew, I was flying through the air. There was a fireball and a loud explosion and then everything went black. I have no idea how long I lay there. When I came around it was carnage. The enemy had mined the breach and had waited until we were all on it to detonate the grenades. Half of my regiment died. MacKinnon died. Fletcher died. Horribly. But I did not. He had begged me to let him go and I dragged him to his death. I used Fletcher's body as a shield.'

Poor Aaron. So consumed with guilt that he could not see past it to the reality. 'It was Napoleon's troops who killed Fletcher—not you, Aaron.'

'But I held him in front of me.'

'You pulled him on to the wall. You did it to save the lives of the rest of your men. He was putting them all in danger. You did not know there were mines there, nor could you have known they would be detonated. Why did you not let Fletcher go as he asked? What difference would it have made if he had run away?'

That question appeared to flummox him and she watched him consider different possible scenarios in his head.

'He would have been left alone.'

'Why did you not want him to be alone, Aaron?'

His handsome face crumpled as he tried to think of some other reason, other than the truth, to punish himself with. In the end, he shook his head violently.

'He died because of me, Connie. The tiny details aren't important.'

Yes, they were. The tiny details were everything. 'Why did you not want Fletcher to be left alone Aaron?'

'He would have been a target.' The words came out in a shudder. 'Alone he did not stand a chance.'

'You were trying to keep Fletcher safe, too, then. He was lazy and he was a coward, but you still *tried* to save him. He would have died alone. You have to remember that, too. Don't punish yourself for what happened Aaron. It was horrible and it was tragic, and I am not surprised that it haunts you still, but it wasn't your fault.'

He let her pull him back down on to the mattress, buried his face in her hair and Connie felt all of that pent-up emotion leave his body as he clung to her as if his very life depended on it. 'Sometimes the nightmares take me when I am awake, Connie. The present disappears and I am back in Spain. I have no control over it. I seriously think I might be going mad.'

She kissed his head and rocked him gently. 'Does that happen every day, too? Is that why you shut yourself away?'

He shook his head. 'Just twice. You have been present for both of them.'

The blood. He had seen blood and he had frozen. 'Those episodes passed quickly, Aaron. I do not think that you are going mad. You really need to give yourself a bit more credit. Not only have you lived through all of the horrors that the war could throw at you, life has not been particularly easy for you since you returned home. It is no wonder that it has all felt a little overwhelming at times. Lack of sleep, your father's health, the estate, having to marry me.'

He was silent for a moment, as he absorbed her words. 'Do you think this madness is temporary, then?'

Absently, she twined her fingers in his hair. 'I do. It might take months for you to feel normal again—perhaps a little longer—but I have no doubt that you will bounce back in time. Please stop being so hard on yourself.'

That seemed to calm him and she finally felt him relax. After several minutes, he propped himself up on to his elbow and gazed down at her adoringly. 'I thought that you would hate me if I told you.'

'I could never hate you, Aaron.' She smiled up at him, amazed to know that he could be as insecure as she was. This appeared to please him.

'That is good because your opinion of me matters more than anyone else's. You are the best thing that has ever happened to me, Connie. I love you with all of my heart.'

That was the second time that he had claimed to love her. There was such longing in his eyes that she almost believed him.

Almost.

A lump formed in her throat that made speech impossible. She wanted to tell him that she loved him, too, but the words would not come. As much as she wanted to believe him she had to be realistic. He was vulnerable and upset and he might not truly mean them. And she was too vulnerable and wanted it all to be true so desperately that she was genuinely terrified that it might not be. Connie was not sure that her fragile heart could take that. All she had ever truly wanted felt as if it might be finally in her grasp—a place to belong, a proper home, a family, someone to love who loved her in return—and yet still she was too scared to reach for it. What if he regretted his declaration in the morning? How could she pretend her heart was not broken if he knew how much he filled it?

Until she was certain, it was best to leave things as they were. There was every chance that, once he was over his crisis, Aaron might still wish to be released from the marriage. Instead of saying the words, she tried to show him how she felt with her body, making love to him until he finally collapsed exhausted in her arms and slept. Only then did she dare whisper what she had been certain of for some time.

'I love you, too, Aaron Wincanton. I always will.'

Chapter Twenty-Seven

They were eating breakfast when Deaks announced the arrival of the Earl of Redbridge. Unsure of what to expect, they both entered the morning room with some trepidation. An Earl of Redbridge had never so much as set foot on Wincanton soil before. Something was clearly very wrong. Her father stood ramrod straight with his back to them, staring out of the French windows. Sat in a chair was her younger brother, Henry, his expression haughtily indifferent as he examined his cuffs and refusing to meet either of their eyes. As if he had not just betrayed his sister as Aaron had predicted he would, choosing her father over her and dashing all of her hopes for her future.

Instinctively, Aaron wrapped his arm around his wife's waist. Whatever mischief was about to befall them; they would face it together. He would be her rock as she had been his last night.

'To what do we owe the pleasure?'

Connie's father appeared to be furious. He turned to them angrily, shooting Connie a special look of disdain before he fixed his gaze on Aaron. 'My son has informed me that you intend to build a quarry on the land adjacent to my property.'

While this was news to Aaron, he shrugged arrogantly. 'What of it?'

'I will not allow it!' Tiny flecks of spittle had gathered in the corner of the earl's mouth and they sprayed outwards as he spoke, like liquid hatred.

'The land is mine to do with as I see fit.'

Connie's brother stood up then and walked towards his father. 'Harsh words will not fix this. Tell him civilly what you propose.'

The old man began to practically vibrate with anger. He shot Connie another frigid look, blinked and then cleared his throat awkwardly.

'I have come here to offer to buy the land from you. Five thousand pounds should cover it. That is well over what it is worth.'

It was a tempting offer. Aaron felt Connie inhale in shock. This must be torture for her. She loved her family and desperately wanted to be reunited with them, but now she had been betrayed by her brother, too. It broke his heart to see her so silent and submissive. Her one and only hope of going back home was slipping away in front of her eyes.

'I have a counter-offer. How about I keep the land for myself, but promise never to disturb it in return for something *other* than money?'

Three heads whipped in his direction. The earl's eyes had narrowed and he was watching Aaron like a hawk.

'What do you propose?'

It was the right thing to do, he knew it in his heart. That did not mean that saying it would shatter his heart into tiny pieces. But he loved Connie and he owed her. It had not escaped his notice that she had not claimed to return his love. Twice he had told her how he felt about her last night and twice she had remained silent. Although the truth had wounded him he understood it. She had never wanted this marriage. Or him.

'Let Connie live at Redbridge House. As long as she is happy and well cared for, you have my word that I will not quarry that land.'

Oh, good grief! He was such a stubborn and honourable man. Only a person truly in love would propose such a selfless and noble thing.

Connie's heart was positively brimming with so much joy that it was almost impossible to contain. She had wanted true proof of his affections and now she had it. He was sacrificing his own happiness for hers. Again.

And it needed to be nipped in the bud.

'Aaron—if I might have a word?'

His wife was glaring at him with such animosity that it brought Aaron up short. She marched stiffly from the morning room, forcing him to trail behind, wondering why she was so very annoyed when he was doing his level best to make her happy. She led him into the room next door, closed the door behind them and then promptly grabbed him by his lapels.

'How dare you! I have a good mind to go upstairs and get *The Complete Farmer* so that I can beat some sense into your thick skull.'

That was not the reaction he had been hoping for. 'This is a chance for you to be with the people you love most, Connie,' he replied, somewhat bewildered by the fire in her eyes. 'You have repeatedly asked to be free of this marriage and have wished for the day when you could go home again. This expedites the process. I thought it would please you.'

'Then you are a fool, Aaron Wincanton. I only wished for those things when I thought you married me out of obligation and certainly before I realised that you loved me. I might have neglected to tell you last night, but you happen to be the person I love the most in the whole world, silly man, so your selfless and noble gesture is misplaced.' She actually shook him then. 'I want no more ridiculous talk of annulments or of sending me back to live with my horrid father. You've seen what a nasty piece of work he is. What on earth makes you think that I would rather go back and live with him? To him I am a disappointment. Here, I am *adored*. I *want* to stay with you and if you think that you can get rid of me that easily then you are sorely mistaken. I am a Wincanton and Wincantons live at Ardleigh Manor. Do. I. Make. Myself. Clear?'

She loved him! He had stopped listening as soon as she had said that and had simply enjoyed watching the spectacle of her flouncing and venting. It was such a glorious sight to see. Aaron could not prevent the huge grin from spreading over his face or from kissing her until they were both breathless. Looking delightfully rumpled, Connie made a valiant effort to fix her hair before she waved her finger at him as if he was an errant schoolboy.

'Let me deal with my father. Clearly you have no head for doing business.'

At that she flounced back into the morning room like a warrior queen—his own personal demon slayer—off to slay the Earl of Redbridge. He almost pitied the man.

'We want ten thousand pounds for the land.'

The Earl of Redbridge balked. 'That is preposterous. Ardleigh only paid seven!'

'I suspect that Mr Thomas cost the Wincanton estate significantly more than the three-thousand-pounds difference, therefore I believe that ten thousand is a reasonable sum.' Connie folded her arms across her chest and regarded her father with haughty disdain. 'You were paying that wastrel Deal twenty thousand to take me off of your hands. Aaron is only asking half of that.'

'I won't pay it!'

'Then leave and let us quarry the land in peace. We will soon make more than ten thousand. Unless Sir Gerald makes us a more tempting offer for it. He has already expressed an interest and holds me in the highest regard.'

'You have allowed this Wincanton to seduce you and turn you against your own family, Constance.'

'Don't flatter yourself, Father. The only person I have turned against is you. If you cannot pay, then I wish you good day. We are done.'

She spun on her heel and stalked towards

Aaron slowly. Only he could see the slight smile that touched her lovely lips. She was enjoying herself. The minx.

'Wait...'

Connie stopped walking, but did not turn around.

'Ten thousand it is, then. Devil take you, Constance!'

'The money needs to be with my husband before this week is out or the deal is void. We shall have *our* solicitor draw up the agreements.'

Ours. Aaron liked the sound of that. The Earl of Redbridge didn't.

'Henry, our business here is concluded. Let's go.'

Henry Stuart turned towards his father. 'I shall be out in a moment. I wish to speak to Constance first.'

The older man was practically quivering with rage. 'I said *now*, Henry!'

'Go and wait in the carriage, Father.' The younger man delivered this with such icy calmness that his father stood gaping at him for several seconds before he marched out of the front door.

Connie went to her brother and hugged him. 'How did you get him to come here?'

'It was quite simple really. I merely informed

him of the twenty, ugly, smoke-billowing lime kilns that you were going build to block his view and lamented the fact that there would be *trade* going on right on our doorstep. He nearly had an apoplexy.' Henry turned towards Aaron, smiling and held out his hand. 'Connie has told me a great deal about you and I trust her judgement implicitly. I cannot vouch for my father, but you have my word that I will not continue this silly feud.'

Aaron shook his hand gratefully, completely bowled over by the peculiar events of the morning, and then walked him to the door with Connie. 'I realise that you are still in mourning, Aaron, but with your permission I would like to bring my mother here to visit you both tomorrow, if that is convenient. I know that she would like that.'

'Father will never allow it, Henry.'

Connie's brother simply smiled at her indulgently then. 'Oh, I think he will. Especially as I shall inform him that if he forbids it, both Mother and I will move into Ardleigh Manor and never speak to him again. What is the worst he can do? He cannot disinherit me, can he, Aaron? The estate is entailed.' Connie had been clearly confiding quite a bit to her younger brother. And she had been quite right. Henry was not a typical Stuart any more than he supposed he was a typical Wincanton. They might be the sons of their fathers, but that did not necessarily mean that they were destined to be enemies.

'You are welcome to move in whenever you see fit, Henry. We are family now.'

After the Redbridge carriage disappeared down the drive, Aaron enjoyed a moment of unexpected triumph. He was no longer in debt, thanks to Connie, and he was beginning to believe that he might not be a murderer or a madman after all. As long as she was there beside him, no mountain was too high to climb and no demons were too ferocious to slay. His father might well be dead—but he had died happy and that was due to Connie, too.

The one constant in all of it was Constance.

Steadfast and resolute.

His wife.

Who loved *him* back.

Yes, she might be a bit of a handful at times and prone to the odd temper tantrum, but she was also the most magnificent, wonderful and beautiful wife a man could wish for—so he would indulge her whims and enjoy her passion. Passion was certainly something she had in abundance.

'Why don't you go and put on that glorious green riding habit?'

Connie beamed back at him. It was one of her genuine smiles. One of the smiles that made him feel as if the most glorious sunrise had been created only for him to enjoy

'Do you want to go for a morning ride, Aaron?'

His russet eyes burned wickedly and he watched the vivid blush bloom on her perfect cheeks as realisation dawned.

'In a manner of speaking, *Mrs Wincanton*, I rather think I do.'

* * * * *

If you enjoyed this story, you won't want to miss this other fantastic read from Virginia Heath:

THAT DESPICABLE ROGUE